MW00573267

The
Sapphire
Daughter

BOOKS BY SORAYA LANE

Soraya
LANE

The
Sapphire
Daughter

bookouture

Published by Bookouture in 2024

An imprint of Storyfire Ltd.
Carmelite House
50 Victoria Embankment
London EC4Y 0DZ

www.bookouture.com

Copyright © Soraya Lane, 2024

Soraya Lane has asserted her right to be identified as the author of this work.

All rights reserved. No part of this publication may be reproduced, stored in any retrieval system, or transmitted, in any form or by any means, electronic, mechanical, photocopying, recording or otherwise, without the prior written permission of the publishers.

ISBN: 978-1-83790-973-5
eBook ISBN: 978-1-83790-972-8

This book is a work of fiction. Names, characters, businesses, organizations, places and events other than those clearly in the public domain are either the product of the author's imagination or are used fictitiously. Any resemblance to actual persons, living or dead, events or locales is entirely coincidental.

For Lisa. Thank you for everything you do for me every single week. I honestly don't know what I'd do without you!

PROLOGUE

SUMMER RESIDENCE OF FLORIAN LENGACHER

Delphine stretched out beside the pool, her silk robe slipping from her shoulder and leaving it bare as she lay in the sun, smiling as she heard Florian's footsteps coming closer. She held out her hand for the drink he'd promised, but instead of a glass, he slipped his palm against hers.

She opened her eyes, sitting upright when she saw his serious expression and turning to face him. In the distance the lake shimmered, the late sun reflecting off the water.

'You look worried,' she said, reaching out her other hand to cup his smooth cheek as he lowered himself to the seat beside her, his dark hair falling forward as he leaned in. 'Tell me—what's wrong?'

'Nothing's wrong,' he replied, smiling as he squeezed her hand. 'On the contrary, I have something to show you.'

Delphine smiled back, only too happy to play along. Their stolen moments together brought her such joy, made her forget all the heartbreak that had come before, and she patiently waited for him to continue.

Her curiosity was piqued when she realised he was holding a box in his other hand. 'What do you want to show me?' she asked.

'This,' Florian said, dropping her hand in order to take the lid off the box, 'belonged to the former queen consort of Italy. I had a feeling you might be familiar with it?'

'The pink sapphire tiara,' Delphine said, her breath catching in her throat as she looked up at him, hardly able to believe what she was looking at. 'I know it well. In fact, I admired it when the queen wore it to a wedding I attended after the war. I don't think there's a woman in Italy who wouldn't recognise it.' She shook her head, leaning forward to better see the stunning jewels. It took her back to her time in Italy, of the years she'd spent going to glittering parties and rubbing shoulders with Italian nobility during the early years of her marriage. 'How has it come to be in your possession?'

'The family discreetly sold some unique pieces from their collection after they left Italy, and my personal curator made certain I was the successful buyer. Most of the other pieces were entrusted to the Bank of Italy in Rome for safekeeping, which makes the few pieces they sold even more special,' he said, holding it up between them so Delphine could look at it more closely. 'I've collected many beautiful diamonds and pieces of art over the years, but this tiara? There is nothing in the world to rival the history and the beauty of such a piece.'

It was certainly unique, and the fact that he'd been able to purchase it reminded her just how well-connected Florian was. The stones caught the light as he turned the tiara in his hands, the sapphires appearing the most vivid pink one moment, and then almost purple the next, made even more brilliant as the sunshine reflected against them. He was right that it was perhaps one of the most coveted and stunning pieces of jewellery he could have invested in.

'This tiara was held in the Italian royal family from the

1800s until they were forced into exile five years ago,' Florian said. 'And now it shall remain in my family for generations to come. This is one of those pieces that I never intend to part with.'

'I hugely admire the former queen,' Delphine said. 'I recall her saying that her only regret during the war was not killing Adolf Hitler herself when she was in the same room as him, and I've always presumed she was quite capable of it. She's one of those rare women who is both feminine and forthright, so it's fitting that you've chosen her favourite tiara. I imagine it's absolutely priceless.'

'I couldn't agree more,' Florian said. 'And you're right, it is priceless. It is to be the jewel in my personal collection, for want of a better expression.'

'It's stunning, Florian. Thank you for showing it to me.' She tucked her legs up beneath her as Florian smiled at her, his expression hard to read.

'I showed it to you for a reason, Delphine,' he finally said, placing the tiara beside him and reaching for both her hands. 'I would like you to choose one of the sapphires so that I can have an engagement ring made for you.' Florian kissed her knuckles, his dark brown eyes never leaving hers as his voice lowered to a whisper.

'Florian—' she began.

'I want us to spend the rest of our lives together, Delphine. I don't want to hide any more. I want the world to know you are to become my wife, and this is my way of showing you what you mean to me.'

Tears filled her eyes, a solitary drop sliding down her cheek as she looked away, wishing it were so easy, wishing she was free to make her own decisions in life. The tiara caught her gaze, and she wondered what heartbreak it had seen, what love it might have been witness to; what sorrow.

'You know it's not so easy as my simply saying yes. If it

were...' She couldn't bring herself to finish the sentence. When they were together like this, it felt as if they were the only two people in the world. But outside the walled gates of his compound, of the beautiful, secluded property by the lake that had been their private oasis these past few months, they couldn't be seen together freely.

Florian nodded, his hands guiding her closer until she was curled on his knee, her arms around his neck, tucked tightly to his chest. The tiara would be nothing without one of its sapphires, its value hugely diminished if it were ever to be offered for sale with a missing stone, but she knew that was what he was trying to tell her: that he would break up the most valuable piece in his collection, the piece that meant the most to him, for her. It was abundantly obvious that he had the funds to buy her the most expensive diamond from Tiffany's, and yet he was willing to sacrifice one of the precious sapphires as a gesture of his love.

'I am nothing without you,' Florian murmured into her hair. 'Please, say yes. Let me find a way for us to marry.'

Neither am I, Florian. Without you, I too am nothing.

Delphine looked up at him, her fingers grazing his cheek as she pressed her mouth to his in a long, slow, warm kiss.

'Yes,' she eventually whispered against his lips. 'I will marry you, Florian. If you can find a way, then I promise you. I will marry you.'

1

LONDON, 2022

Georgia stepped out of the taxi and hurried down the narrow London street, double-checking the address on her phone. Older-style buildings stretched down both sides, with the exception of a modern, glass-fronted design sandwiched between the brickwork at the very end, bearing a discreet sign announcing that it was the law firm she was looking for—Williamson, Clark & Duncan. She'd told herself all morning that she wasn't going to go, right up until the moment she'd walked out of her office, convinced the letter she'd received was a hoax. *And yet here I am.*

She inhaled, squared her shoulders and marched into the lawyer's office, giving the receptionist her name and taking a seat in the chair closest to the front desk. She was surprised to see that there were other young women also waiting, and one glanced up at her before quickly looking back down to her magazine.

When Georgia had received the letter, stating that her presence was required to collect something left to her family's estate, she'd been somewhat caught off-guard. But as the last remaining family member, she'd decided that it would be foolish not to go, especially when her assistant had assured her that the law firm was legitimate.

What she hadn't been expecting was for her name to be called along with five others soon after she'd arrived, and for them all to be ushered into a conference room together. Her heart began to race as she glanced around at the other young women and she shifted uncomfortably. *They weren't all about to be told they were related, were they?*

Georgia took a sip of water from the glass on the table to soothe her suddenly dry throat as she sat, glancing around the modern office as a well-dressed woman stood and introduced herself as Mia Jones. It wasn't that she was uninterested in what the woman standing before her was saying; she simply needed to be elsewhere, and when her phone vibrated in her bag, she knew there was no way she'd be able to stay for more than fifteen minutes. Georgia picked up the bag and placed it on her lap, hoping she might be able to disguise the sound. But even with her arms pressed onto her bag, it was impossible not to hear the vibrations.

Would it be rude to ask to come back another time?

Georgia started to tap her foot as the man who'd introduced himself as the lawyer cleared his throat and began to speak. She recognised his name as the lawyer who'd sent her the letter and, as distracted as she was, she was also very curious about why she'd been summoned. She looked around at the other women there, still not sure what the connection was. There was the pretty brunette with freckles across her nose who'd glanced at her in the waiting area, another brunette and a very attractive blonde, who had both been quick to smile at her across the table when they'd sat down. One of the other women had dark blonde hair and a big smile, emphasised by a shock of bright red lipstick; and then there was another woman, with hair almost as dark as Georgia's, who kept her head down, her fingers worrying the edge of the table.

It wasn't until she looked away from the last woman, as Mia began to place little wooden boxes that were perhaps twice the size of a ring box on the table in front of them, that Georgia had an inkling as to why she was there. Her eyes were drawn to a name that was familiar to her, a name she hadn't seen in years, tied to a piece of string, which was in turn attached to one of the small boxes. *Cara Montano.* Was that why she was here, to receive the tiny box? She glanced at the other women, wondering if they'd recognised the name, too, but no one else appeared to have seen it, or if they had, it didn't seem to mean anything to them.

Georgia sat a little straighter as the woman named Mia, the woman clearly responsible for summoning them all, continued to place the small boxes out on the table, lining them all up in a row as she spoke.

'As you've just heard, my aunt's name was Hope Berenson, and for many years she ran a private home here in London called Hope's House, for unmarried mothers and their babies. She was very well known for her discretion, as well as her kindness, despite the times.'

Hope's House? Georgia had no idea what that had to do with her, but she couldn't take her eyes from the little box, from the name of her grandmother—Cara Montano—staring back at her as plain as day. Her spine stiffened and she involuntarily dug her fingernails into her palms. If she'd known this was about her grandmother, she may not have come at all.

After all these years of wishing she'd come for me, of wishing she wanted me, her name still has a way of hurting me.

She continued to ignore the vibrations from her phone as she listened to Mia, who was telling them about how she'd found the little boxes beneath the floorboards of her aunt's house, and her decision to reunite them with the descendants of the women they'd been intended for. It was fascinating, and if it had been another day, she would have loved to have heard more about it.

Georgia dragged her eyes from the little handwritten label and looked up at the lawyer as he spoke again.

'When Mia found these, she brought them straight to me, and we went through all the old records in her aunt's office. Hope's documentation was meticulous, and although those records should have stayed private, in this case we chose to search for the names on the boxes, to see if we couldn't reunite them with their rightful owners. I felt an obligation to do what I could.'

'Did you open any of them?' asked one of the women seated across from Georgia.

'No.' Mia's voice lowered, much softer now than when she'd spoken before. 'That's why I asked you all to be here today, so you could each choose whether to open them or not.' Her eyes filled with tears, and Georgia watched as she quickly brushed them away. 'To keep them hidden all these years, they must have held such importance to my aunt, but what I don't under-stand is why she never reunited the boxes with their intended during her lifetime. I felt it was my duty to at least try, and now it's up to each one of you whether they remain sealed or not.'

'What we don't know,' the lawyer said, planting his hands on the table as he slowly rose from his chair, 'is whether there were other boxes that were given out over the years. Either Hope chose not to give these seven out for some reason, or they weren't claimed.'

'Or she decided, again for reasons of her own, that they were better kept hidden,' Mia finished for him. 'In which case, I may have uncovered something that was supposed to stay buried.'

The lawyer cleared his throat as Georgia's phone started to buzz again. She sighed and finally reached for it, seeing that it was Sam, her business partner. *Of course, it was Sam.* She was only going to keep calling if Georgia didn't answer—it was shaping up to be one of the most exciting days of both their careers, which was the reason she hadn't intended on coming to the meeting at all—which in turn meant she needed to go. Georgia listened to the conversation, waiting for a break so she could excuse herself.

'Yes,' the lawyer said. 'But whatever the reason, my duty is to pass them on to their rightful owners, or in this case, to the estates of their rightful owners.'

'And you have no idea what's inside any of them?' another woman asked from across the room.

'No, we don't,' Mia replied.

Georgia stood then, taking her chance and slipping her bag over her shoulder as she cleared her throat. No matter how fascinating this was, she had to go.

'Well, as interesting as all this sounds, I have to get back to work,' she said, hoping she didn't sound as rude as she felt. But when she looked at the other women seated, she realised that was exactly how she came across. 'If you could pass me the box labelled Cara Montano, I'll be on my way. I'm sorry I can't stay longer.'

'Thank you for coming,' the lawyer said, nodding to her. 'If you have any questions, please don't hesitate to contact me. We will be more than happy to discuss the matter with you at a later date.'

Georgia nodded, signing the piece of paper that Mia nudged towards her and rummaging in her bag for her wallet so she could show her identification. Her cheeks heated a little as she felt everyone's eyes on her, but she didn't look up from the task at hand.

'Thank you,' she murmured to Mia, touching her hand to the other woman's arm. 'I can see how much this all means to you. I'm only sorry I can't stay longer.'

Mia gave her a small smile before passing her the box, and

Georgia took it and dropped it into her bag, before crossing the room and pushing open the door as she reached for her phone.

Sam answered in a tone as clipped as Georgia's heels on the tiled floor.

'G, where have you been? I need you! The investor—'

'I'm on my way,' Georgia said as she waved down a taxi and stamped her feet against the cold as it circled round for her. 'I'll be back in the office in twenty minutes. I'll come straight in to see you, I promise.' She ended the call, sliding into the taxi the second it pulled up to the kerb and giving the driver the address.

Georgia rested her head back and took a breath then, trying to process what had just happened. Sometimes she felt as if she hadn't truly rested in years, every minute of every day filled with work and her nights spent answering emails and sitting up in bed until she fell asleep with her laptop, before it started all over again. It was as if she'd been exhausted for as long as she could remember.

She leaned forward and reached into her bag for the little box she'd just been given. Georgia turned it over in her hand, blowing away a little dust that had gathered against the string as she wondered whether she even wanted to know what was inside. She'd spent the past ten years accepting the fact that she didn't have a family, proving to herself and to the world that she could succeed despite everything she'd been through, that she could move past the grief of her teenage years. And yet the idea of opening the box felt almost as if she'd be unravelling the carefully constructed barriers she'd so painstakingly built around herself.

Just open it. Don't overthink it, just open it.

It took her a moment to untie it, her nails catching on the string as she tried to pull the knot. Eventually it gave way and she discarded it along with the tag, lost to the depths of her oversized bag, before pulling back the lid and finding an enormous gemstone resting inside. She gasped, not having expected anything quite so extravagant, especially knowing the decades the box had spent hidden beneath floorboards, gathering dust in an old house. She put the box on her lap and took out the stone, turning it over in her fingers, marvelling at the sheer beauty of it and wondering whether it was a rare gem or possibly even a diamond, its pink hues so radiant they were almost purple as it caught the light. The size was almost impossible to comprehend —it was at least twice the diameter of the largest engagement ring she'd ever seen.

Beneath it was a newspaper clipping, and she reluctantly put the stone back inside the box and took the yellowed paper out. It was in a language she didn't recognise, and so she folded it again, taking out the stone so she could place it all back carefully inside. Her grandmother had been wealthy—that was one of the only things she really knew about her—and she'd held that wealth as tight as could be until her death. But this stone was possibly something her grandmother didn't even know about; or if she had, was it something she'd been searching for throughout her lifetime? Had her grandmother even known she was adopted?

'Miss, this is as close as I'll be able to get you,' her driver said.

Georgia looked up, having lost all track of time as she inspected the little box, realising they were almost at her office. As her phone began to vibrate again, she quickly secured the box and put it back in her bag, nodding her thanks to the driver as she paid him at the same time as answering the call.

'Sam, I'm here. I told you—'

She touched her hand to her bag, her mind still on the stone she'd found as her best friend and business partner positively squealed down the line, her excitement palpable, and told her that they'd been called in for a final meeting within the hour to discuss the proposed buyout of their company. Georgia crossed

the road and hurried towards her building, deciding to grab
them both very strong coffees at the café downstairs before
going up, even though Sam had insisted she come straight to her
office. But despite Georgia's excitement at what they were about
to achieve, for once it wasn't work on her mind as she stood and
waited for their espressos. After all these years, all that time
yearning to have more reminders of her family, to discover more
about the loving parents she'd never stopped mourning, and
now she'd finally been given one.

She only wished that the one reminder she'd now been
given didn't belong to the one family member she'd have
preferred to forget.

2

EIGHTEEN MONTHS LATER

Georgia walked through the auction house, admiring all the jewellery on display. She nudged Sam's shoulder when they passed a necklace dripping with diamonds so large it was almost impossible to believe they were real. She couldn't imagine who would buy these things to wear; or perhaps she was wrong, and they simply went into safes throughout London, investments that were never intended to be worn.

'When you said we needed to treat ourselves, I was thinking of something a little smaller,' Sam whispered.

They both laughed, heads bent together before moving along to an arrangement of designer handbags. After years of doing not much apart from work, Georgia had decided it was time to indulge in a luxury purchase, and it hadn't taken much convincing to get Sam to join her.

'You know, when we started out in my parents' attic, I never would have thought we'd be here,' Sam said with a sigh, as she gestured to a bright pink snakeskin Birkin bag. 'I'm still not ready to part with this much money, but even the fact that we're here looking, that we *could* buy something if we wanted to...'

Georgia linked her arm through Sam's, thinking back to

those early years, remembering the fire inside her, that she wouldn't be held back by the tragedy that had marred her life. The fire in her belly was still there, only now it was more about proving to *herself* that she could achieve everything she set her mind to.

'I know exactly what you mean. I feel like I've been window-shopping for years, and suddenly we can walk into the shop. I actually can't believe it.' Just like she couldn't believe they had no work to do over the weekend, when usually her every waking moment was spent glued to her laptop.

They kept strolling, neither of them stopping for long, until Sam came across a Cartier love bracelet that caught her eye. 'I think this is what I came here for,' she announced, waving one of the assistants over. 'Isn't it gorgeous?'

Georgia nodded, but it wasn't the rose gold bracelet inset with diamonds that she was looking at anymore. In a glass box a few paces away, a pair of earrings was on display. They were each made of an enormous pink stone, which hung from a circle of diamonds and smaller, matching pink stones, and Georgia couldn't take her eyes off them. The pink almost turned purple as the light caught it; a colour she'd only ever seen once before in a stone, and she moved around the box the better to look at them.

'Georgia?' Sam called. 'What do you think?'

Georgia turned her attention back to Sam, walking over to look at the bracelet on her wrist as she held it out to her. 'It's gorgeous. I think you should definitely bid on it.'

'What are you looking at over there?' Sam asked, nodding to the assistant to take off the bracelet. It needed a little tool to unscrew it, and Georgia imagined how claustrophobic she'd feel if she couldn't easily slip something off when she wanted to. 'Just a theory, but I think the items in locked glass boxes with alarms fitted might be out of your budget.'

Georgia laughed, they both did, before the woman helping them cleared her throat.

'You're referring to the pink earrings?' she asked.

Georgia followed the other woman's gaze back to the display. 'Yes. They're absolutely stunning, aren't they? The colour caught my eye as I walked past, but I can tell they're most definitely out of my league.' Even if she had that kind of money, they weren't her style. Georgia wore a small pair of solitaire diamond earrings in her lobes that had belonged to her mother, and a smartwatch on her wrist—she was more practical than extravagant when it came to style.

'The stones are pink tourmalines, and they're unique, given their size,' the assistant said, securing away the bracelet Sam had been trying on before walking towards the glass case.

Georgia followed, admiring the earrings again. Clearly the woman was going to tell her about them, despite her having made it clear that she wasn't buying.

'They belonged to the Italian monarchy, and were held by the royal family since the late 1800s. They were actually worn by the former queen herself shortly before the king's abdication of the throne. When they went into exile, relocating to London, rumour has it that a few pieces were discreetly sold to the wealthiest of collectors in Switzerland and London, with a strict caveat that they weren't to be put on display for at least half a century.'

The other woman moved around the glass box, leaning forward, which made Georgia do the same.

'Many people who remember the family's jewels expect these to be pink sapphires, to match the famous Italian pink sapphire tiara that hasn't been seen since the abdication, but they were made at different times, and from different stones. They were each thought to be prized pieces from the monarch's collection, though.'

'So those people, the collectors who purchased the

jewellery, have had to keep the pieces hidden all these years? After paying what I can only presume was an exorbitant amount of money for them in the first place?' Georgia asked, trying to imagine owning something so breathtaking, yet having it hidden away for so long.

'Correct,' the assistant said. 'These earrings are being offered on the open market for sale for the very first time at our upcoming auction, and many people are curious to know whether other investors will come forward when they see them advertised. It might finally answer the question, once and for all, about how many other pieces there are throughout Europe in the hands of private collectors. Or perhaps the Italian royal family themselves will be impressed with the interest we generate, and decide to offer some of their other pieces for sale, too.'

'Wow, I can see why these caught your eye. It must have been heartbreaking for them to part with so many of their pieces,' Sam said, peering over Georgia's shoulder.

'We understand that they retained most of their collection, unlike other European monarchs who sold everything when they went into exile. But what they did sell would have been worth a small fortune, even back then.'

Georgia smiled as the other woman excused herself to help another customer, dragging her eyes from the earrings.

'Have you found anything to bid on?' Sam asked, as she started to walk away. 'I don't think I can live without that bracelet.'

'No,' Georgia said, sighing as she linked her arm through her friend's. 'I just...' Her voice trailed off.

Sam stopped walking and groaned. 'Do you want the bracelet as well? Was that your pick, too? Trust us to both—'

'No, it's not the bracelet. It was gorgeous on you, Sam. Truly it was.'

Sam's eyebrows lifted in question.

'Those earrings, they just...' Georgia wondered if she was

actually going mad, but if she was going to tell anyone it would be Sam. 'Do you remember that day, when we were in the middle of negotiations to sell the company, and I had to go to that meeting at a lawyer's office? You kept calling me because it was all so exciting and they'd called to ask us in for one final meeting while I was out? It was about eighteen months ago.'

'The meeting about your grandma's estate, or something?' Sam asked as they began walking again. 'Sure, I remember. It's crazy to think it took us so much longer to finish the negotiations and close the sale after that.'

'We were so busy at the time, we were barely leaving the office even to sleep, and I just put it all out of my mind. I honestly haven't thought about it since, there was just too much else going on, until I saw those earrings just now.'

Sam squeezed her arm. She was the only person who knew the truth about Georgia's family, which meant she didn't have to explain why anything to do with her grandmother was traumatic for her. Sam had been there when she'd received the news that her grandmother wasn't coming for her, when her family's lawyer had talked to her about the reality of her situation, of a minor with no immediate family to step in as her legal guardian. Georgia would never forget how protective Sam had been, how fiercely she'd insisted that Georgia would never be alone, that she'd be able to stay with them.

'I don't think I'm seeing the link,' Sam said, when Georgia didn't continue. 'What does that meeting have to do with those earrings?'

'The lawyer gave me a little box that day, which had been intended for my grandmother. It had a stone inside, one that looked the exact same colour as those tourmalines.'

'The same as those earrings?' Sam asked.

'The *very* same as those earrings. I mean, I tucked it away in my bedside drawer and I haven't looked at it since, so I could be wrong, but—'

'Why didn't you tell me all this back then?' Sam asked. 'Was there anything else in the box?'

'A clipping from a newspaper, although I couldn't read it. I think it was in Italian, or maybe French?'

Sam stopped walking again and stepped in front of Georgia. 'Let me get this straight. You received a mysterious little box, with a pink stone and a newspaper clipping inside, and you never thought to tell me about it until now? You truly haven't thought about it since?'

Georgia shrugged. 'I honestly haven't, I just put it out of my mind. Although when you say it like that...'

'Come on. I'm going to register to bid, and then we're going out for drinks and you can tell me all about what actually happened at that meeting. I can't believe you've been sitting on this for so long.'

Georgia knew better than to argue with Sam. They'd been like sisters since she'd moved in with her family as a fifteen-year-old, when her world had turned upside down and left her an orphan, and when Sam wanted something, she stopped at nothing until she got it. Even if it meant coercing Georgia into telling her all her secrets.

'But before we go, can you please just find something you like? I can't be the only one bidding.'

Georgia nodded and steered Sam back towards the handbags, deciding that if she didn't want jewellery, she would at least try to find a vintage designer handbag that might even go up in value as it aged.

That night, Georgia stood in front of her bathroom mirror, pressing night cream into her face and staring back at her reflection. Whenever she talked about her family, even to Sam, it brought back so many memories she'd spent a lifetime trying to forget. But as she looked at herself now, she could see her mother's eyes staring back at her; recognised the dimple on the left side of her cheek as belonging to her father. She brushed her fingers across her cheek as she remembered him, wondering if it was a memory or simply an imprint of a photo in her mind when she tried to recall what he looked like. Usually she kept herself busy, constantly moving and working to avoid thinking about her past or her feelings about what had happened, but now that she had time to breathe, everything seemed to be resurfacing.

She wandered from the bathroom to her bedside table, crouching down and opening the drawer and reaching to the very back where she'd left the little box all that time ago. Her fingers connected with it and she took it out, closing the drawer and sitting on the bed. She tucked her legs beneath the covers and settled back against the pillows as she opened the box, her breath catching in her throat as she looked at the pink stone nestled on top of the newspaper clipping.

It was exquisite; easily as stunning as the stones in the earrings from earlier in the day, and she wondered what the stone could be—a tourmaline, a sapphire, or even a pink diamond. It wasn't for lack of being eye-catching that she'd hidden away the pink stone and the little box. She knew, deep down, that she'd done so because of all the feelings that came with it, not because she hadn't been interested or that the little box of treasure hadn't impressed her at the time. Sometimes, when it came to reminders of her family, it was easier to bury the feelings than confront them.

Georgia placed the box beside her and leaned down to reach under her bed for the Harry Potter bag she always kept there, a bag she'd saved after visiting the studio tour with her parents the year before they died. As a teenager sharing a room with Sam, she'd kept it beneath her bed and often reached for it during the night, needing the reassurance of the past, and now as a woman of thirty with her own flat, she still kept it there.

Even after all these years, Georgia was convinced that her father's jumper still smelt like him, and she took it out now and held it to her nose, inhaling and pressing it to her chest, as if she could imagine he was there simply by holding the garment. She always took everything out in order, and next was a soft cashmere scarf that her mother had worn every day in winter, then photos, her old teddy bear and finally a letter. The letter was always at the bottom, and every time she read it, she wanted to tear it into little pieces; but somehow every single time she packed it back into the bag with everything else.

Because that letter from so long ago had lit a flame in her heart; it had given her the determination to build the company she'd started with Sam when she was barely twenty, had fuelled a desire to rebuild what she'd lost, to create a home and a life that no one could ever take from her. Despite not being wanted by the one family member who could have taken her in, she'd still managed to build a full life.

She read the letter now, her eyes travelling slowly over the words, even though she could have recounted it by heart, she'd pored over it so many times.

To Whom It May Concern,

I do not feel that it would be in the best interests of Georgia to live with me, despite me being her biological grandmother, and I would like to advise that I will not be coming forward to claim guardianship. Her father and I were no longer in contact, and I made it very clear to him when he chose to marry that I did not approve of his choice. As such, I proceeded to disinherit him from my will as I had instructed him I would do so, and I do not intend to change my mind, despite the circumstances. This means that his daughter will not receive anything from the family estate either now or in the event of my death, and it will therefore be necessary for the child to be

*placed into alternative care, or to find a family willing to take
her in. I am, however, prepared to fund her education if necessary, and any application for such assistance is to be made
through my lawyer. I believe that education is the key to any
young person's success, and I can only hope that she chooses to
make the most of her life despite the hardships she now faces.*

*I wish Georgia all the best, although I request that no
further contact be made with me directly.*

Yours, Cara Montano

As a young child, Georgia had received a small gift each
year from her elusive grandmother, always imagining her father
to be the one preventing her from being in their lives. It wasn't
ever the type of present she'd hoped for, with her grandmother
choosing to send her twenty-five pounds in shares each year,
although it was still something. All those years she'd created a
picture of a delightful, white-haired woman taking her out for
ice cream and to the movies after school or at the weekend,
wanting to hear everything about her only granddaughter, had
Georgia's father let her be part of their lives.

But that illusion had been promptly shattered when her
parents had died in a car accident just after her fifteenth birthday, leaving her an orphan with only an estranged grandmother
to turn to. And when the letter had arrived, she'd known that
the grandmother she'd imagined couldn't have been further
from the truth. Her father had never spoken badly of his
mother, but Georgia had grown up knowing that her grandmother hadn't approved of her mum. She remembered him
telling her that his family had wanted him to marry someone
from a more prominent family, that they'd been horrified her
mother had dropped out of university—pregnant—and even
more horrified when her father had told them they were getting
married. And from what she'd discovered from her mother's

affairs after the tragedy, it had been her who'd stopped Georgia's grandmother from seeing her. Her mother had written to her to say that she either accepted them as a family and became a proper part of their lives, or she stayed away, and it seemed Georgia's grandmother had chosen the latter.

Georgia blinked away tears, tears that came every time she read the letter, no matter how hard she tried to fight them, and folded the paper back into the small square she'd found it in. She took a deep breath, about to put it in the bag before changing her mind.

She'd kept it to prove her grandmother wrong, to show her that she had succeeded without her: without her love, without her compassion, and certainly without her money. She'd founded a business that had been bought out by one of the biggest cosmetics companies in the world, but even that still didn't seem enough. *Now I know how you felt, Dad. Nothing you did could ever live up to her expectations, or the expectations you had for yourself.* Her grandmother had passed away a few years earlier, something Georgia only knew about after receiving an email from a lawyer advising her of the fact, but somehow she still had the power to hurt her.

Georgia scrunched the paper in her palm and threw it to the floor, not sure whether she'd retrieve it in the morning or scoop it up with the rubbish. She held the scarf, her teddy, and then the jumper one last time before carefully placing them all in the bag, and turned her attention back to the stone.

Tomorrow she would take it to the auction house and see if they could value it and put it up for sale. Her grandmother hadn't wanted her, so she didn't want the jewel, it was as simple as that. And once she'd had the stone appraised, she would find someone to translate the newspaper clipping, just in case it contained important family information that had a link to her father, and then she could forget all about the meeting she'd had and her grandmother's potentially illegitimate past.

Georgia put everything back in the box and placed it on her bedside table, turning off her lamp and snuggling down under the covers.

It was the right decision, getting rid of the stone, just as it was the right thing to do to get rid of the letter after all these years. She'd felt melancholy all day thinking about the grandmother she'd never even met, and the best thing for her was to dispose of anything that made her feel sad or unworthy. She'd worked too hard to put her past behind her to let it catch up with her now.

Georgia laughed to herself as she shut her eyes. It was probably a worthless fake anyway, nothing like the tourmalines she hadn't been able to keep her eyes off at the auction house. After a life of being miserable with money, there was no way her grandmother could have left behind a valuable jewel for her granddaughter to claim. Or was there?

3

ITALY, JUNE 1951

Delphine was surprised to see her husband, Giovanni, taking breakfast with the children when she came downstairs. Often, she took her breakfast in bed, but today she'd wanted to come down and sit with the children before they left for school. Her husband had been absent for almost two weeks, and although it still astounded her that he could disappear for so long, she was starting to become used to it.

'Good morning,' she said, gliding past the children and pressing a kiss to first her son's head, and then her daughter's as she did so. She looked to her husband, who gave her a polite nod and a smile. 'It's lovely to have you back, Giovanni. Did you arrive home late last night?'

'Indeed, I did,' he replied, without looking up again.

Early in their marriage she'd wanted to take the paper from his hands and beat him about the head with it each morning, so desperate was she to get more than a simple nod from him when it was just the two of them. She'd wanted him to look at her, to talk to her, to have a lively conversation to start the day, to give her something to look forward to each morning. It hadn't been any better when he came home for dinner at night— he would kiss her cheek when he returned for the day or sometimes the top of her head in the same way she now greeted her children, and they would eat dinner in a silence that she would not have described as companionable.

When she'd given up on hoping that he would love her, Delphine had wondered if any reaction would be better than the bland way he greeted her each day. Once she'd imagined throwing her coffee cup at his head to see if he was at least capable of anger if he wasn't capable of love. But, of course, she wasn't that childish. Or stupid. She was painfully aware that some husbands had fiery tempers that left their wives with black eyes and hidden bruises. But she also knew that many more husbands loved their wives in ways that hers simply wasn't interested in. He hadn't visited her bedroom since they'd conceived Isabella, their youngest child, and she'd long ago given up hope that he ever would again.

'How is everyone this morning?' Delphine asked brightly, taking her seat and looking first to her son, Tommaso, who was seated across from her.

His almost black hair was damp and brushed back from his face, curling slightly behind his ears, so like his father in looks although nothing like him in temperament. Her darling, sensitive boy.

'I am well, Mama,' he said with a smile.

She nodded and turned to her daughter, who was eating the same milk with bread as her brother. It irritated her husband that the children still ate what he considered either baby's food or a peasant's meal, depending on the day, but she was of the mind to let them eat whatever brought them joy.

'Isabella?' she asked her daughter.

'I don't want to go to school,' her daughter said, but with a smile so sweet that Delphine found it impossible to scold her.

'You will have a new school to go to soon,' Giovanni announced, folding his paper and smiling over at them all.

Delphine's blood ran cold. She'd been desperate for him to speak to them for so long, and now that he finally had, she wished he'd stayed silent.

'Gio,' she said, with a tight, forced smile. 'Is that not something we should discuss further in private?' *Why would he have arranged a change of school for them? They were both settled and happy.*

'Not at all,' he said, impatiently holding his cup in the air as one of their maids hurried over with a pot of fresh coffee. 'It has already been decided. We are to leave at the end of the month on a new adventure.'

'An adventure to where, Papa?' Isabella asked, her eyes wide as she positively beamed at her father.

Giovanni might have been an unloving husband, but he'd certainly managed to make his daughter adore his attention. When he was there, Isabella was the kind of little girl who would do anything to win her father's affections.

'To Geneva,' he said. 'We are going to expand our business, and Switzerland is the perfect place for our family to be based.'

But I don't want to move. I've come to love Italy. It's my home now.

'Could the children and I not stay here?' Delphine asked. 'You travel so much anyway, and you could—'

'We are moving to Geneva,' he said, putting down his cup with more force than she'd heard before, making the porcelain saucer rattle.

Delphine looked to her son, who was much quieter and more easily upset than Isabella. He would hate the change, just as Delphine would. Their lives were in Italy; their friends, their house, their schools... she felt her hands begin to shake and quickly clasped them before anyone noticed.

'I will be spending much of my time in London from now on, and Geneva will be a convenient location for us to reside in.

Not to mention your family has many useful business acquaintances there, Delphine.'

She lowered her gaze, knowing precisely what he was trying to tell her. They'd married for a reason, their families benefitting from their union, and he was about to make use of the connection. Delphine also knew that it wasn't her place to question his decision; he was head of the family and whatever he decided was law. If his wife didn't like it? She doubted he'd so much as give it a second thought.

'Papa, when do we leave? Can I say goodbye to my friends?'

'Of course, Isabella,' Giovanni said. 'You and Tommaso can even have a party to say goodbye to your friends, right here at the house. Would you like that?'

'Yes, Papa,' they both said in unison, although Delphine saw the way Tommaso glanced at her, could see the creases in his face echoing the way she felt, her stomach turning at the thought of leaving their beautiful home behind. Of leaving the life she'd created for herself and her family.

When he rose to leave, Delphine looked up and caught Giovanni's eye, saw the set of his jaw and the way he nodded to her a little more stiffly than she'd noticed before. Was she imagining it, or was there something different about him today? Was there something he wasn't telling her? A reason why he wanted to uproot his family from the only home they'd ever known? They might not be intimate, but she'd spent long enough studying him to know when something was wrong.

'Gio!' she called out, hurriedly pushing back her chair and running after her husband. 'Please wait!'

He turned, running his hands down his lapel as if to smooth away creases. Delphine knew there would be none though, because she'd had the suit pressed for him only days earlier, had inspected it and made certain it was perfect before one of the maids had taken it to his dressing room.

'Gio, may I ask if there's another reason that we're

moving?' she said, hesitantly reaching for him, placing her hand over his arm. 'If it's money, if something has happened that you don't want to tell me, we can always ask my parents—'

'We are moving because I have decided we're moving,' he said, his tone curt. 'I don't expect you to understand the intricacies of business, as you don't expect me to understand how to run a household. And you are never, *ever* to mention our finances again. Is that clear?'

She withdrew her hand, as if she'd been slapped.

'Is that all?' he asked.

'I, I...' She took a deep breath, looking into her husband's eyes and wishing she saw something, *anything* reflected there other than impatience at being stopped in the hallway. 'What arrangements must I make?' she asked, lowering her voice. 'When will we leave?'

'I will be leaving in a fortnight,' he said. 'You and the children can enjoy the start of summer and join me after that.'

Delphine cleared her throat, not certain what she hoped the answer would be to her next question. 'You will be living with us, won't you, Gio? You won't leave us entirely on our own?'

He smiled and chastely kissed her forehead, before patting her shoulder. 'Of course, I'll be living with you. The children are very important to me.'

His words stung as she watched him leave the house, the door closing with a heavy thud behind him.

'Mama?' She turned and saw her son standing there, his eyes filled with unshed tears. 'Can't we stay? Can you change Papa's mind? I don't want to go.'

She opened her arms and held Tommaso in a long, warm hug. He was eight years old, but she'd always said it was as if he'd walked the earth before. He was her sensitive child, the one who worried about everything and anything, and she knew how hard he would find leaving Italy behind. He didn't even like the cover on his bed being changed to a different colour, let alone the home he lived in.

'When your father makes his mind up, there is little I can do to stop him.'

'But will you try?'

Delphine didn't tell him that she already had, that she didn't want to go any more than he did. 'Yes, my love, I will try. But if we are to leave Italy for Geneva?' She smiled and kissed his cheek. 'We will find a wonderful home and meet new friends. It will be every bit as wonderful as our home in Italy, I promise. And we have family there, too.'

'Mama, Mama!' came an excited call, before little Isabella came running down the hallway, her long plait bouncing behind her.

Delphine reluctantly let go of her son and bent to fold her daughter against her in a warm hug. Isabella's eyes were bright when she held her at arm's length, her smile contagious.

'Mama, when are we travelling? When can we go on our adventure?'

'Soon, darling,' she said, smoothing her daughter's hair as Isabella pulled away. 'But for now, you need to get ready for school.' She turned to Tommaso and gave him a gentle smile. 'Both of you. You let me worry about when we might be moving, and what the arrangements are.'

It wouldn't have been an understatement to tell the children that she would be doing enough worrying for the three of them combined.

Delphine watched them go; her heartstrings pulled taut as she caught her breath.

'Coffee, Signora?'

She straightened her shoulders and smiled when one of their maids spoke to her. 'I shall have coffee and a *cornetto*. Please have them sent up to my room.'

Delphine walked up the stairs, grateful that the children

were now on their way to school, her husband gone for the day, and her house filled only with servants who would move quietly about until their jobs were done.

Within minutes, one of them knocked and entered her room, placing a tray beside her bed.

'Will that be all, Signora?'

Delphine studied the younger woman, the way her lower lip trembled, and she couldn't tell whether it was from nerves or whether she was trying to stop herself from smirking. Was she terrified of her mistress, or was it something else? Or was she simply overthinking everything today?

'I require my stationery,' she said, looking the young maid up and down and trying to decipher her expression. 'Is something the matter?'

'No, Signora,' she said, her voice barely a whisper as she bowed her head.

'Send Signora Martina to me when she arrives,' Delphine demanded. 'Other than that, I'm not to be disturbed for the rest of the day.'

She would write a letter to her sister and tell her that she would be travelling home to Switzerland. And as much as she hated the way Giovanni had told them about the move, she felt a flutter of hope deep in her stomach.

Perhaps a change is just what we need.

4

PRESENT DAY

Georgia had her bag tucked tight to her shoulder when she walked back into Christie's auction house the following day. She knew it was terrible timing—she expected they would be busy preparing for that evening's auction—but she hadn't been able to wait.

I'm probably wasting my time. I'm probably wasting everyone's time even thinking this is worth something. But despite her thoughts, she found that she kept walking until she found someone who could help her. At the very least, she'd discover what the gem was and whether it was worth selling or not. Either way, she'd decided she no longer wanted it in her possession.

'Excuse me,' Georgia said, clearing her throat. 'I'm hoping to speak to someone about having a stone appraised.'

The attendant smiled. 'We usually don't have time for walk-ins, our business is predominantly by appointment only, but'— she smiled—'what is it you would like appraised? If you're wanting us to sell it on your behalf, you've missed the deadline for our upcoming jewellery auction...'

Her voice trailed off as if she was almost indifferent, but

Georgia reached into her bag anyway, taking out the little box
and opening it.

'I thought it might be a tourmaline,' Georgia said, as she
held the stone in her palm. 'I saw the display you had yesterday,
and I thought—'

'Please come with me,' the woman said, her voice suddenly
hushed. 'Right this way.'

Georgia followed, realising that she'd been prioritised given
the size of the stone. There was no other way to explain the
sudden interest.

'I'm happy to leave it here, or to pay whatever's required for
an appraisal, but I thought—'

'I'm sorry, what was your name?' the woman asked, waving
an older man over.

'Georgia,' she said. 'Georgia Montano.'

'Ms Montano,' she said, gesturing to the man who'd
appeared. 'I'd like you to meet Thomas Kent. He's our most
experienced appraiser of rare and antique jewellery.'

'How can I be of assistance, Ms Montano?' he asked,
looking puzzled as to why he'd been called over with such
urgency in the first place.

The woman backed away, leaving Georgia with Thomas. 'I
was just explaining that I have this stone in my possession,
something that has been passed down to me from a grandpar
ent. After viewing your collection yesterday, I thought it was
worth bringing it here for an appraisal.'

She placed the gem on her palm again and Thomas took a
soft cotton glove from his pocket, putting it on before reaching
out.

'May I?'

Georgia passed the stone to him, watching as he turned it
back and forth in his fingers.

'This is a large stone, Ms Montano. Do you know the
authenticity of it?'

'I know nothing of its history or even what type of stone it might be.' She cleared her throat. 'If it's not of any value, I understand you won't want to spend time appraising it, but if it is valuable then I'd very much like to entrust you with its sale.'

He kept hold of it, turning it into the light. Georgia felt a pang of regret then, as if perhaps she should have simply asked for a valuation and then had it reset into a piece of jewellery she could wear herself. But she pushed those thoughts away as she saw the furrow of the man's brow, imagining that he was perhaps trying to establish whether it was worthless or not.

'I suggest you come with me and fill out some paperwork,' he said. 'We have a busy few days ahead with the auction tonight, but I'll complete a report just as soon as I can, and perhaps we could aim to include it in our next catalogue?'

Georgia nodded, surprised he was offering to appraise it so promptly. 'Thank you. I appreciate your assistance.'

She followed him to an office and filled out her details, watching as he photographed the stone and made her sign the form beside its size and weight, before telling her she could leave.

Georgia looked at it one last time, and as she walked away, she reached into her bag for the little box that was now empty, rattling around in her too-big bag, wondering if perhaps the stone was more valuable than she'd expected.

It was only an hour later, while she was in a café, when Georgia's phone rang. She didn't recognise the number, but answered it anyway.

'Ms Montano, it's Thomas Kent here from Christie's.'

She sighed. He was no doubt calling to tell her that the stone was made of glass. 'I'm so sorry if you spent time on the stone only to discover that—'

'Ms Montano, are you nearby? I was hoping we might be able to discuss this in person.'

'O-*kay*,' she said slowly, wondering why he'd want to see her again. 'You're certain you can't just tell me over the phone?'

'It would be best if you could come back.'

She found herself nodding, even though he couldn't see her. 'Sure. No problem at all. I'll be back within the hour.'

Georgia ended the call, still staring at her phone, lost in thought when her coffee order was called out. Thankfully, she'd ordered it to go.

It took her almost forty minutes to get back to Christie's, and when she stepped through the door she knew something had changed. The attendant who'd spoken to her earlier with such disinterest now greeted her by name and ushered her to the back of the building, and to say that Thomas Kent was pleased to see her would have been an understatement.

'Ah, Ms Montano, thank you for making the trip back.'

'Georgia, please,' she said. 'There's no need for such formality.' She smiled and followed him into a room.

There was no sign of the pink stone, until a security guard entered and placed a secure box on the table. Georgia watched in surprise as the guard left, and only once they had the room to themselves did Thomas press numbers into the keypad and open it. It was even more of a shock to see the now-familiar stone sitting there, carefully placed on what looked like a small black cushion.

Georgia looked up and into the older man's bright blue eyes, which were positively twinkling as he gazed back at her.

'I have a feeling the stone isn't worthless,' she murmured as he leaned forward, putting on the white cotton glove she'd seen him use before as he carefully picked it up.

'Georgia, I'd very much like to know how you came to be in possession of this item.'

She laughed, but it was a nervous laugh that sounded too

high-pitched to belong to her. Georgia glanced over her shoulder, suddenly feeling uncomfortable and not entirely sure why.

'Well, two years ago I was summoned to a lawyer's office,' she began, deciding that she may as well tell this man the entire story, since he seemed so enthusiastic. 'It transpired that my paternal grandmother was adopted, from a place for unwed mothers and unwanted babies called Hope's House, here in London.'

'I remember hearing about that place,' he said. 'I think there was something in the newspaper about the house being demolished and the proceeds of the sale being left to a charity?'

Georgia made a mental note to search for the article. 'I only know what I discovered that day, unfortunately,' she said. 'But to cut a long story short, some of the women who gave birth there left something behind. In case their child was ever to come looking for them, I suppose.'

Thomas was listening to her every word, leaning forward as if eager to hear the rest of the story. 'You're telling me that this was what was left behind? For your paternal grandmother?'

Georgia nodded. 'Yes. I was given a small wooden box with my grandmother's name tied to it, and the stone was one of two things inside.'

'You don't happen to have this box with you, by chance?' he asked, as he set the stone back down. 'I would very much like to see it.'

Georgia reached into her bag and took it out, passing it to him and watching as he turned it over in his hands and eventually opened it.

'May I?' Thomas asked, his fingers hovering over the newspaper clipping.

'Of course. I can't read it, but—'

'Italian,' he said, almost triumphantly. 'This is a clipping from an Italian newspaper.' He looked up, his eyes positively shining now. 'I can't believe it. It's all quite extraordinary.'

'Extraordinary?' she repeated. Extraordinary because the paper was Italian? 'I'm not entirely sure I follow.'

'Ms Montano, it's obvious that you have absolutely no idea just what you're in possession of.'

She waited, eyebrows arched as he set the box down and picked up the stone again, holding it out towards her.

'I believe that this stone is more than just valuable,' he said, as he placed it in her palm. 'If I'm right, I believe that you could be the custodian of the missing royal pink sapphire.'

'*Missing*?' she asked. *Royal*?

He gestured for her to stand and pointed to the glass box that had so entranced her the day before, his hand gently closing over her shoulder as they both looked through the window. 'You've seen the pink tourmaline earrings we have displayed? You understand the history of them?'

'They belonged to the Italian monarchy,' she whispered, starting to realise what he was trying to tell her, her palm closing over the stone in her hand. 'They were in the royal family for decades.' *There was a tiara. That's what the lady told me yesterday. There was a tiara made of sapphires that looked almost identical to the tourmalines.*

'One of the greatest mysteries in the world of rare and historically important jewellery is why the famous sapphire tiara, purchased by a private collector in the early 1950s, is missing one of its sapphires.'

'You think,' Georgia said as she slowly opened her palm, staring down at the pink stone as it winked to her beneath the bright lights, 'that I am in possession of it?'

'I don't just think, Ms Montano,' he said, 'I am almost certain of it.'

She met his gaze, his as triumphant as hers was shocked. 'What do I do with it then? If it belongs with the tiara, does that mean I could be holding stolen property? I—'

'There was a reason your grandmother was given this

sapphire, and whatever that reason was, I would guess it had absolutely nothing to do with theft,' he said. 'But you are indeed the owner of something very rare, and with a value that it is almost impossible to ascertain. To the right collector...'

'We're talking in the thousands?'

He cleared his throat. 'My dear, I'd say we're in the realm of many, many tens of thousands.'

Georgia laughed. She couldn't help it. She'd held something of great value for more than a year, and hadn't even known it!

'What do you suggest I do with it?' she asked. 'Is it something that should be auctioned, or—' *Or what? Offered to a museum? Reunited with the tiara it was taken from?*

'While I was awaiting your return, I did some research, because I recalled information crossing my desk a few years ago.'

Georgia waited, not sure what to do with the sapphire—whether to keep hold of it in her palm or return it to its little wooden box.

'There was a collector putting out feelers, following on from the work of perhaps his father or grandfather, in his search for the missing sapphire. If you bear with me a few minutes, I'll find his information for you.'

'You think I should contact him?' Georgia asked. 'With the intent of selling it to this collector?'

Thomas paused what he was doing, looked up and, studying her intently, glasses perched on the tip of his nose, said, 'I think it would be a very good starting point, and he may be the only person able to confirm its authenticity.'

'What about the newspaper clipping? You mentioned it was in Italian. Are you fluent in the language?'

'Unfortunately, not fluent enough to translate it, but I would keep both the clipping and the sapphire safe and in your possession. Perhaps contact an Italian language school or even the Italian Embassy to see if someone could assist you with the translation, and then I might suggest a genealogist as well, to help you understand how your family is connected to the stone. Who knows? It could be the clue that enables you to piece everything together.'

The trouble was that she had no idea what she was piecing together. She'd grown up without knowing her grandmother, had very little in the way of family mementos or records, and there was no one she could even turn to, to ask about the past, no matter how badly she wished otherwise.

'Aha! Here it is. The man you're looking for is a Luca Kaufmann,' he said, scribbling on a piece of paper and passing it to Georgia.

'He's not in Italy?' she said, surprised as she looked over the address and saw he was in Geneva.

'Most of the pieces that were sold were to collectors in other European countries, as was the case with the fall of many European monarchies over the years,' he said. 'If you have the resources to travel to Switzerland, then that's where I would begin.'

Georgia swallowed. 'Well, it appears I have no excuse not to contact this'—she reread the name—'Luca Kaufmann.'

'Good luck, my dear. And please, do let me know what transpires.' He beamed at her as she placed the sapphire back in the little box, deciding to keep hold of it rather than put it in her bag, now that she knew how valuable it was. 'I have a feeling you might just be on the cusp of solving a mystery more than half a century in the making.'

5

ITALY, JUNE 1951

Delphine sat at her desk, her back straight as the woman she'd trusted her entire married life stood across the room, facing her. If anyone was prepared to tell her the truth, it would be her lady's maid, Martina, the one person in her household who felt more family member than staff. The longer she'd waited for her to arrive, the more determined she'd become to ask her questions that had for some time been burning inside of her. It was time for her to understand precisely whom she was married to.

'Please, come and sit,' Delphine said. 'We've known each other long enough to forego formality.'

'Signora—'

'Delphine,' she insisted. 'I'm certain you've already heard that my family is moving, no doubt it's all the staff can talk about, so if this is to be our last month together, it's time you called me Delphine.'

Martina looked uncomfortable, which wasn't what Delphine wanted at all, but she was starting to see that perhaps there were questions she should have asked many months, even years, before this.

'You've heard the rumours of our impending departure?' she asked.

Martina nodded. 'I have. I don't know what I'll do without you, Signora, I mean, *Delphine*. It's been such a pleasure working for you all these years.'

Delphine nodded, feeling the familiar prickle of tears but refusing to acknowledge them. Martina had been there when she'd first moved into the house, a new bride who'd been alone and frightened, with a husband who rarely came home. Martina had comforted her when she'd cried for her family, counselled her about how to run the household with a firmer hand than came naturally to her, and had been the first to know when she was expecting. To say she trusted her would have been an understatement.

'I have a very sensitive question to ask you, Martina, and I want you to answer me truthfully, no matter how difficult the response might be,' she said. 'I also want you to know that I understand why you might have kept certain things from me.'

She noticed the other woman positively wringing her hands, but Delphine knew there was no point in stopping, not now she'd decided to come out and ask her.

'Is there anything I should know about my husband?' she asked, her voice low and breathy, the question almost impossible to expel. 'I've had a feeling for some time, I just... and one of the maids before...' Delphine stopped and pressed her fingers to her temples. Perhaps she was going mad. Perhaps she was imagining things. Perhaps... 'I feel as if there are things I should know, things that perhaps everyone else in this household knows, except me.'

Martina lowered her voice. 'You are asking whether your husband has been unfaithful to your marriage?'

Delphine's intake of breath was sharp. 'Yes, Martina, that is precisely what I'm asking. I would like to know if there are any rumours you're aware of, any particular reason that he would be so insistent that we move away. Are you personally aware of any... *indiscretions?*'

Martina held her gaze, woman to woman, and Delphine knew she was finally going to hear the truth. 'Signor Giovanni has always been very respectful to all members of your household, but I am aware of some talk that he may have a mistress, or mistresses, in London.'

'In London?' Delphine's heart ached. She'd always known he didn't love her in the way a husband was supposed to love a wife, but she hadn't thought he would hurt her in such a way. She closed her eyes for a second, realising now why the maid had looked at her sideways earlier, horrified that her staff were talking about her, gossiping about the poor lady of the house as her husband gallivanted about.

She straightened her shoulders, refusing to appear embarrassed. 'And this is the first time you've heard of such a rumour, or is this simply the latest...' She paused, finding the word hard to utter. '*Infidelity?*'

'Signora, your husband is known to be a very different man at home to the man he is, well, when he's away.'

'You're telling me that this isn't the first time?' Delphine asked. 'That I am the last to know that my husband has been unfaithful throughout our marriage?' How had she been so naive as to not see what he was doing? 'You're saying that he has had mistresses before?'

Martina looked away, as if this last part was perhaps the hardest to break. 'Yes, Signora. I understand that your husband—'

Delphine held up her hand, feeling she could not stomach any more information. 'Thank you for your honesty, Martina. I won't be needing to hear any more, I think that's quite enough for one day.' This time the tears were impossible to fight, and they escaped and began to slip furiously down her cheeks.

Martina stood and came closer, holding her as a mother

would a child, as Delphine cried for what she'd lost, but what she'd known in her heart was the truth. They had married for convenience and nothing more, and despite her best efforts to be a doting and attractive wife, his feelings had never developed into anything deeper despite all the years they'd been together.

'Any man would be lucky to have you as his wife, Delphine,' Martina whispered as she rubbed her back. 'It's always been a mystery to me why that man doesn't love you in the way...'

'That a husband should?' Delphine asked, looking up at her, blinking through her tears. 'Is that what you were going to say?'

Martina nodded, and Delphine wondered what it was that she didn't have, what it was that made her the desired wife to bear his children, but not to fall in love with. Why he would go to another woman's bed, and not the bed of his young wife who sat up night after night waiting for him, hoping that he'd finally choose to love her. Was she not pretty enough? Was there something about her that repulsed him? Something she didn't know that she was supposed to do?

'Would you come with us?' Delphine asked as she straightened, quickly wiping her cheeks and clearing her throat. 'Is there any way I could persuade you to come to Geneva, even if only to settle us into the new house? It would mean the world to me, and to the children.'

'It would be my pleasure,' Martina said, patting her shoulder as she stepped back. 'Since my Salvatore passed away, I'm happy with any excuse to keep busy, and I've always fancied travelling outside of Italy. Until my children have children of their own, I'd very much like to stay with you and your family.'

Delphine studied her kind, loyal lady-in-waiting, the way her face had changed when she spoke of her late husband. Clearly theirs had been a very different marriage to the one Delphine had been bartered into.

'Martina, may I ask you a personal question?'

Martina nodded.

'Throughout your marriage, did you and your husband share a bed? Did he come to you, well, *willingly*?' Delphine's cheeks burned, but she was simply a married woman asking another woman's advice.

'Yes, Signora. I could not have imagined not sharing a bed with my Salvatore.'

Delphine inhaled as she thought of the way she'd waited for so many weeks and months after Isabella's birth for her husband to come to her quarters again. Six years later, and she was still waiting. *It appears that I should not bother waiting any longer.*

'Do you think it is strange that my husband does not, that he—'

'I think your husband has rocks in his head when it comes to his stunning young bride, Signora, and I have thought that for a very long time. But then I think that there are husbands throughout the country who probably behave in the same way, who don't realise how fortunate they are for the wife at home waiting for them.'

'So, I am not alone, that is what you're trying to tell me? That my loneliness is not unusual?'

'*Sì.*'

'Thank you for your honesty, Martina. I know I don't have to ask, but if we could keep what has been discussed between us...'

She received a nod and a kindly smile in response.

Martina left her then, and Delphine resumed writing the letter she'd started to her sister. It seemed that the only thing she had to count on in this world was the love of her children, and the support of the women closest to her.

There's nothing to be embarrassed about, she told herself. *Plenty of Italian men have mistresses. It's perfectly normal.*

But as her hand began to shake, making it almost impossible to hold her gold-nibbed pen, she knew that nothing about her husband taking up with another woman, or *women*, was normal, at least not to her. In fact, the very thought made her want to be sick right there at the priceless antique desk he'd bought for her as a wedding present. She hadn't been *in love* with him for a very long time, but until now, she'd thought they were, at the very least, faithful to their wedding vows.

Delphine drummed her fingers against the wooden desktop. She would never dare to confront him, but she wasn't going to give up on her marriage without a fight.

6

PRESENT DAY

Georgia was nothing if not exceptionally ambitious when it came to her work. At age seventeen, she'd realised she had a knack for business and writing software, and had a highly paid part-time job with a tech firm that meant she was earning more than someone twice her age while she was still studying. She'd left university with a business plan, refusing to accept that there was a problem she couldn't solve; lost every penny with a terrible tech start-up that had failed miserably within its first year. But by the day before her twenty-seventh birthday she'd made the 'Forbes 30 Under 30 Europe' list, sitting one place higher than her best friend and co-founder, Sam. Their idea to create a company within the beauty space, with its patented colour-match technology and their make-up range, had grown faster than either of them had expected, and her second attempt at launching a company had most definitely *not* been a failure. They'd sold the company just after their thirtieth birthdays.

It had been a decade of extreme ups and downs, and she'd realised along the way that she'd been as determined to prove herself despite her past as she was to do well for Sam's parents—to prove to them that they'd been right to take her in and give her a chance, to have given her a home and an education that she might not have otherwise received.

But now, having sold the business and with plenty of time on her hands, she was ready to launch herself into full investigative mode when it came to her great-grandmother and the mysterious sapphire. Part of her was still convinced it was all a hoax, but still, she was too intrigued not to find out more now.

She clicked on the link to an article about Hope's House, reading with interest how the property had been left to a women's refuge charity. *Would it be strange if I contacted the lawyer or even Hope's niece, Mia, given it's been two years since the meeting at the lawyer's office?* Georgia sighed as she scrolled through a few other articles, until an obituary about Hope caught her eye.

If history has told us anything, it's that unwed mothers were the subject of much shame, regardless of their situation. Wealthy families often had the means to hide such a scandal, but poorer girls and women were usually sent to convents, where they were treated as second-class citizens. But Hope Berenson was different. She treated every woman in her care with kindness and compassion, regardless of whether they had the money to pay for her services or not, finding suitable adoptive homes for almost every baby born at her dedicated residence, Hope's House.

She was highly skilled at birthing babies, calling on the services of a kind-hearted doctor only in the most difficult of cases. Despite not opening her doors for many years, she will be dearly missed, and remembered forever for her service to the community.

Georgia hadn't really given it all that much consideration, but reading the article made her think about what her great-grandmother must have endured. To have been pregnant back then... She thought it over, counting backwards and estimating that it must have been in the 1950s when her grandmother was born. It would have been a horrible time to be pregnant—post-war and within a generation that looked down on unwed mothers—and given the circumstances, her great-grandmother must have been young and unmarried. Had she come from a poor family, or one that had refused to accept that she was pregnant? Her father had told her that one of the reasons he didn't speak to his mother, other than the fact that she'd been so rude and disrespectful towards Georgia's mother, was because she'd wanted them to have Georgia adopted when she was born. Her father had recounted a very traditional upbringing to her, formed around a strict set of rules and expectations, which made her think that her grandmother most likely had no idea that she was adopted herself.

Georgia closed her browser and looked up her emails, going back to find one from the lawyer that she'd received after the meeting where she'd been given the stone. It had confirmed receipt of the box, and included their details in case she needed to make contact with anyone at the firm. Unfortunately, it didn't have details for Mia, who was the person she really wanted to talk to, but she decided to email the lawyer anyway and see if perhaps he might release at least Mia's phone number. After so long telling herself she didn't care about that side of her family, perhaps she did want to know more about where she came from. *And it might even give me some answers about why my grandmother was the way she was right up to her death.*

She eventually closed her laptop and sat back, pausing before lifting the lid again. Patience wasn't her virtue, and she decided to just google Mia and see if she could find her that way instead of waiting to hear back from the lawyer. When she finally found her on Facebook she sent her a message, before shutting her laptop again and walking away from it. All she could do now was wait.

.   .   .

It had only taken a few hours for Mia to reply to Georgia's message, but it wasn't until three days later on Saturday that she'd been able to meet. She'd suggested they meet that afternoon at Dalloway Terrace, and Georgia was on her way to the restaurant now. Part of her was wondering if she'd actually gone mad, but she wasn't going to stand Mia up, so she was committed to going.

She touched her palm to her bag as she stepped through the door, subconsciously checking to make sure the little box was still there. Since she was meeting Mia, she'd thought she should bring it with her, to show her what was inside, just in case she knew more about what had been left behind than she'd let on at the lawyer's office.

Georgia was early, and she was shown to an alfresco table out the back with a wall of fresh flowers and a black and white awning above. It was perhaps the quaintest setting she'd ever seen, and as she gazed around and admired it, taking a quick video to send to Sam, two women approached her table.

'Georgia?'

She dropped her phone back in her bag and half rose, not sure whether to hug Mia or stay seated. Mia made the decision easy, embracing her without hesitation.

'Thank you so much for agreeing to meet with me,' Georgia said, taking her seat as Mia gestured to the heavily pregnant woman beside her.

'This is Ella,' Mia said. 'I hope you don't mind, but I thought two heads might be better than one to help solve your mystery.'

'Lovely to meet you, Ella, and I don't mind at all.' Georgia caught her bottom lip beneath her top teeth. 'You look familiar, have we met?'

'At the lawyer's office,' Ella said. 'We were seated close to each other.'

'You were there to receive a box?'

'I was.'

'Well, before we order I'd like to offer you both an apology,' Georgia said, looking between them. 'I want you to know that I'm not usually so rude, and I've felt terrible for the way I just upped and left that day. It wasn't my intention to appear so uninterested.'

Mia nodded and Ella just smiled back at her.

'I imagine you had somewhere else to be,' Ella said. 'And if I'm completely honest, I was convinced it was all a scam that day anyway.'

'Did your clues make sense to you at all? I mean, what were you able to glean from what was in your little box?'

Ella laughed and exchanged glances with Mia. 'I think we need to order drinks first, because we have a lot to unpack!'

Mia rose. 'Let me order while you two get acquainted. Wine for us, and a mocktail for you, Ella?'

Georgia nodded as Ella said yes, and as soon as Mia had gone, Georgia turned to Ella, eager to hear more.

'Did you start searching for your connection right away? Tell me what you discovered?' Georgia asked.

'I discovered a grandmother living on the most beautiful island in Greece,' Ella said, her eyes sparkling, 'and because of the clues I crossed paths with my new husband. My box contained an old photo and a folded sheet of music.'

Georgia laughed when Ella touched her stomach, having immediately warmed to her.

'And this little peanut on the way is all thanks to that little box, too. It completely changed my life.'

Mia returned then, and Georgia considered them both before reaching into her bag. 'Can I show you what was in my box?'

'Yes!' both women replied.

'I didn't give it much thought at the time, I had so many other things happening in my life and my connection to my family is complicated, but this past week I took the box out. It's consumed me ever since.'

She opened it, and Ella and Mia both gasped when they saw the stone.

'Oh my gosh,' Mia whispered.

'It's incredible,' Ella said.

'There was also an Italian newspaper clipping, but I haven't found anyone to translate it yet.'

'May I?' Mia reached for the stone and carefully picked it up, turning it over in her hand as the sun caught the colour. 'It's absolutely stunning.'

'I just, I suppose I just want to know if I'm putting my energy into what will end up being a wild goose chase. It doesn't seem real to me, the idea that something like this was hidden all that time, for decades, just waiting to be found.'

'Georgia, I felt exactly the same, truly I did,' Ella said. 'But honestly, following the clues that were left behind, discovering my family's heritage? I will forever be grateful that I went to that meeting and started on this journey.'

'What do your family think? Were they not interested in finding out more?' Mia asked.

Georgia looked up and smiled as the waiter brought their drinks, thankful for the reprieve. It meant she had a moment to think about how to reply.

'Unfortunately, I don't really have any family,' she said, as they all took a sip. 'My parents died in a car crash when I was a teenager, and I don't have any siblings.'

'I'm so sorry,' Mia said. 'I shouldn't have asked.'

Ella reached for her hand. 'I'm sorry, too. I can't imagine what that must have been like for you.'

'It was a long time ago, and I don't dwell on it, but it is

strange not having a connection to my family, especially when we were so close. I was very fortunate to have gone to live with my best friend's family, and I'm as close to them now as I was to my parents, but I just don't have anyone to ask about all this. I suppose it's why it all seemed so strange to me.'

'You don't have any grandparents still alive?' Mia asked.

'My maternal grandparents died when I was much younger, as did my paternal grandfather, and both my parents were only children,' she said, taking another sip of wine. 'But my dad's mother, the one who this box must have been left for, she was a mean old woman who I didn't want anything to do with.'

'Ah,' said Ella. 'It makes sense now why you buried the box away and forgot about it.'

They all sat back in silence and Georgia wondered if she'd said too much. But both women seemed so warm and genuinely interested in her story.

'Could this box change how you feel?' Ella asked. 'I mean, could it be the key to you feeling closer to the family you lost?'

'Honestly, I don't know,' Georgia replied. 'My intention was to sell this stone and get rid of it, to never think about any of this again, but—' She decided not to tell them what she'd discovered, wanting to know for sure first whether it was all true or not. 'But I think that perhaps I was being too hasty in my decision-making.'

'Keep it,' Ella urged. 'You never know where it could lead you, or how special it might be to someone you haven't even met yet.'

Mia cleared her throat then and Georgia turned to her, seeing the conflicted look in her gaze. 'When I gave you all those boxes, I didn't know if I was doing the right thing. I still wonder sometimes if they were supposed to stay hidden or whether they were meant to be shared.'

Georgia glanced between Ella and Mia, sensing the two had a real connection. She was so happy they'd come to meet her, because just seeing them made it all seem more real, told her that she wasn't mad in her quest to find out more about the stone.

'You did the right thing, Mia,' Ella said, her voice low, tears caught in her lashes. 'I truly found myself because of your decision, so please don't second-guess yourself again. You absolutely did the right thing.'

'So, you're telling me that I should try to discover the connection between this stone and my family?' Georgia asked. 'You think it's worth it?'

'If I were you, I'd be having that newspaper article translated and booking a flight to wherever in Italy it points you,' Ella said. 'For the first time in my life I made an impromptu decision and went to Greece.' She touched her stomach and laughed. 'And look how that turned out!'

Georgia laughed along with her. 'Well, babies aren't part of my ten-year plan, but I wouldn't say no to the holiday romance.' She turned to Mia, who had reached for the little box on the table and was turning it over in her hands. 'What do you think? Should I try to find out more?'

'I don't think you'll be able to stop yourself,' Mia said with a wry smile when she looked up. 'I've heard from two other granddaughters as well, and they all said their little box changed their lives, that once they started on the journey of finding out more about their family, it was impossible to stop until they'd discovered the truth.'

Georgia shook her head. It was hard to believe so many of the secret boxes had been left behind.

'What about your box, Mia?' Ella asked. 'Have you discovered anything helpful yet?'

Mia shook her head and sighed. 'Nothing. I don't know where to start, it's an absolute mystery to me.'

'Wait, there was a box left for you, too?' Georgia felt her eyebrows rise as she studied Mia.

'Well, it was a box similar to the ones you were left, and it had my aunt's name on it,' Mia told them. 'On her one, the name was etched into it rather than having a little note attached, but when I opened it, there was nothing inside.'

'She'd already opened it?' Georgia asked.

'She must have. I only wish I knew what she found inside it, or why she kept the box all these years,' Mia said. 'She was a very private woman in many ways. She held the secrets of so many others, and I'm starting to think she had her own secrets, too. Secrets she never shared with the rest of our family.'

'I think her box must have inspired all the ones you discovered,' Ella said. 'I think she held on to her little box because it meant so much to her, and because of it, she encouraged other mothers to do the same.'

Georgia sat back as Mia checked the time on her phone and Ella placed a hand on her stomach, groaning as she moved.

'When is baby due?' Georgia asked, as Ella shifted her weight again.

'Four weeks,' she said. 'I was perfectly fine until a few days ago, and then she seemed to take up acrobatics. Uncomfortable doesn't even begin to describe it.'

'I can't even imagine,' Georgia said. She wasn't one of those women who knew they wanted to be mothers, or who dreamed of what their children might be like, but looking at Ella she couldn't think what it would be like to be pregnant and know you had to give your baby up. To know that so many women had passed through Hope's House, so many mothers who had no choice but to give up the child they were carrying.

She reached for her box and looked down at it. Being with Mia and Ella, looking at the tender way Ella kept touching her stomach, it had suddenly given her a much deeper appreciation of what had been left behind. And she couldn't help but wonder if her grandmother might have had a different outlook on life if she'd been given the box during her lifetime, if she'd known she was adopted, as the records at Hope's House had confirmed. Because all signs were pointing at the adoption being a complete mystery, since the box had just recently been discovered, and she couldn't believe that back then families would have openly discussed adoption. She only wished her dad was alive to ask, to show the sapphire to. *He would have loved the mystery of it all.*

'It's been so lovely meeting you again, Georgia,' Mia said, as they all finished their drinks and stood. 'If I didn't have some-where to be I'd suggest dinner, but maybe next time?'

'I'd love that,' she said, realising just how much she actually would like to see Mia and Ella again. 'It's been really nice connecting with you both. I just hope you don't think I'm awful for not looking into all this sooner.'

Ella gave her a quick hug and Mia did the same.

'Not at all. In fact, my advice to all of you at the meeting was to make sure you wanted to go down the road of discovering family secrets,' Mia said. 'It's important to be prepared, to know that you can find out things that perhaps you wished you hadn't.'

'I think I might have left before you had time to say that,' Georgia said with a grimace, pleased to see that Mia was laughing it off. 'But I promise I won't ever run out on you like that again.'

'It's fine. We all have those days, and I would never judge you. I'm only happy you have the box in your possession. I still have one that wasn't claimed,' Mia said. 'Actually, not claimed isn't quite true. We weren't able to find any contact details for the name listed. The lawyer is still trying, but he's not holding out much hope.'

'What a mystery,' Georgia said. 'Let us know if you manage to find who it belongs to.'

'And you make sure you let us know if you solve *your*

mystery,' Ella said. 'I can't wait to find out how your family is linked to that striking stone.'

'Dinner, once you have more to share?' Mia asked.

'Preferably before my bump is born,' Ella added. 'So don't take too long.'

Georgia grinned. 'Deal.'

They walked to the door together, Mia and Ella going in one direction and Georgia the other. She found that she couldn't stop smiling. *What a day.* In fact, what a *week.* Part of her wished she'd opened up to them a little more about what she'd already discovered, but until she had some sort of confirmation of what she'd been told, she wasn't sure about discussing it with anyone.

The sun was shining as she walked, and Georgia picked up her phone as she strolled away from the restaurant. As with everything that happened in her life, her first reaction was to tell Sam all about it. She was starting to miss her—they'd gone from living together as teenagers, sharing a room at university and then working together every day as adults. Even when they'd first gone into business together, they'd worked from Sam's parents' house, falling asleep at their makeshift desks in the attic half the time. Georgia realised she didn't even know whether Sam had bought the Cartier love bracelet at the auction. Before, they'd never have gone an entire day without speaking. Georgia also hadn't teased Sam lately about her preoccupation with her new man. Smiling to herself, she opened her screen to call Sam, going straight to her favourites, but her phone began to ring with an unfamiliar number before she'd touched her friend's name.

Switzerland.

She swallowed, suddenly realising just how invested she was in the whole mystery of the little wooden box and its contents, especially after being with Mia and Ella. *So much for not wanting to connect with my father's side of the family.*

Her finger hovered as her stomach did a little flip, but she made herself answer.

'Hello?'

'Am I speaking with Georgia Montano?'

Georgia hesitated as she listened to the heavily accented, deep male voice at the other end of the line. She'd started to think the Swiss jeweller wasn't going to call her back, as it had been days since she'd left a message for him.

'Yes, this is she.'

'I understand that you have information on the missing royal sapphire?'

She cleared her throat. 'May I ask who I'm speaking with?'

'I'm sorry, I was so excited to receive your message that I've lost my manners. My name is Luca, Luca Kaufmann.' He paused. 'You called me and left a message, but I was away on summer holiday. I've only just received it.'

Georgia took a deep breath, about to speak, but he beat her to it.

'How soon can we meet?'

7

GENEVA, 1951

It was one thing to know her husband was being unfaithful, and another entirely to confront him about it.

Delphine looked at her appearance in the mirror, turning her face from side to side as she studied her complexion. She was only twenty-seven years old, and as far as she could see there was little that had changed about her face from when she'd married her husband almost nine years earlier. Other than puffiness around her eyes from the tears she'd cried into her pillow the night before, her skin was still smooth and plump, her lips full, her hair thick and lustrous. She tilted her head forward to inspect her parting line, pleased to see there were no early grey hairs showing.

As a girl, she'd been lauded for being the prettiest in the neighbourhood, and later complimented for her beauty as a teenager attending events with her parents. She'd often see boys looking at her; even men closer to her father's age would run their eyes over her admiringly, leaving her red-cheeked and embarrassed by the heat in their gaze, not quite certain why they looked at her in such a way. But she'd been promised to Giovanni since childhood, their families making the decision to unite when she was still young enough to be playing make-believe with her dolls. So, no matter how many boys smiled at her or asked her to dance, she always knew that she would marry a man already chosen for her; that she was to rebuke any advances made by anyone who wasn't Giovanni. She was not to have a hand laid on her before marriage.

This meant that her experience with boys, and indeed men, was limited to her family, to her father and cousins, until she came of age. And then, on her eighteenth birthday, her engagement had been announced, followed by an extravagant party in her native Switzerland. One year later, two days after she turned nineteen, she was married in Rome, and then barely ten months later she'd welcomed her first child, her son Tommaso.

Delphine hadn't known what to expect from marriage—her husband was kind to her and made certain she had everything she needed. She'd grown up in a household where her parents never slept in the same room, so she hadn't thought it unusual for her and Giovanni to have separate wings in their large home, and when her children came along she'd forgotten all about how lonely she'd felt in those early months of her marriage. His chaste kisses had been warm, but not particularly loving, almost as if she were a sister he was fond of, and when they'd consummated their marriage it was an act she'd have described as uncomfortable and deeply embarrassing. It had only happened a few times, enough for her to get pregnant, and then she'd wondered if it was something that would ever happen again, or if perhaps it wasn't for pleasure at all, which is what she'd heard her older sister whispering about with her friends when Delphine had been just a girl.

But now, as she stood in her new bedroom, surrounded by all the things she'd chosen to bring with her from Italy, that yawning, painful loneliness was starting to creep back in, the ache almost bone-deep. And she knew in her heart that there was something very wrong with a husband not seeking out his wife's love in the marital bed. Regardless of whether they shared the bed each night for the purpose of sleeping, it was unusual that he didn't come to her to seek out comfort, to want to touch her body.

Delphine gave herself one last, long look, before dabbing her new Eau d'Hermès perfume to her wrists and neck and hoping Giovanni would like the scent. She walked downstairs, still getting used to the smaller size of their flat compared to their rather palatial home in Rome. Today was the day she was going to put her marriage back in order. She would make her husband forget all about whatever other women he was spending time with, and find a way to make him fall in love with her. Perhaps the fault hadn't been entirely his; perhaps she should have spent more time trying to understand how to keep a man content, but that ended today.

'*Buongiorno*,' she said, as she walked into the breakfast room.

'Good morning,' her husband replied, giving her a quick smile before turning his attention back to his paper.

She kissed both her children on the tops of their heads, lingering a little longer at her son's chair and placing a hand to his shoulder. He was sad to have left Italy, but with Martina and their cook coming along with them, the children were at least eating the same food they were used to. She expected any diversion from their usual milk and bread wouldn't be favoured, just as she very much doubted they'd be willing to deviate from their favourite spaghetti for dinner.

'I thought you'd be taking your breakfast in bed today,' Giovanni said, without looking up from what he was reading.

'Quite to the contrary,' Delphine said, hoping her enthusiasm would be contagious. 'It's such a treat to have you here with us. I was hoping we might explore Geneva together as a family, perhaps take the children to the lake where I spent so much of my childhood summers?'

Giovanni looked up then, but she saw that instead of the smile she was hoping for, she received a hovering frown instead. Clearly, he had other plans. It was like their last breakfast in Italy all over again, when he'd announced their move.

'That sounds like a very pleasant idea, Delphine. Children, what do you say about cancelling your lessons today and having a day adventuring with your mother? It is your first proper day in Geneva, after all, and I've heard the Bois de la Bâtie animal park is wonderful.'

She fixed her smile as the children cheered, hoping she'd misheard. 'You mean with your mother *and* father, don't you, my darling? I was hoping we could be together as a family.'

Giovanni made a noise that was halfway between a sigh and a grunt, before downing his coffee. 'I'm afraid I have business to attend to. It's why we've moved here, after all. But you have fun, and tell me about it tonight.' He winked at the children. 'I can't wait to hear about all the smelly little piglets and other animals you see.'

The children laughed as he copied the sound of a pig snorting, which only made Delphine's feelings more difficult for her to understand. She couldn't deny he was a kind father; he made the children smile and was never short-tempered with them, but other than when he was in residence for breakfast, they never saw him.

Delphine watched him go, moving towards her seat in the hope that he'd smell her perfume as she intercepted him and look down at her; that he'd actually *see* his wife for once. Instead, she received the forehead kiss that had become so customary in her marriage. He liked her to be placid, and nothing more.

'Can we expect you home for dinner tonight?' Delphine asked, keeping her voice light, not wanting him to think she was nagging.

'You can,' he replied. 'I leave for London on Monday, so I shall be enjoying dinner with you every night until then.'

'London?' she asked, her voice quavering. 'So soon?'

'I have pressing matters to deal with there, but I'm sure you will all be well settled by then.'

Giovanni kissed his children goodbye as his wife watched him go, feeling as though in that moment he was walking out of their lives forever.

'Mama, can we truly have the day off?' Isabella asked. 'Can we go to the Bois de la Bâtie place that Papa spoke of?'

But it was to her son that she looked, those soulful eyes of his telling her that he knew, that he could sense that something wasn't right, that his mother was in mourning.

Papa isn't coming home once he goes to London, is he? That's what she imagined Tommaso to be asking her with his eyes, and if he'd voiced his question out loud, she knew there was no way she could lie to him and tell him otherwise.

She walked to the window and looked out at the street below. She loved Geneva, it was the place of her birth; but she'd also come to love Italy, and most especially their country house. And her heart yearned for the acres that had stretched as far as the eye could see, the vineyards peeking at her in the distance, the very air that she'd breathed.

This is home now. This was home before I moved to Italy, and it will be my home again. I have no choice but to make it the place of my heart.

That evening, with the children in bed and the house silent, Delphine did something she hadn't been brave enough to do before. In the past, as a young bride eager to be everything her new husband might expect, she'd waited in her bedroom every night in the event that he might come to see her. She'd brush her hair, change into a pretty lace nightgown, and press perfume to her wrists and decolletage, before arranging herself against the pillows and waiting, listening out for his footfalls, holding her breath as she heard him coming, and then feeling crestfallen when he kept on walking past.

In the very beginning, Giovanni had come to see her, and she'd learned quickly what was expected of a woman when it came to matters of the flesh. But never had she gone to him, even when weeks had stretched into months since his last visit to her bedchamber. She'd simply waited, prepared each night for him in case he decided he wanted to see her.

Tonight, though, Delphine lifted her hand, her knock tentative. She knew he'd heard it by the sound of his boots crossing the floor, and within seconds the door to his quarters was opened.

Giovanni stood there, his expression puzzled as he looked back at his wife, as if she were the last person he could possibly be expecting. 'Delphine? Is something the matter?'

She moved past him into the room, not asking permission. *I am his wife and this is our home. I do not need permission to come into his quarters. I have every right to be here.*

Giovanni spun round as she stood before him and slipped her silk robe from her shoulders, braving his gaze as she stepped out of it and lifted her fingers to the straps of her nightgown. She took a tentative step backwards, towards the bed, hoping that he'd follow, hoping that she'd see something in his eyes that told her he desired her, that he finally wanted her in the way she knew a man could want a woman. That he'd change his mind about going to London.

'Delphine,' he scolded, quickly crossing the room and taking her hands, stopping her from undressing. 'Stop that!'

'Is it so wrong for me to want my husband?' *After all this time? After being lonely for so many years?* 'I only wanted to spend the night with you before you left for London, so that you remembered me.'

'Please,' Giovanni said, bending to retrieve her robe from where it had pooled on the carpet, looking dreadfully embarrassed. 'Cover yourself.'

Delphine lifted her chin, refusing to let him tell her what to do. She'd spoken to Martina, she knew other wives went to their husbands, that she didn't have to wait like a virgin bride. This was her right, to seek out pleasure with the man she'd married.

'What's wrong with me, Gio?' she asked softly as she studied his face. When she'd understood as a teenager that they were to marry, she'd looked often at a photo of him, pleased that she wasn't betrothed to a beast of a man. And now, as she looked over his features, she found that he was as handsome now as he'd been on their wedding day, if not more so. 'Is there something so wrong with me that you cannot even stand to see me naked? Am I truly so ugly?'

The way he looked at her could have broken her heart if she'd let it. Pain mixed with embarrassment, perhaps—the worst kind of look she could have imagined. Or perhaps it was pity, which was even worse. It was then she realised what a terrible, terrible mistake she'd made in coming to him.

'Delphine, you are everything I could have wanted in a wife,' he said, taking her hand in a rare show of affection. 'You've given me an heir to my family's company and a beautiful daughter, but—'

She swallowed. *But.* Of course, there was a *but.*

'We were chosen for each other as children, perhaps before we were even born. Our union was a business arrangement and nothing more, something our families decided for us, to unite two great companies by blood, which we have done.'

To you, it was an arrangement. To me, it was a marriage. I thought my husband would fall in love with me, I thought we would be happy together.

'You wouldn't have chosen me, if you'd been given the

choice?' she whispered. 'Is that what you're trying to tell me, Gio?'

He let go of her hand and walked away a few steps, before eventually turning back to her. 'The truth is that I wouldn't have chosen anyone,' he said. 'Marriage wasn't something I wanted. I loved being a bachelor, and if I'd been the younger brother, if the weight of expectation wasn't on my shoulders...'

He didn't have to finish his sentence for her to know what he was about to say. He'd done his duty as the heir and eldest son, and now that duty had been achieved, he wouldn't be seeking out her affection ever again.

'I understand. This life was chosen for me, too,' she said. 'But can we not find a way to—'

'Delphine, we will always be married. You are my wife, and I am your husband.' Giovanni took a breath as his face slowly hardened. 'But I will be leaving for London on Monday, and I don't know when I'll return. I need you to be here to show that my family is serious about expanding our business into Switzerland, and I'll come to visit, but I think we both know that our marriage is one for show only. A match of convenience.'

He may as well have punched her in the stomach, and it took every inch of her willpower not to run across the room and pound his chest, demanding that he stay, demanding that he give their marriage at least a chance to succeed. Demanding that he give her the chance to be what he needed.

'So, you're leaving us?' she whispered. 'You're actually leaving us, after making us leave Italy? After making us move here with you?'

'I'll return to visit for the holidays, and for important occasions. It's why I wanted you close to London.'

'But you don't want us in London, by your side?' Delphine found it impossible to hide the pain in her voice this time. 'Not even your children?'

'I'm giving you your freedom, Delphine, don't you see?' he

asked, going to sit on the bed and taking off his boots. 'You've given me everything I needed from this marriage, everything *we* needed, and I'm grateful for our wonderful children, but you must know that it was only an arrangement between us. There is nothing unusual about us living separate lives, it's not something you need to be upset about.'

'What do I tell my family?' she asked, as tears made her voice quaver.

'You tell them that your husband is living abroad for work,' he said. 'They will understand.'

'And our children?'

'I will talk to them,' he said. 'But they will be away at school soon. I've organised the best school in Geneva for them to attend, and they'll be so busy they'll barely notice I'm not living here.' He smiled. 'It's not as if we will ever divorce, so there's nothing about our arrangement that will affect the children. And when Tommaso is older, he will spend time with me at all our offices, here, in London, and in Rome. You have nothing to worry about.'

She nodded. So that was it then. Her marriage, it seemed, was beyond saving.

'What if I want a divorce?' she asked, tilting her chin, tired of not standing up for herself, feeling as if she'd finally found her voice. 'What if I don't want to live a lie? Do I not get a choice in all of this? What if I don't want to live separately from my husband?'

'Divorce?' Giovanni laughed. 'We will never divorce, Delphine, that is the one thing I can promise you. We will remain wedded. It's how it's always done, and it's how we will do it. I will not bring any shame on this family.'

She shook her head. So, she was to be bound to her husband forever, despite the fact that he didn't love her? Despite not wanting to live with her anymore? It was to be a marriage in name only? She wondered how it was shameful to divorce, but not shameful to live separately. How it wasn't shameful to be seeking comfort with other women.

'I implore you to be discreet, as will I, and when we're together, we'll be as we've always been,' he said, smiling as if he hadn't just broken her heart into a million tiny pieces. 'There will be times when we need one another, expectations to attend certain things and such, but most of the time we can live our own lives as we want.' He frowned. 'I thought you'd be happy to have your freedom? It was always my intention for you to live the life you wanted after birthing and raising our children. Now that they're almost at school, you will be as free as a bird, and I'll ensure you have a generous monthly allowance.'

Delphine stared at him for a long moment, but she had no words to answer him. Instead, she walked away, her head hanging and her heart heavy, clutching her robe to her chest, understanding that she was stuck in a loveless marriage of convenience for the rest of her life.

My marriage is over. I'm to live the rest of my life alone, with only my children for company.

She closed the door to her bedroom and sank down against the timber until she reached the floor, drawing her knees to her chest and crying as she hadn't cried since she was a girl. Her mother would have told her there was no point in crying over spilt milk, that she was fortunate to be given free rein to live her life as she wanted, albeit without her husband. But that was the problem; Delphine didn't want to be alone.

She wanted Giovanni to love her.

8

PRESENT DAY

'Georgia?'

She looked up, happy to hear Sam's voice.

'In here!'

'What are you doing in your bedroom?' Sam asked. 'And what's going on? Your message didn't make any...' She paused, kicking off her heels and looking at the mess in the room. 'Sense.'

Georgia willingly took the coffee Sam passed her, grimacing when she turned in a circle, clothes strewn everywhere as if a bomb had gone off in her wardrobe.

'Excuse the mess.'

'Mess?' Sam laughed. 'This isn't a mess, G, it's an explosion. What's going on? I don't remember you being like this even when we were teenagers!'

Georgia sighed and sat down with Sam on the bed. 'I think I'm going mad.'

'Well, I can see that!'

'Ever since I took the stone in to be valued, I just can't stop thinking about it. About the mystery of it all.' She took a sip, thankful for the combination of caffeine and sugar. 'I've become obsessed with finding out everything I can.'

'So, two things,' Sam said, tucking her legs beneath her and leaning back into the assortment of pillows Georgia had on the bed. 'First, I think that perhaps you might have replaced your work obsession with a family history obsession. You've transferred all your energy and time into solving the mystery of your grandmother's past.'

Georgia held up one hand in the air. 'You're not wrong. Guilty as charged.' Her brows shot up. 'What's the second thing?'

Sam sighed dramatically and inched her shirtsleeve back, turning her wrist from side to side. 'Second is that I'm wearing a Cartier love bracelet, and you haven't even noticed.'

Georgia set her coffee down on the bedside table and shook her head, her hands covering her mouth as she looked at the bracelet. 'It's amazing, Sam. Absolutely, without a doubt, the most gorgeous bracelet I've ever seen. I'm so pleased you bought it.'

Sam grinned. 'It *is* gorgeous, and I've been dying to show it to you, but I'm actually far more interested in what you're doing. Why the luggage?'

'Because I'm going to Geneva.'

'You're going to *Switzerland*?' Sam asked. 'I don't believe it.'

'Well, believe it, because I've booked my ticket and I leave tomorrow.'

Sam's jaw dropped. 'You, Georgia Montano, are leaving London and travelling to Switzerland? I've never, ever known you to travel for pleasure.'

She groaned and flopped back beside Sam on the bed. 'I know. I'm having palpitations just thinking about it.'

Whenever they'd travelled for work, Sam had had to practically drag Georgia onto the plane—she certainly hadn't ever gone willingly. It was more being on the plane than leaving the country that she hated. Thankfully when they were younger, Sam's family had taken all their holidays by car or train, which meant she'd been perfectly fine.

'What made you decide to go? What have you discovered that you haven't told me?'

Georgia closed her eyes, trying to visualise herself getting on the plane, foreseeing sitting there and gripping the arm rest, her knuckles white. Her eyes flew open then, wishing she hadn't imagined it. *I'm going to be fine. There's nothing to worry about.*

'You know you're going to be fine, right?' Sam said, as if she could read her thoughts. 'Completely, one hundred per cent fine?'

She took a deep breath. 'Logically, I know that. But telling you just now has made it real.' Georgia sat bolt upright. 'Why don't you come with me?'

'Can't,' Sam said. 'I'm, well—'

'Samantha Bradshaw, are you blushing?' Georgia laughed.

'I'm going to meet Harry's parents. There! I've said it.'

'Wait, you're ditching your best friend and business partner for a man?'

'Yes,' Sam said. 'But only because I knew nothing about this trip when I agreed to a weekend in the Cotswolds with his family, and in case you've forgotten, we're no longer business partners, so you're released from having to spend every day with me.'

Georgia gave her a look that she hoped she understood. She would never get tired of spending time with Sam; she was the sister she'd never had.

'I'm happy for you, Sam,' she said. 'You know that, right? I couldn't be happier that things are working out so well with Harry.'

Sam reached for her hand and squeezed it. 'I know. But your family mystery is far more exciting than me pretending I like being out of the city for the weekend. Now, explain to me why you're going to Geneva and not Italy?'

Georgia got off the bed and began to reach for her discarded clothes, holding them up and waiting for Sam to either shake her head or nod, before putting them away or placing them in her luggage.

'I still haven't had the newspaper clipping translated. To be honest, I haven't looked into it, but the man from Christie's told me to call a jeweller in Geneva, a Luca Kaufmann, who has apparently been searching for a missing sapphire for many years.'

'Which is potentially the sapphire in your possession,' Sam clarified.

'Precisely,' Georgia said, surveying how many things she'd already packed. 'I mean, I don't really believe it could be the missing stone, but if it is, then I thought I should travel with it rather than send it to a stranger, no matter how legitimate his business might be.'

'I agree,' Sam said. 'It's no different to when we took all our samples to show retailers because we were scared the competition might somehow intercept them.'

Georgia grinned. 'Exactly.'

It felt like a lifetime ago that they'd been a start-up company, peddling their samples to retailers in the hope that someone would pick up their products and put them on the map. Their business had been twofold: first they'd developed software to match the foundations and lipsticks of big brands, to allow their customers to easily shop their more affordable products online and work out which colour they wanted; and then they'd created the same technology in-store for their biggest retailers. A woman could walk in wearing her favourite lipstick from another brand, and with facial recognition they could match the pigment and shade, with the sale made in minutes. Their technology had set them apart more than their make-up;

the ability to provide a service that made shopping easy and affordable. And it was the reason they'd been courted by one of the biggest cosmetic companies in the world, selling the controlling shares to their business before their thirtieth birthdays. Georgia still wanted to pinch herself sometimes, and she knew Sam felt the same.

'So what do you know about this Luca Kaufmann?' Sam asked, draining her coffee and dropping the takeout cup in the bin beside Georgia's bed. 'Have you looked him up?'

Georgia shook her head. 'No, but I've spoken to him.'

'And then you ran home, booked a flight, and started packing?'

She knew how impulsive that sounded, especially for her. 'Correct on all counts.'

'How about I research him while you finish packing then?' Sam asked, lying back down on the bed and taking out her phone. 'Also, I think you need to pack a dress or two. What about that little black dress you wore out for my birthday earlier in the year?'

'Why would I need a dress like that?' Georgia asked.

Sam turned her phone around and sat up, holding it out to Georgia. 'Because this is Luca Kaufmann.'

Georgia dropped the jumper she was folding and took a few steps closer to inspect the photo. Handsome would have been an understatement. He had eyes that were such a light blue she wondered if they were grey, and dark hair that was just a smidge too long, curls almost brushing his collar. And he was tall, with broad shoulders that suited the jacket he was wearing.

'Just because he looks like Henry Cavill doesn't mean I have a reason to take the dress.'

'What if he asks you out to dinner? Wouldn't you want to have that in your arsenal?'

Georgia laughed. 'You're being ridiculous. Now tell me

something about him, other than showing me photos of how gorgeous he is.'

'It says here,' Sam said, lying back down again as Georgia resumed her packing, 'that he worked as a curator for a museum for some time, specialising in gems and jewels, before taking over the business that he currently owns. It sounds like a family business, but I'll have to—'

'The Christie's man said something about this Luca taking over the search from someone else, perhaps his father. It sounded to me very much like a family business.' She mulled over this information. 'Does it say exactly what he does? I had the impression he was a collector, but perhaps not.'

'Hang on,' Sam said, as she continued scrolling. 'It says here that in addition to running the family business, he also manages some significant collections on behalf of investors. Perhaps he's carrying on the search on behalf of one of those investors?'

Georgia shrugged. 'Maybe. All I know for certain is that I'll be able to ask him any questions I have tomorrow. He's asked me to come straight in to see him when I land, so I'll take a taxi from the airport.'

'Are you excited?' Sam asked.

'About meeting Luca Kaufmann?'

'Well, yes, that, but I mean are you excited to learn more about your family? I know it was a shock being given this box, but—'

'Yes,' Georgia said, not waiting for Sam to finish her sentence. 'I went from not wanting anything to do with it at all, to thinking that it would be nice to have that connection. I mean, if my family truly was connected to this stone, if it is the missing sapphire...'

'Then you might meet a relative you never even knew existed,' Sam said softly.

Georgia nodded. 'Exactly.' She looked away and blinked back tears. It had been a long time since she'd been emotional about her parents, but the last week seemed to have brought everything to the surface. It was as if she were fifteen again, coming to terms with being an orphan. But rather than the grief she'd experienced then, this time she felt a sense of hope. If there were other family members out there, or even simply a family mystery to be solved, then it was something she knew she had to do.

Sam stood, leaving her phone on the bed as she crossed the room, gently touching Georgia's shoulder as she passed before taking out a short black dress from the wardrobe. 'Please take this?' she asked. 'For me?'

'You truly think I need that dress?' Georgia laughed as she dabbed at her eyes. Sam always had a way of knowing how to make her feel better.

'I do. If you get asked out for dinner, you can wear this and let your hair down. You deserve to have the time of your life on this trip, G, so please, say yes to every opportunity. Do *not* stay in your hotel room.'

Georgia's eyes flitted between her friend and the dress she was holding.

'You do realise that I'm meeting him strictly in a business capacity,' Georgia said, 'and I'm not sure that dress is necessarily appropriate.'

'Then ask him out for drinks and dinner!' Sam said, her eyes sparkling as if she were about to meet the handsome jeweller herself. 'Because this dress is definitely appropriate for *that* purpose. He's gorgeous, you're gorgeous, so just see what happens. And if not him, then another gorgeous Swiss man. The place is full of them.'

'If he didn't look like a Hollywood actor, I don't think we'd be having this conversation.'

'Fine,' Sam said, holding up her hands in surrender. 'But if you don't want to talk about the handsome man you're flying to another country to meet, how about you tell me what the two women were like? The ones you had a drink with? Did you find out anything useful?'

'Nothing specifically about my clues, if that's what you mean, but they did encourage me to find out more,' Georgia said. 'And it also made me realise just what the clues in my box must have meant to the woman who left them behind. Whether I liked my grandmother or not, I feel an obligation to see this through.' She sighed and closed the lid on her case, turning to face Sam. 'I mean, imagine leaving a baby behind and trying to decide what to place in a little box that the child may or may not find one day. It's heartbreaking.'

Sam took out another dress and folded it, putting it into her luggage. 'You know, if it truly is worth some huge sum, don't you find it interesting that this woman left it behind? I mean, if you were penniless and had to give up your baby, wouldn't you sell it?'

'I've thought that, too,' Georgia said. 'Which made me wonder if she wasn't penniless at all. Perhaps there were other reasons she had to give up the baby?'

'Or perhaps she cared more about her daughter having something of value, in case *she* ever needed it?'

'Actually, thinking of how valuable it could be, aren't you nervous about just carrying it around in your bag?'

Georgia shrugged. 'Not really. I mean, it might not even be the famous stone.'

She took out the dress Sam had just put in her case, receiving an arched-brow glare from her friend.

'Do I need to cancel my weekend away just to make sure you have fun in Geneva?'

Georgia sighed and put the dress back in. 'No, you do not need to cancel your loved-up weekend with Harry. I do remember how to have fun.'

'Really? Because you could have fooled me.'

Georgia glowered at her, but she couldn't stay mad at Sam for long. Especially when she started to talk business.

'When you get back, I was thinking we could start working up some new ideas. I think I'll go mad if I don't have something to work on soon.'

'Music to my ears,' Georgia replied. 'Now get back to researching Luca Kaufmann while I finish packing, would you?'

Sam grinned. 'It would be my pleasure.'

Later that evening, when Sam was long gone and Georgia was packed and ready for her flight in the morning, she opened her laptop and sat up in bed. When they'd sold the business, she'd thought about buying a bigger flat, but she loved her cosy one-bedroom place, and although she'd splurged on an expensive bed and new sofa, the only other thing that had changed in her life since then had been the amount she spent on a nice bottle of wine.

She had a glass of rosé beside her now, and a romcom playing in the background, but ever since Sam had started researching Luca, Georgia hadn't been able to stop thinking about him, which meant that her mind wasn't on the movie. She typed the name Luca Kaufmann into her search engine and found the same photo Sam had shown her earlier. He was handsome, Sam had been right about that, but what interested Georgia most was how he was connected to her sapphire. She'd begun searching for information on the royal tiara before dinner, and she'd come across an article dated ten years previously. A well-known Swiss jeweller had been interviewed on the various collections of jewels from European monarchs, and he'd made special mention of the missing sapphire. It seemed that it had puzzled collectors around the world for many years, which made it all the more unbeliev-able that her family could be connected to it in some way.

Just as she was scrolling to another article, she heard a ping and glanced down at her emails. She clicked off the article, her heart pounding as she saw who it was from. She'd found a translator earlier in the day and scanned the article through to them, hoping she might get it back in a few days, but to her amazement, it was there already.

Georgia reached for her wine glass and took a sip, surprised by how nervous she was. The newspaper clipping must have been at least seventy years old, so she knew that whatever information it contained might not mean anything to her, but it might also tell her the link between the stone and her great-grandmother.

Please find the translation below. There's no date on the article unfortunately. Thanks for the work and let me know if there's anything else you need assistance with!

Georgia quickly skimmed across the message, holding her breath as she began to read the translation.

Financier and philanthropist Florian Lengacher has died at the scene of a tragic car accident near his summer home in Lake Geneva. It is understood that his motor vehicle was struck by another vehicle travelling in the opposite direction, killing both drivers.

Lengacher was recognised as being one of the most successful financiers in Switzerland. During his lifetime, he amassed a personal fortune in excess of forty million francs, and was known for being an avid collector of priceless artefacts and artwork. Despite his great wealth, he donated many historically significant pieces of art to Swiss galleries, fulfilling his desire to see art enjoyed by all. When he was interviewed recently to discuss his acquisition of a finance firm, he was asked what his advice would be to young men wanting to follow in his footsteps. 'I had a working-class upbringing, and was the first in my family to attend university. It doesn't matter where you come from, but more so the hunger you have to succeed, to provide for those you love. I tell my son not to waste any opportunity, to be passionate about his schooling and his work. My family sacrificed so much to give me the opportunities they didn't have.'

Lengacher is survived by his wife and son. He will be remembered in a private service, and his family has pledged to make a charitable donation in his name to a museum. Before his passing, he established a foundation to provide university education for underprivileged students, and his family intend on honouring that commitment.

Georgia read the article again, in case she'd missed something in her first read-through, but as interesting as the words were, they didn't mean anything to her. She googled *Florian Lengacher* in the hope that she might find a photo, but other than a few hits in Italian, she couldn't find anything to help her discover more about who this man was.

She eventually closed her laptop and put it on her bedside table, sinking back farther into her pillows. Could he have been her great-grandfather? The article had said he had a wife and son, which made the situation even stranger. Was her great-grandmother his wife? But if she were pregnant when he died, wouldn't she have had the means to keep the child, given his great fortune? Or had she been pregnant by another man, and not wanted anyone to know?

Georgia turned off the television, her mind racing at all the what-ifs. Reading the article had given her more questions than answers, and she doubted she'd get a wink of sleep before her flight in the morning.

Who are you, Florian, and what on earth is your connection to my family?

9

Georgia had started to second-guess her decision the moment she'd boarded the plane, and now she was having those doubts all over again as she stood on the street outside a high-end jewellery shop. It looked as if it could have been there for a hundred years, in a heritage-style building with windows just large enough to display a small collection of earrings and rings, and a well-dressed man standing at the door who was clearly a guard. *Why did I think this was a good idea?*

She was also suddenly acutely aware that she was carrying around a very expensive sapphire, which was making her nervous. Even if it wasn't the missing royal sapphire, it was still worth a great deal of money, and she felt as if it should be under lock and key somewhere, not rattling around in a little wooden box inside her bag.

'Georgia?' said a deep voice with a French accent, startling her.

She spun round and came face to face with a very hand-some, very familiar-looking man. Luca looked exactly as he did in the photos Sam had found online, despite Georgia insisting that he was probably much older and less attractive in real life. It seemed she'd been very, very wrong.

'Yes,' she said, holding out her hand. 'You must be Luca?'

He placed his palm to hers and shook her hand, and she liked that he didn't squash her fingers. Her pet hate was men who seemed to think a handshake was an excuse to show how strong they were.

'I'm so pleased you were able to travel here so promptly. Please, come in.'

Luca stepped around her and held open the door, and she realised then that he had a coffee in hand. She must have eyed it because he smiled as if he knew precisely what she was thinking.

'You're in need of caffeine?'

Georgia laughed. 'I am. I didn't have a coffee before my flight as I'm a nervous flyer.'

'Ah, I see.' Once they were inside, Luca called a younger man over, before turning back to her. 'Your order?'

'Oh no, please don't go to any trouble.'

'It's no trouble at all. Espresso?'

She nodded. 'Double espresso with one sugar, please.'

'Get two of their Aprikosenwähe, too,' he said to the man whom she presumed was his assistant.

'Aprikosenwähe?'

'Swiss apricot tart,' Luca said, gesturing for her to follow him. 'We have a coffee machine here, but the place just across the road has the best coffee and even better pastries. Trust me, you'll love it.'

Georgia's stomach growled in response. She wasn't going to say no to a delicious sweet treat, given that she hadn't eaten breakfast before she left home either.

Her head turned right, then left, as they walked through the shop. The diamonds were dazzling, and the size of some of the rings and earrings on display were so large, she almost thought they couldn't be real. But, of course, this was one of the most prestigious jewellery stores in Geneva, so she didn't doubt their authenticity for a second.

She found herself being ushered into a private room, with a table in the middle and four chairs around it. There was something on the table with a lens that she presumed was used for looking at diamonds and stones up close.

She turned as Luca moved to close the door behind her.

'Do you mind, or would you rather I left it open?'

'Ah, no, it's fine closed.' *Or at least she thought it was.*

'When we look at something that has this kind of value, we usually keep the door shut,' Luca said, pulling out a chair for her, before going around to the other side and sitting across from her. 'But if you feel uncomfortable at any stage, I can open the door or ask one of my female staff members to join us.'

Georgia appreciated the gesture. 'Thank you, but I'm fine. If I look nervous, it's only because I'm looking forward to hearing your thoughts on the stone.'

Luca was waiting patiently, but she imagined that he was very keen to see what she had with her, so she reached into her bag and took out the box.

'I understand that you will be able to recognise the sapphire when you see it,' she said. 'If it is indeed the sapphire you think it is.'

'Yes,' he replied, placing the strange instrument on his head, the little magnifying lenses turned up so they appeared to be attached to his forehead. 'I've studied the tiara more times than I could count, and it's been in my care for years now, so I'm confident I'll recognise it if it's the missing sapphire.'

She opened the box and reached for the stone, placing it in his hand. Luca's sharp intake of breath was impossible not to hear, and she found herself leaning forward as he studied it, the lenses down over his eyes as he turned it left and then right, and then left again.

'What do you think?' she asked.

'I think,' Luca said, as he held it up to the light, a broad smile taking over his face as he set the stone down between them and took the contraption off his head. 'That after many decades of searching for answers, the mystery has finally been solved.'

'You're certain?' Georgia asked, as he lifted one hand to his face, his knuckles against his lips as he leaned forward to look at it once more. 'You truly believe this is the missing sapphire?'

'Georgia,' he said, as his eyes slowly met hers. 'I have never been so certain of anything in my life.'

She reached for the sapphire herself, holding it up and looking at the way the colour caught the light. 'Your mystery might have been solved, Luca, but my search has only just begun.'

Right then, the assistant from earlier appeared, a coffee in his hand, as well as two brown paper bags. He apologised for the interruption, and as he bustled in, Georgia couldn't help but notice the way Luca casually placed his hand over the sapphire, as if he didn't want it to be seen.

'Thank you. Please close the door behind you,' Luca instructed.

When they were alone, she spoke. 'You didn't want him to see it?'

'I don't want anyone to see it,' he replied. 'This sapphire is priceless to me, just as it was to my grandfather, and everyone in this industry knows that. I won't be disclosing its existence until it's under lock and key.'

'Providing I let you keep it?' Georgia asked.

She wished her words weren't quite so abrupt as soon as she'd said them, but Luca seemed unfazed. Instead, he smiled at her across the table, and she reached for the coffee cup for something to do, taking a quick sip and wishing she hadn't, as she immediately burned her tongue.

'How about we take an early lunch, so you can tell me all about your connection to the sapphire, and I can tell you all about mine?'

'What about the pastries?' Georgia asked, as her stomach rumbled.

'Take them as a treat for later,' he said. 'But I must ask you, may I please put the sapphire in my safe? I can have an agreement drawn up in minutes that confirms your ownership of the sapphire, and it will simply state that you are entrusting it into our care for inspection.'

Georgia nodded. 'Of course. I have to confess I'm suddenly quite nervous about carrying something so valuable in my bag.'

Luca touched her hand as he stood, taking her by surprise. She glanced up and into his pale blue eyes.

'Thank you for coming here. In time, I hope you will understand how much this sapphire means to me.'

Georgia just nodded, not sure what to say.

'If you're comfortable leaving your luggage here as well, I'll ensure that no one else has access to the room,' he said. 'You will join me for lunch, won't you?'

Georgia found herself nodding again as Luca whisked out of the room to get the paperwork, hearing him call to someone that they were to make him a booking for two at Café du Centre. But all she could think, as a wry smile caught her lips, was that Sam had been right.

Perhaps packing the little black dress hadn't been such a bad idea after all. She only hoped that his obvious lack of a wedding ring was indicative of him not being married, because she was finding herself very much looking forward to lunch.

They took a taxi through town to the restaurant, and Luca pointed out landmarks and architectural buildings of significance along the way, which made the journey pass quickly. She was acutely aware of him beside her in the back seat, although he'd been nothing other than a perfect gentleman, opening the door for her and positioning himself far enough away that they weren't in danger of bumping knees.

They were there within minutes, and she waited as he paid the driver before she opened her door and stepped out onto the pavement.

'This is one of my favourite places to come,' he told her. 'Café du Centre is one of the oldest restaurants in the city. My grandfather came here in the 1930s when they first opened, then my father after him and then me.'

'You truly didn't need to take me out to lunch,' she said. 'I would have been more than happy with the pastries.'

Luca arched a brow. 'Clearly you couldn't hear your stomach rumbling then, because it was telling me that pastries simply weren't going to be enough.'

She laughed and followed his lead as they walked down the cobbled street, seeing the white awnings up ahead with the name of the restaurant emblazoned in black lettering.

'Would you like to sit outside? It's such a nice day,' Luca said.

'Of course.'

Georgia stepped in front of him as he gestured for her to walk ahead, his hand brushing her lower back and sending an unfamiliar tingle down her spine.

He spoke to a waiter in German, and she stood and waited as they conversed before being ushered to a table for two. She looked around as she took her seat, admiring the old building the restaurant was housed in, loving the way so many people could be accommodated outside. Tables with white cloths and matching white awnings stretched as far as the eye could see around them, and she could only imagine how popular it must be.

'It'll be ridiculously busy soon, but for now we can enjoy the quiet,' he said.

'It's gorgeous. I can already tell I'll like it.'

Luca took the drinks menu and turned it over, looking up at her. 'Wine? Or is it too early in the day?'

She went to decline, but then changed her mind. 'Why not? If you're having one, I'd love to. It's not every day that I'm in Geneva for lunch.'

Luca waved their waiter over and ordered, before settling into his seat and training his gaze on her. 'I have to say that I'm surprised you were able to travel here at such short notice.'

'Let's just say that my schedule is currently wide open.'

'You're out of work?'

She smiled. 'I've just sold my business, actually. So when you asked me to come here, it was quite a relief to have something to do.'

'You'd rather be working?'

'I'd *much* rather be working,' she said, pausing as their drinks arrived. 'I've been working towards something for such a long time, with a goal in mind, and now that I've achieved it, I miss it.'

'I understand. I would be the same if I didn't have my work.' Luca held up his glass. 'To the sapphire that brought you to Geneva.'

She grinned. 'To the sapphire.' *And to meeting you.* Sam was going to be beside herself when she told her that Luca was as charming as he was handsome.

'Georgia, I don't mean to be rude, it's not my nature to ask questions—how do you say? To be nosy?'

She laughed. 'You want to ask me how I came to be in possession of the sapphire.'

He smiled back at her. 'I do. It's all I can think about.'

'Could you tell me first why you're so interested in this

particular stone? I'd love to know what made you start searching for it in the first place.'

He nodded, appearing relaxed even though she'd turned the questions on him.

'I come from a family of jewellers and I recently took over the business from my father,' Luca said, sitting back with his wine glass in his hand. 'I've lived and breathed diamonds and fine jewels since I was a boy, growing up in the back of the shop and then working there to put myself through university when I was older.'

'Did you join the business out of duty, or love?' she asked.

'Love,' he responded, without hesitation. 'I can't imagine doing anything else.'

They sat in silence for a minute, and when Luca looked away, Georgia indulged in running her eyes across his profile, feeling as if the wine was going to her head as she studied him.

'Our family is known for sourcing the best diamonds from all over the world, and making the finest pieces of jewellery, but my great-grandfather also spent much of his time finding rare and vintage pieces for some of his wealthiest clients.'

'He was a curator of private collections?'

Luca nodded. 'He was. And that is something else that has been passed down through the generations. Our family name opens doors that are closed to many, and I don't say that to be pretentious. It is not we who invest, but our clients, who are some of the wealthiest Swiss, and we are known for having the right connections, and the right eye.'

'So how did you end up with the tiara? Your family has held it for decades, is that right?'

'We have. But we've held it on behalf.'

Georgia wasn't certain she understood. 'On behalf of who?'

'My great-grandfather passed away suddenly, before he was able to share that information. All we know, all anyone in my family knows, is that we must protect it for its rightful owner.'

'How will you know who that person is?'

'My grandfather always said that he believed the rightful owner would have the missing sapphire.'

Georgia gulped. 'So that person would have been my great-grandmother.'

'Perhaps,' Luca said. 'Although we'd have to find out how she came to have it in the first place. We'd also have to contact the legal firm holding the letter that was stored with the tiara when it came into my family's guardianship.'

'A letter?'

'Yes, a letter. But it's still sealed and I haven't personally seen it or who it's addressed to. We'll have to wait until Monday to find out.'

Georgia turned that over in her mind, imagining how it would feel to see her great-grandmother's name on the envelope, if it was, and how she'd ever possibly figure out the link between her family and the stone, even if her great-grandmother had been given it lawfully. To think she might have stolen it, which would in turn mean she, Georgia, was in possession of stolen goods, was enough to make her stomach flip.

'Now,' Luca said, 'it is your turn. I want to hear everything you know, from start to finish.'

Their waiter came back then, granting Georgia a short reprieve for which she was very grateful.

'Are you ready to order?' the waiter asked.

'Anything you don't eat?' Luca asked.

'Pickles and veal.'

'Huh,' he said, raising his eyebrows as he glanced at the menu. 'We'll have oysters to begin, then the special of the day, the pan-fried king prawns and the Cajun spiced chicken burger. All to share.'

Once their menus were gone and they were alone again, Luca turned to her.

'Why veal?'

'Because I don't want to eat a baby cow that has been taken from its mother.'

'Hmm, well, I can understand that,' he said. 'Now—'

'Back to the mystery,' she said, taking another sip of wine before telling him how she'd come to be in possession of the sapphire, and how she'd ended up making contact with him. 'As you can see, I wasn't expecting it to be anything of value.'

'So you are prepared to donate it, then?'

Georgia couldn't help but smile back at Luca, who also couldn't keep his face straight. 'Luca, I'm a businesswoman. If the sapphire holds great value, then my great-grandmother would have known that. That tells me she had a reason for leaving it behind, that she wanted her daughter to have it, to prosper from it even.'

'May I see your little wooden box again?' Luca asked.

'Of course.' Georgia reached into her bag and passed it to him, staring at his hands as he turned it over. His fingers were long and tapered, as if perhaps he'd been a pianist in another life.

'May I open it?' She liked the softness in his gaze when he looked at her.

Georgia nodded, watching as he set it down and took out the newspaper clipping.

'You speak Italian?'

'No. But I had it translated.'

Their oysters arrived, served on ice, as he read the article. He'd been smiling when he began, but his smile quickly disappeared.

'The clipping is as much a mystery to me as the sapphire. I don't know the connection,' she said.

Luca raised his eyes and stared at her, as if trying to decide whether or not she was telling the truth.

'You have no idea who this is? Why you were left this clipping about the death of Florian Lengacher?'

She shook her head. 'I have absolutely no idea at all.'

Luca set down the article and reached for his wine, taking a very long, very slow sip.

'Do you remember how I told you that my grandfather gave my father the tiara, to look after? That it had been passed down through our family for generations?'

'I do.' He'd only just told her about it; of course, she remembered.

'Well, my grandfather had a dispute with the family of Florian Lengacher. When they discovered that my family held the tiara, they tried to mount a claim against it. They insisted that it belonged to his estate.'

'Your family won the claim?'

'Florian's wife passed away before it went to court, and his son wasn't interested in pursuing the claim. But it caused a divide between two families who'd once been so close.'

'This Florian, how were he and his family connected to yours?'

'My great-grandfather, Andreas, was Florian's godfather, so when he was accused of stealing the tiara, you can imagine how well that was received.' Luca stared at the piece of newsprint again, as if he'd seen a ghost. 'Florian has to be the reason your grandmother was given that sapphire, her connection to him.'

'Let me get this straight,' Georgia said, taking an oyster and using a little fork to scoop it into her mouth. She sat relishing the taste as she thought over what Luca had just told her. 'Your great-grandfather somehow had the sapphire in his possession, despite the fact that it may or may not have belonged to Florian Lengacher, who happened to be his godson. But while he was custodian of it, one of the stones went missing.'

'Correct. Although my family believe the stone went missing before it was under our care,' he said. 'Another fact that was disputed at the time.'

'So this Florian,' she said, pointing to the paper, 'is the link between my mystery and yours.'

He reached forward to take an oyster. 'The question now,' Luca said, 'is who was he to your great-grandmother? And how did she end up with a stone from one of the most iconic European tiaras in history?'

10

GENEVA, JULY 1951

'Come on, children, we're going to have lunch and then ice cream,' Delphine said, trying to sound bright for their sake. Giovanni had gone that morning, and although he hadn't told the children what was happening, they seemed to sense that something was wrong. Which was why she'd decided to take them out for a day of fun, and to show them how beautiful the lake was. It might be just the three of them from now on, but she was determined not to stay at home and mope. Perhaps it would be better just the three of them, anyway, or at least that's what she'd decided to tell herself. Her only regret was that her sister hadn't been there to join them—they'd gone away for an extended summer holiday to Greece, where her husband was from.

Tommaso stayed close to her, but Isabella ran ahead, skipping between the strangers despite Delphine's constant pleas to keep near. As usual, she was in her own little world, not caring that she was no longer within eyesight of her mother and brother.

'Isabella,' she called, when she disappeared from sight. 'Isabella!' Delphine tugged on Tommaso's hand and hurried through a small crowd of people near an ice cream stand when she realised she could no longer see Isabella, furious with her daughter for disobeying her. But when she spied her, she couldn't give her the sharp telling-off she deserved, because it seemed that the little girl had found someone to talk to.

'I'm terribly sorry,' Delphine said, grabbing hold of Isabella's hand. 'One second she was just ahead of me, and the next she'd disappeared completely.'

'You have nothing at all to be sorry about,' said a tall man with warm dark eyes and a wide, even warmer smile. He was wearing a suit, but the top button of his shirt was undone and his tie was pulled down slightly lower than it should have been, as if he'd just arrived home from work at the end of the day. 'The young lady has been telling me which ice cream she'd like to order.'

Delphine could feel her cheeks turning what she imagined would be a very dark shade of pink. 'I can't apologise enough, she—'

'Would like the strawberry flavour, it seems,' he said, his mouth turning up slightly at one corner as if he was terribly amused. 'I made it very clear that we would have to ask her mother first though, because she did declare that she hadn't yet had lunch.'

Isabella turned to her then, with a devilish smile, somehow having wrapped this stranger around her little finger. Tommaso leaned into Delphine and kept hold of her hand, reminding her just how different her children were.

'I think my daughter needs a lesson in manners,' Delphine said, gesturing to Isabella that it was time to leave and that she should come and stand beside her. 'Thank you for your kindness, but—'

'Can I not buy you all ice cream?' he asked. 'I have to confess that I think ice cream before lunch sounds like a fantastic idea. I don't know why I haven't thought to do it before.'

Delphine hesitated, but even Tommaso was looking at her with pleading eyes now. 'Well...'

'I'm Florian,' he said, stepping closer and holding out his hand. 'Now it's me who's the one forgetting their manners. Florian Lengacher.'

'Delphine,' she replied, as he held her hand firmly, yet gently. 'And this is my son Tommaso and—'

'Your daughter Bella, short for Isabella.'

Her cheeks heated again. Isabella had managed to tell this stranger her name *and* her favourite ice cream all within the few minutes she'd been missing. They were definitely going to have words.

'Favourite flavours?' Florian asked, with a twinkle in his eye that told her he was enjoying every moment of their exchange.

She was able to observe him as he bent to speak to her son, and she found herself drawn to the easy way he conversed with her children.

'Banana, please,' Tommaso said from beside her, before walking over to join his sister.

'And for you?' Florian asked.

'Oh, I don't need one, just the children, but I can't let you—'

'Please, let me treat you all,' he said. 'And I can highly recommend the strawberry, your daughter was very smart with her choice. If I can twist your arm to try something, that is.'

She laughed. Despite how ridiculous it was that she was standing talking to a very handsome gentleman outside an ice cream stand, she laughed. 'Well, then, strawberry it is.'

Florian grinned, holding her gaze a second too long and making her feel heat in places other than her cheeks. How long had it been since a man gave her such an appreciative gaze? Her husband certainly hadn't ever looked at her like that, and she couldn't help but wonder if he was already in the arms of his mistress in London. The thought had made her desperately sad only the day before, but she'd almost become numb to it now, accepting after her humiliating attempt at seducing him that there truly was nothing she could do to save her marriage.

She stood and waited as Florian ordered, not sure whether to feel flattered or uncomfortable that he'd taken such an interest in them. Did he feel sorry for her because she clearly had such little control over her daughter, or did he feel unexpectedly drawn to her in the same way she was feeling drawn to him?

'First one for the little lady, second one for the handsome young man,' Florian said, before turning to her with a smile. 'And lastly, one for their beautiful mother.'

She took the ice cream he held out to her, pleased to see that he also had one for himself. Delphine tried to lick hers in the most ladylike way possible, while stealing glances at Florian, wondering where he was from and what his story was. He certainly looked like a man who'd have a stunning wife at home waiting for him. Unless, of course, he was a widower? She had so many questions and no intention of asking any of them.

She glanced at his finger to try to catch sight of a wedding ring, but he wasn't wearing one. It wasn't conclusive though, as many married men didn't wear jewellery. She wondered now if that was why Giovanni never wore his—did it make it easier for him to meet women?

'Shall we sit or stroll?' Florian asked, interrupting her thoughts. 'Are you holidaymakers here to see the lake? It's certainly a lovely day to enjoy the view.'

'We've just moved here,' Isabella said, before Delphine had time to answer. 'But Papa has left for London and he's not coming home.'

Delphine choked on her ice cream, spluttering as she glared at Isabella. Clearly her daughter was becoming far too precocious; she would be having a word with Martina when they got home, and would make sure they were both harder on her manners from now on.

'Papa *is* coming home,' Delphine said, firmly.

'But I heard—'

She gave her daughter such a sharp look that she stopped speaking immediately.

'Your husband works abroad? And yet you've just moved here? From...'

'Italy,' she said. 'Rome, to be precise. But my family is from Switzerland, and both my family and my husband's family have business interests here in Geneva.'

He nodded, and they went back to eating their ice cream as they strolled.

'How have you found it? Moving back to your home country?'

Delphine cleared her throat, looking away as she tried to think of how to answer. *Lonely. Sad. Heartbroken.* But, of course, she wasn't about to tell him the truth.

'It's been an adjustment. I'd lived in Rome since I was nineteen, and I thought it was where I'd live for the rest of my life.' She smiled. 'And yet here I am, back in the country of my birth.'

He smiled, and she realised they were getting to the end of their ice cream. Delphine didn't want their walk to end, was liking the company, and particularly the attention of Florian. She only wished it was him they were talking about, and not her.

'Are you a tourist?' she asked. But the second the words left her mouth, she knew it was a silly question. He was dressed for business, and his accent sounded as if he was a native Swiss.

'Not at all. I have a house near here.'

'Overlooking the lake?'

He nodded. 'Yes, overlooking the lake. I grew up in Annemasse, so I'm French-born, but my parents worked here and I always knew that this was where I wanted to be. After I graduated, I went looking around the lake for houses, and I decided then and there which house I wanted to own one day. It took me a decade, but when I had the money, I knocked on the door myself and offered to buy it.'

'I'm impressed,' Delphine said. And she was. He was clearly successful, but he was telling her almost matter-of-factly rather than boasting. 'And I'm also impressed that you have time for ice cream in the middle of the day. Your boss must be very understanding.'

Florian laughed, and she knew she would do anything to see him laugh like that again; to see his eyes crinkle at the sides and his head tip back. It was a real laugh, and it made her want to laugh, too. When had she last been herself like this? Had a conversation with another person without worrying that she was saying the right thing? Laughed without being self-conscious?

'Thankfully I am my own boss. I work in finance,' he said. 'But I have to confess that I wasn't looking for ice cream. I had a business meeting earlier, and I was walking to my favourite restaurant on the lake for lunch when I crossed paths with your delightful daughter.'

'My precocious daughter,' she corrected. 'I have no idea how she became so wilful.'

'She has a captivating smile, just like her mother. There's nothing precocious about her at all.' He laughed. 'Perhaps you were the same at her age?'

Delphine sighed. Perhaps he was right, although it had been so long since she was a little girl with dreams that she'd almost forgotten. 'I'm sorry we ruined your lunch. Is there any way I can make it up to you?'

Florian stopped walking for a second, his ice cream long gone as he smiled at her. They stood for a short while, the remnants of her ice cream in her hand still as she watched him in return.

'Would you like to join me?' he asked. 'For lunch? Have you eaten?'

Delphine shifted her weight from one foot to the other. They had been looking for somewhere to stop and eat, but she knew that it would be very improper to have a meal with a complete stranger, especially when that stranger was a man. Even if they had ruined his day and already let him buy them ice cream.

'The soup is particularly good at the restaurant I was going to. If you're partial to soup, that is?'

She realised she was holding her breath and she slowly let it go before answering him. 'That does sound very appealing, but I'd better keep the children moving. But thank you, for the ice cream. It was most unexpected.'

Florian nodded. 'I understand. But just in case you're in the area tomorrow at this time, perhaps without your children, I'll be at the Beau-Rivage. It's just a stone's throw from the ice cream vendor.'

Delphine stared at him for a second, wondering if she'd misheard, because it sounded awfully like he'd just invited her on a date. His gaze didn't waver, which told her he was most definitely serious. *I'm married. I have a husband. I cannot have lunch with you.* They were all things she should have said, but nothing came out of her mouth.

'It's been a pleasure meeting you today, Delphine,' Florian said, holding out his hand.

She lifted hers and let him take it, finding that she was holding her breath again until he finally let it go. There was something about his palm being pressed to hers that made her want to hold on and not let go.

'Thank you,' she murmured. 'It's been a pleasure meeting you, too.'

As he nodded and began to walk away, she found herself staring after him, wondering what had just happened. The only thing she knew for certain was that she absolutely shouldn't go to the restaurant the following day, no matter how badly she wanted to.

I'm a married woman.

Yet here she was, in Geneva, alone with her children, without a husband.

And Delphine had the strangest feeling that, for evermore, her life would be divided into before she met Florian Lengacher and after.

11

GENEVA, JULY 1951

Delphine knew she shouldn't go. All morning she'd told herself that she wouldn't, that she would stay home and forget all about the alluring man she'd met the day before. But the closer the time came, the more she knew that she couldn't abide by her own rules. Giovanni had made her feel small their entire marriage, had made her think something was wrong with her, but Florian... Florian had made her feel alive in the short time they'd spent together. So, despite her guilt, despite knowing better, she decided to go back to the restaurant by the lake where she knew she would find him.

Leaving the house was simple enough; she had no one to explain herself to. She told her children she was meeting a friend, and for the first time in her life, she lied to Martina. She might have been her closest friend in Geneva, but she wasn't ready to tell anyone about Florian yet. Besides, she didn't even know if there was anything to tell.

Delphine went to her room and closed the door behind her, touching up her make-up and going through her entire wardrobe before settling on a pretty summer dress. She glanced down at her ring finger, at the diamond band there, but refused to feel guilty. She could only imagine that Giovanni wasn't thinking twice about whatever he was doing, or with whom, and she needed to learn to do the same.

By the time she was ready to leave the house, and had kissed both her children goodbye, she was beginning to feel less and less guilt, and more and more excitement. Her heart raced as she stepped down the path to the waiting car, and she thought she might explode as she sat in the back seat on the short drive, back towards the lake, back towards where she'd met Florian the day before. Something about the way he'd looked at her, the way he'd spoken to her, had been impossible to forget.

She'd gone to sleep the night before thinking about him, and she'd woken with him on her mind, and all she could think of was that he'd told her where he'd be, that he would be at his favourite restaurant at the same time as they'd met the day before, and that he very much wished they would cross paths again. Delphine had half a mind to think that she'd made a mistake, that he was only being polite when he'd said that to her, but something about the way he'd held her eye, the way he'd smiled at her, told her that it was more than just politeness. He'd looked at her in the way she'd waited her entire life for a man to look at her—there had been no mistaking his intention.

Which was how she found herself walking alone in her pretty summer dress, looking out at the water and wondering whether she had the courage to stop, or whether she'd simply end up going home without seeing him at all. In the end, she hesitated outside the restaurant and then kept walking, her nerves getting the better of her.

I can't do it. What if he's not there? What if he doesn't want to see me?

'I was starting to think you'd stayed home today,' Florian said. 'But now I've seen you walk past the restaurant without going in, I'm wondering if you've decided to have ice cream again first?'

Delphine's body flooded with relief when she heard his deep, warm voice, although she didn't look up immediately, letting his words wash over her as she stood. 'Something like that,' she eventually said, turning to look at him. 'And you? You came back for the soup again?'

He laughed, and she found herself glancing up and catching his eye. 'Something like that,' he said, repeating her words back to her. 'Although there was something about the view yesterday that I was particularly fond of, too. I very much hoped that I would be seeing it again.'

Their eyes met, her stomach fluttering and her hands trembling. *What am I doing? I should never have come, I should have stayed home and forgotten all about him, not come back looking for trouble.*

'Will you be joining me for lunch?' Florian asked, although he obviously saw the look on her face and thought better of his invitation. 'Or perhaps we could just walk.'

She hesitated. 'I'm cautious of being seen. I wouldn't want to...' She wasn't quite certain how to tell him that she wasn't used to having lunch dates with men.

'It would only be lunch,' he said. 'And in plain sight. Friends sharing a meal.' He smiled. 'You do have to eat, after all.'

It seemed he was very good at twisting her arm, because only minutes later she found herself being ushered to an outside table and being seated across from Florian. She was careful to keep her seat well away from his, and when he asked what wine she liked, she was quick to shake her head.

'I couldn't,' Delphine said. 'Water will be fine.'

He raised a brow and smiled at her across the table, making her stomach flutter again. 'One glass? Surely you'll join me? It's such a lovely day, after all.'

'One glass then,' she said, her resolve fading. 'But—'

'Delphine, there is nothing wrong with two people having

lunch,' he said. 'Perhaps we could make this a business lunch, so you don't feel uncomfortable?'

'A *business* lunch?' She laughed. 'And how do you suppose we do that? I don't think I look like a woman doing business.'

He grinned. 'Well, that way, if anyone were to see you and ask, you can confidently tell them that you were meeting me to discuss your investments. Perhaps you have family money you'd like me to invest for you?'

Delphine laughed. 'And how many female clients do you have, Florian? I suspect that you very rarely discuss *investments* with women.'

He shrugged. 'On the contrary. I have some widows who trust me implicitly with their fortune, although I deal mostly in company finance.'

If his goal was to set her at ease, he'd certainly achieved it. 'Fine,' Delphine said. 'One glass of wine, and only because I very much feel like one after my little walk in the sun.'

His smile was contagious. 'Of course.'

By the time their lunch arrived—fillets of perch served with a squeeze of lemon, and a side of French fries that Florian had insisted upon—she'd almost forgotten all about her nerves at being seen with him. He'd kept up an easy conversation, asking her about her children and mentioning his work, and when they paused to taste their food, she found herself glancing up at him to study his face between mouthfuls. He was handsome in a traditional way, with brown hair and eyes to match, his skin slightly tanned, evidenced by the way he had his shirtsleeves rolled up, his forearms golden. He'd clearly shaved that morning, but already she could see a light stubble forming, and her fingers ached to reach out and touch his cheek or stroke along his jaw.

'So tell me, where in Switzerland did you grow up?'

'We lived in Lyon when I was younger, but as my parents' business became more successful, they bought a summer house here by the lake,' she said, wondering if her accent still sounded as laced with French as his did. 'My family had a house with views of the water, and my sister lives there still.'

'She's the oldest?'

'No,' Delphine said, 'I am. But I was married off to a suitable prospect, and we moved to his native Italy, so she was left the house.' *Not to mention being allowed to choose the man she was to marry.*

'Do you miss Italy?' he asked.

'I do. I miss my home, I miss the friends I'd made, the children's friends...' Her voice trailed off. 'But enough about me, tell me about you.'

'I grew up in Annemasse, but moved to Geneva to attend university and I never left. I found it was the perfect place for me to conduct my business, although it was the lake I truly fell in love with.'

'Do you have children?'

'A son. Daniel is studying law at university, although at present he's in Paris with his mother.'

They were silent as the waiter came and cleared their plates. They both had a mouthful or so of wine left in their glasses, but it seemed that neither of them was in a hurry to empty them. Delphine found herself stroking the stem as she smiled at Florian across the table.

'It's been wonderful seeing you again, Delphine,' Florian said when they were alone. 'I would be lying if I said I wasn't hoping you'd come. Imagine my good fortune when you suddenly appeared.'

She didn't tell him that she felt the very same way, or that she'd been about to walk off when he'd seen her and called out. Perhaps he already knew and had decided not to mention it.

'I come here most Fridays, if you ever need a companion for lunch again, and I've heard they have *excellent* ice cream nearby.'

'I happen to have heard of the same ice cream place. I may have even been there yesterday.' She lifted her glass then and finished it, surprised by her sudden boldness, her fingers playing up and down the stem as Florian drained the last of the wine from his glass, too. 'Well, it was a pleasure seeing you, Florian, but I must be going.'

The last thing she truly wanted was to leave, but she knew she'd already been out long enough. It was time for her to go home.

Florian stood and pulled out her chair, and she accidentally grazed her arm against his as she stood. He stared at her in a way that made her entire body flood with heat. She trusted that no one else had noticed, or at the very least that he hadn't.

'I would very much like to see you again, Delphine,' Florian said quietly, as he lifted her hand and pressed a kiss to her skin. 'My house is very private. Perhaps you could join me for dinner one evening?'

Delphine wanted to say yes, to tell him that she very much wanted to see him again, too. That he was most likely all she was going to think about for the rest of the day. But her voice stuttered in her throat, her worry about someone seeing them together, about what would happen if Giovanni found out, rising inside her.

'I could send a car for you tomorrow evening,' he said, holding her gaze even as he let go of her hand.

Say no. You're married, and just because you're living separately, that doesn't mean you can see another man. But then she remembered what Giovanni had said when he'd told her he was leaving, when he'd given her her freedom. *Be discreet.* That's what he'd said, as if he presumed that she would take a lover outside of their marriage, almost as if he *expected* it. *Just as he's been doing for God only knows how long without my knowledge.*

'Florian, I'm married,' she eventually murmured, knowing

that at some point she had to come out and say it. It might as well be now, before things went any further between them.

'I'm well aware that you're married,' he replied, his voice as low as hers had been. 'As am I. And yet we're both here alone, seeking out each other's company. It seems that we're in the same predicament.'

She swallowed. 'You live separately from your wife?'

'I do. We've lived apart for almost a decade, in different countries for that matter. And you? Where does your husband reside?' His face gave nothing away. 'Do you expect him to return?'

Delphine didn't want to talk about her husband, she didn't even want to think about him, not when her heart was racing as she stood in front of Florian. 'We also live separately. He's in London now, and no, I do not expect him to return. Not for me, anyway.'

Florian's gaze was a question, the heat in his eyes telling her that he was still waiting for her answer. It seemed they had more in common that she'd realised, and a flutter of longing ignited deep inside her, a sense that perhaps what she was feeling was real.

'Was that a yes to me sending a car, then?' he asked.

She lifted her chin and squared her shoulders, looking boldly at Florian, as if she wasn't withering inside with nerves, as if she was used to behaving in such a way with a man who wasn't her husband. 'I shall arrange my own car,' she said, speaking confidently in a way she never would have if she'd been addressing Giovanni.

The twinkle in Florian's eye as he smiled back at her and gave her his address told her that he was very happy with her decision, and she only wished that he still had hold of her hand so she could feel the warmth of his skin against hers one last time.

'Until tomorrow night, then,' he said.

Her pulse raced as she smiled back at him. 'Until tomorrow.'

'It would be an understatement to say that I'm already looking forward to it.'

And as she turned to walk away, trying to resist her smile and failing, all she could think was that tomorrow couldn't come fast enough. But she would have to be careful. The last thing she wanted was for anyone to see her with Florian, for a rumour to start, or for anyone in her household to guess that she was spending time with a man. If she was going to do this, she would be more than just discreet—it would be a secret that no one would ever discover.

Tomorrow. Delphine glanced over her shoulder before the restaurant disappeared from sight, and it sent a thrill of excitement through her when she saw that Florian was still watching her, that he hadn't—it appeared—taken his eyes off her.

12

PRESENT DAY

Georgia looked out of the window of her hotel, admiring the view as the light began to fade. She'd checked into the Beau-Rivage for her stay, although she was starting to realise that four nights might not be long enough. The hotel was stunning, but Luca had told her that she absolutely must stay longer and check into the La Réserve Hotel and Spa for a few nights, as well. It wasn't as if she had anything pressing to return to England for, and she did love the idea of indulging in massages and lazing about by a swimming pool for a few more days. Not to mention that Luca seemed very interested in showing her around. After their long lunch the day before, that had stretched well into the afternoon, she had no intention of declining if he wanted to see her again.

Her phone rang then and Georgia reached for it, knowing exactly who it would be. *Sam.* They'd texted since she'd arrived but not had the chance to speak, and she knew that Sam would be wanting to hear all about Luca. She'd already updated her on the sapphire, but she had a feeling it wasn't the stone Sam wanted to hear about.

'I was just thinking about you,' Georgia said when she

answered, seeing Sam on her screen. Her friend appeared to be dressed in a dark green woollen jumper, which was very unlike her. 'What are you wearing?'

'Please don't ask. Apparently Harry's family like to go grouse shooting together at the weekend.'

'Well, it sounds like you're really moving out of your comfort zone. I'm impressed.'

Sam groaned. 'Please can we just talk about you?' She leaned towards the screen and dropped her voice to a whisper. 'I wish I'd come with you. It's horrible here! I thought we'd be sipping gin and tonics in the sun, but instead they have me out marching around the countryside day and night!'

Georgia laughed at the pained expression on Sam's face. 'I'm sorry it's not the weekend you expected.'

'Tell me about your trip. What's happening? Is Luca as divine as he is in his photo?'

Georgia smiled to herself. 'He's gorgeous, and his accent is divine. Even the way he says my name sends a shiver down my spine.'

'When are you seeing him again?'

'Monday morning. He's coming to take me to a lawyer's office, to see if a letter there is addressed to my great-grandmother.'

'Ooh, the plot thickens,' Sam said. 'But didn't he offer to take you out over the weekend? It's not every day a girl travels to Switzerland.'

'I imagine he already had other plans,' she said, hoping she was fooling Sam with her nonchalance. 'But honestly, the strangest thing is not having the sapphire with me. I've become used to having it in the little box with me, but Luca thought it was best to keep it in a safe, given the value.'

Sam leaned closer into the phone again, her face taking up the entire screen. 'They're calling me again. Save me, G. *Please* save me!'

Georgia laughed as Sam kissed the air, before the screen went blank. She was still laughing when the hotel phone rang, nearly causing her to jump out of her skin.

'Hello?' She pressed the receiver to her ear.

'Ms Montano, I'm calling on behalf of a Mr Luca Kaufmann.'

Her pulse ignited. 'He's in reception?'

'He requested that you meet him in the lobby at your earliest convenience. He will be waiting at the bar.'

'Thank you.'

She hung up the telephone and stared at the open wardrobe where she'd hung all her clothes. The little black dress was staring back at her, and despite her protests when Sam had told her to pack it, suddenly it felt like the most appropriate attire.

If he was only stopping by for a drink or to give her information, she could pretend she was dressed to go out elsewhere. But if he wanted to take her out for dinner? Then she would be perfectly dressed for the occasion. *At least I hope I will be.*

Fifteen minutes later, Georgia stepped out of the elevator and crossed the lobby to find Luca sitting with a drink in his hand. She hesitated, watching him, but he seemed to sense she was there and turned.

'Georgia,' he said, putting his drink down and standing.

She couldn't help but notice the way his eyes danced down and then back up her body. *Thank you, Sam.* Georgia felt like a million dollars in her dress, with her long dark hair falling over her shoulders and a pair of black pumps on. She had a blazer caught over her arm, an excuse in case it became cold, but in reality she'd brought it down with her to slip on if she felt the dress was too much. But Luca was wearing a tailored suit with an open-necked shirt underneath, which made her pleased she'd dressed up instead of coming down in jeans.

'It was presumptuous of me to think you wouldn't already have plans,' he said, leaning in to kiss her cheek. 'Hopefully you can join me for a drink?'

Georgia nodded. 'Of course. I don't know anyone in Geneva other than you, so it's nice to see a friendly face.'

Luca gestured for her to take the seat he'd been in, pulling another bar stool closer for himself. 'What would you like to drink?'

'What are you having?'

'Well, I've just had a brandy.' He grinned. 'Tough day at the office, but I'm already starting to forget all about it.'

The way he smiled at her made her wonder if he was meaning that *she'd* made him forget all about it, and she glanced away from the heat in his gaze.

'Difficult customers?' she asked.

'You could say that,' Luca said. 'But tell me about your day. I would have come to see you sooner, but work got in the way.'

'Well, I followed your instructions and visited the old town, and you were absolutely right about the architecture, it's stunning.'

'And you went somewhere nice for lunch?'

'I did, to a charming café. Then I climbed the tower of St Pierre Cathedral, and the view was every bit as incredible as you said it would be, and then I explored the underground archaeological remains before I came back to the hotel.'

He sat back and studied her, grinning as he slowly shook his head. 'You did all that, and yet somehow you've still managed to come down for drinks looking refreshed and beautiful, as if you've been resting all day.'

Georgia couldn't help the blush that she knew was creeping across her cheeks, but she refused to acknowledge her embarrassment. Usually, she would have fobbed off a compliment, but not tonight. She wasn't going to let herself. 'Thank you.'

'Now, back to drinks,' he said. 'Shall we have a glass of champagne? To toast you being in Geneva?'

She smiled. 'That sounds perfect to me.'

Once he'd ordered, he pulled his chair a little closer, and if she'd uncrossed her legs, it would have been impossible not to brush his knees with hers.

'How long are you staying for again?' Luca asked, his face suddenly serious.

'I'm scheduled to leave on Tuesday morning, at this stage.' She held her breath a second before asking, 'Is that long enough?'

'Long enough for us to unravel the mystery of the sapphire?' He shook his head. 'No.'

'I was meaning was it long enough to see Geneva?' she said softly.

'It's not long enough for that, either,' Luca said, passing her the champagne as it arrived. 'I was hoping that I might be the one to show you around. I've organised a few days off work if you can change your travel plans?'

'Of course,' she said, taking a sip, the bubbles tickling her nose as she swallowed them. 'What exactly do you have in mind?'

'Well,' he said, leaning forward a little, his arm braced on the bar. 'I was thinking we could start with dinner out tonight, somewhere nice on the lake, and tomorrow I want to take you on a helicopter ride over the city. It's the best way to see the sights.'

Georgia immediately felt uncomfortable, a bead of sweat breaking out across her top lip at the mention of helicopters. Luca must have noticed her reaction, the way she held her glass too tight, because he reached out and took it from her, replacing the glass with his hand.

'I can see that wasn't a good idea.'

She looked up at him, wishing she didn't react so viscerally to even thinking about being in a helicopter. 'I'm, ah, I'm just not good in the air. Even commercial flights, it's just—'

'You don't have to explain, I recall yesterday you saying you didn't enjoy the flight,' he said, softly, still holding her hand. 'I don't know what I was thinking anyway, it would be *much* more enjoyable to visit the museum. And if you prefer cycling, we could hire bicycles and visit a winery.'

Georgia laughed. 'Could we not just drive there?'

Luca laughed along with her, releasing her hand and passing her the champagne again. 'That's an even better idea,' he said, and she appreciated how quickly he'd made light of her reaction. Laughing with Luca felt better than good; it felt *great*. 'I don't know why I didn't suggest that in the first place.'

'I'm sorry, about before, I just—'

'No need to explain,' he said. 'I will do anything to keep that gorgeous smile on your face. And if that means not mentioning helicopters ever again?' Luca placed his hand over his heart. 'I have already removed the word from my vocabulary.'

She sipped her champagne as he reached for his, realising that the only person who she'd ever been so herself around was Sam.

'I should have asked already, but you don't have a, ah, significant other back in London?' Luca asked.

'I do not,' she replied, trying very hard not to choke on her champagne. 'And you?' *Please say no. Please say no.*

'I wouldn't be sitting in a bar with a beautiful brunette if I did,' he teased. 'I don't think there would be a wife anywhere in Switzerland who'd allow it.'

Warmth spread through her at the compliment, but it also left her completely speechless.

'Do you have plans for dinner, Georgia?'

'I was intending on asking the concierge for recommendations on where to dine tonight.'

'Alone?' Luca asked. 'I thought since you were dressed like that...'

'Alone,' she confirmed.

'Well, we can't have that. Would you like to join me? I have a reservation at Tosca.'

'You were that certain I would say yes to joining you?'

'Well, I intended on telling you how incredible their Italian food is, and that we had many things to discuss about the sapphire.' He grinned. 'In case you were wondering, both of those things are true.'

'So, it would be a business dinner? To discuss the sapphire?'

Luca stood and held out his arm. 'Of course. Strictly professional.'

Georgia looped her hand through his arm, feeling as if she had stepped back in time, holding on to the arm of a devilishly handsome man as they strolled through the hotel lobby on their way to dinner. She was under no illusions that their dinner was strictly business, but she loved that he was willing to pretend it was.

'You're going to love the restaurant,' Luca said, as the concierge opened the door for them. 'It's on the Rue de la Mairie, and their pheasant ravioli is like nothing you've ever tasted before.'

She had no idea where that was, and she'd certainly never eaten pheasant ravioli, but somehow with Luca's French accent, everything sounded incredible.

After dinner, Georgia strolled beside Luca. She'd never imagined how pretty it would be walking by the lake, especially at night.

'There is nothing more beautiful than looking out at the boats after dark,' he said.

'It's magical,' Georgia said, pausing to admire all the twinkling lights in the distance. 'They look like fireflies, dancing in the dark.'

Luca stood close to her; close enough so that she could feel his presence, but without touching her.

'Do you have an aversion to boat rides, by chance?' he asked.

She turned, laughing at the playful look in his expression.

'Thankfully, no. I would be more than willing to go for a boat ride.'

Luca nodded, and although she respected that he hadn't asked, she decided to tell him anyway.

'My parents died when I was a teenager,' she said, turning back to look out at the water, finding it easier to talk about them when she stared into the distance. 'It was years ago now, and I've long since come to accept their passing, but they died on a trip away.'

'A helicopter trip?' he asked, gently.

Georgia sighed, her memories of that day still vivid in her mind, impossible to forget even after all this time. 'They were due to come home that day, and my mum had planned a helicopter flight for my dad. He was an aviation nerd, knew everything about every plane and helicopter ever made, and it was their twentieth wedding anniversary. Mum knew he'd love it.'

Luca moved closer then, standing almost in front of her so he could see her face. She forced herself to look at him, instead of taking the easier option and looking away.

'The crash was fatal, the pilot lost his life as well, and ever since I've found it impossible to even look at a helicopter without a shudder running through me. I don't find any type of flying straightforward, if I'm completely honest.'

He touched his hand gently to her back, as if sensing that she needed to start walking, and they began to stroll again, with the river to their left.

'Thank you for sharing that with me, Georgia,' he said. 'I

can hear from your voice that you must have been a close family.'

Emotion clogged her throat and she quickly cleared it. 'We were. I only wish it were easier to talk about.'

'The passing of a family member is never easy. I don't think it's supposed to be,' Luca said. 'But I can see now why the sapphire must hold a special meaning for you, since it was left for a family member, when you don't have either of your parents anymore.'

'It is special, but restoring it to its rightful owner is important, too. If it wasn't my great-grandmother's to give—'

'I believe it was hers to give,' he said. 'I don't know the details yet, but for a sapphire to be taken from the tiara? It had to be by someone who owned it, or someone who was close to it. If it were stolen, there would have been an uproar, a manhunt even, rather than a great mystery that's lasted for so many decades.'

'You truly believe that it belonged to her?' Georgia asked.

'I think there is much of the mystery that we're yet to uncover, but yes, I believe it belonged to her. I believe that it held a special significance, which is why she left it behind for her daughter.'

'A link to the father of the child?'

Luca shrugged. 'Perhaps. Or perhaps a link to her family, a family that disowned her due to her being pregnant.'

Georgia hadn't thought about that possibility, but now that he'd said it, it would make sense. Perhaps her great-grandmother had been treated unfairly in the same way Georgia's father had, for choosing to marry someone who wasn't from the right family or the right side of town.

'Thank you, Luca,' she said, stopping and watching him as he did the same. 'Thank you for giving me such a great time, for making this trip so special.'

Luca surprised her by taking her hand, his fingers catching

hold of hers as he slowly lifted her palm, pressing a soft, lingering kiss to her skin as he looked into her eyes.

'It's me who must thank you for a magical evening,' he said. 'Had I known my day was going to end like this...'

She swallowed, wanting him to keep hold of her hand, wanting to feel his lips pressed against hers. She didn't know if it was because she was on holiday and away from home, but something about being in Switzerland in the company of a man as handsome and charming as Luca... felt different. Or maybe she was finally relaxing and letting her hair down, allowing herself to just be rather than trying to be what she felt was expected of her all the time.

'This trip isn't turning out anything like I thought,' she whispered. 'I didn't expect any of this.'

'Then that makes two of us.'

His voice was a low whisper, and she found herself tilting her chin to look up into his eyes, imagining what it would be like if he kissed her.

'What did you expect?' Georgia asked, as he linked their fingers and pulled her gently towards him. It was a gesture so light that she could have simply leaned back a little to resist moving at all, but she was only too happy to take a step closer to him.

His eyes met hers, unwavering as he spoke, making it impossible for her to look away.

'I expected someone searching for as much money as they could get,' he murmured. 'A woman that I would have to be nice to, simply because I needed to acquire the sapphire, if it truly was what I was looking for. I didn't expect that woman to be anything like you.'

'So all of this,' she said, gesturing with her free hand to the water behind them, 'drinks, dinner, the walk, it was all part of your plan to win me over? So that I would sell you the stone? So that I would be easier to negotiate with?' Georgia was only teasing, but a little part of her had wondered if he was playing a game, if he wanted her to fall for him so that she would be a softer touch. She couldn't think of anything more humiliating than finding out she'd been duped by a man she was having feelings for.

'Not at all,' Luca said, tugging her a little closer still, his fingers warm against hers, his smile just touching the corners of his mouth. 'I believe that you are a businesswoman who will part with the sapphire for what it is worth. I don't think you came here for any reason other than to establish the facts and find out what those clues mean to your family. And I think,' he said, his voice even deeper, husky now, 'I think that you will be a very astute businesswoman to deal with.'

'Is that so?'

Her breath was ragged now as he lifted his other hand and gently ran his knuckles down her cheek, before leaning forward and whispering a kiss to her skin.

If Georgia had been more brazen, she would have turned her face slightly so that his lips touched her mouth instead, but she didn't. Instead she stood, immobile, as he took a step back and slowly let go of her hand, his fingers holding on to the tips of hers until they finally fell away.

'Thank you for a night I will never forget,' Luca said, touching his hand to his heart. 'Tomorrow?'

She nodded. 'Tomorrow,' Georgia repeated. 'I shall be ready at eleven.'

'Should I get my assistant to change your flights for you?' he asked. 'You truly do need more time here. I have so much still to show you.'

Georgia laughed. 'I'm perfectly capable of changing my flights. But yes, I agree, four nights were never going to be enough.' *If it means spending more time with you, I'll stay another week if I need to.*

Luca's smile was impossible not to return, and as she turned to walk back to the hotel, Georgia fought with every step not to look over her shoulder. But she couldn't help but glance back when she entered the lobby of the hotel, a hand on the door as her eyes met his for one last time.

He was still standing there, his hands in his pockets, looking impossibly handsome in his suit, his white shirt unbuttoned lower than it had been at the start of the night and looking just ever so slightly dishevelled. He held up his hand in a wave, and she waved back to him, with a smile on her face that she knew would still be there when she fell asleep that night. Luca would be impossible not to keep thinking about, and she only wished she'd been courageous enough to ask him up for a drink from the minibar, to draw their night out just a little longer.

Once she was up in her room, the door safely locked behind her, Georgia kicked off her heels and reached for the little wooden box. She'd left it beside the bed earlier, and she suddenly had an overwhelming desire to hold it. She flopped onto the mattress, the box in her outstretched hand as she closed her eyes and relived the past few hours. Without that box, she would never have travelled to Geneva. She would never have crossed paths with Luca. Her grandmother had done nothing to help her when she'd been alive, but the little box bearing her name had sent Georgia on an unforgettable journey that felt as if it was only just beginning.

She'd felt so alone for such a long time, wishing she had her family with her, wishing she had her mother to turn to or her father to laugh with. Perhaps now she'd finally find the connection to her family she'd been yearning for.

13

LAKE GENEVA, JULY 1951

Delphine had been to Florian's house for dinner three times now, and every time filled her with a shiver of excitement. There was something about him that completely captivated her, that made her yearn to see him again. But up until now, he'd been the perfect gentleman, despite the intimacy of their dinners, and she was starting to wonder if it would be her who had to make the first move to develop their relationship. She only wished she weren't so hesitant, but the last time she'd shown a man what she wanted, the rebuff had been quick and painful. The last thing she wanted was to see that same look of horror pass over Florian's face.

'How are you finding the house?' he asked, as they sat at a table by his glistening blue pool. There was a candle burning between them, a bottle of opened champagne and two plates of the finest fillet steak, served with tiny potatoes, green beans, and a sauce that smelt delicious.

'It's amazing,' she said, taking a sip of her champagne. She'd already had a glass, and her head was starting to spin a little from the bubbles. 'Giovanni will most likely be furious, but I don't care. The children have a huge home and grounds to explore, and I feel like I'm in control of my life again, even if it is only for the summer.'

Florian smiled at her. 'I'm proud of you. It was a very bold move, if I do say so myself.'

She smiled back at him. It was the first time in her married life that she'd done anything so bold—her sister had written saying she was welcome to use the lake house in her absence, and Delphine had jumped at the chance, taking only Martina with her. The rest of the staff had been left behind, which she knew would anger Giovanni, but she was beginning to care less and less what her husband thought, and more and more about what she wanted.

'Your cook certainly knows how to make a memorable dinner,' Delphine said. 'I feel like I've come to a Michelin-starred restaurant every time I've visited.'

Florian laughed. 'He'll be very happy to hear that. I think he's starting to wonder who I'm trying to impress. I usually come here for the summer and spend the entire time either alone or hosting business associates.'

'He knows you're hosting someone more personal?'

'He does. And I've made him dine at my favourite restaurant many times to learn the menu, so that I can replicate it for you.'

Delphine didn't know what to say. That a man could be so thoughtful constantly took her by surprise. She was also grateful that she'd met him when she had, as he'd explained that he usually spent the summer in this house, as well as long weekends throughout the year, but the rest of the time he was based in Zürich for work.

'These nights, they've become very special to me,' she said, shyly looking up at him as she moved a small piece of steak around her plate.

'They've come to be very special to me, too,' he said. 'I find myself thinking of little else throughout the day. If I'm not careful, you're going to become detrimental to my business.'

She looked at him, not sure how to take his words.

'Detrimental in the very best of ways,' he said, reaching out to touch her hand, his fingers lingering over hers, as if to gauge her reaction.

Delphine stayed still, her breath catching in her throat, as he smiled at her.

'If you like dinner, you'll love dessert,' he said, removing his hand and picking up his fork again.

Delphine's breath returned and she found it almost impossible to concentrate on her food, thinking of nothing other than Florian's touch, about the way he made her feel whenever she was with him.

And when he looked up at her and smiled, his gaze lingering on hers, she knew that she would never, ever feel this way about another man. She'd fallen in love with Florian, and whether she wanted to admit it or not, it would only take one word, one gesture, for her to fall into his arms.

As they stood at his door barely two hours later, she wished their night hadn't come to an end. Just like the nights that had come before, he was the perfect gentleman, but she wanted very much for him not to be.

'Florian,' she said. 'I...' She cleared her throat as Florian leaned past her, his hand on the door to open it for her.

She didn't know how to read the expression on his face, or perhaps she simply didn't trust herself; didn't believe that he could feel that way about her.

He stopped, so close, his eyes finding hers as she drew upon her confidence, as she summoned a nerve that was slowly disappearing on her.

'I wish I didn't have to go,' she said.

Florian slowly dropped his hand from the door, his gaze unwavering as he stared back at her. She knew he was waiting for her, that he wouldn't cross the line that existed between them without her encouragement, without her being explicit in what she wanted, and she also knew that if she didn't do it now, she might never tell him how she felt.

'I would very much like to...' She swallowed, losing her words but taking a step towards him instead. She lifted one hand and placed it lightly on his chest, lowering her gaze before finally glancing back up at him. *Please don't look at me like my husband did. Please don't push me away. Please don't make me regret showing you how I truly feel.*

Delphine stood on tiptoes and hovered, her mouth close to Florian's, desperately wanting to kiss him, to see what his lips tasted like, to see how they made her feel when they moved against hers. To change their relationship from friendship to lovers.

He pulled back and fear rose inside her. She lowered herself to her heels, mortified that she'd read the situation wrong, that she'd done something so deeply out of character, something he didn't want to reciprocate.

Only she hadn't.

Florian cupped her face with his hands, staring down into her eyes with such a hopeful expression, she could tell he wanted it as much as she did. His hesitation wasn't the same as Giovanni's; she could see that now. He was wanting to make sure, to savour the moment.

'Delphine, if we do this, if we take this step...'

She smiled up at him, and immediately Florian lost his composure and kissed her, his palms still against her cheeks as his mouth met hers, forgetting his words. It was a slow, soft kiss the first time, but as she pressed herself against him and his hands fell to her waist, her arms looping around his neck, their lips began to move with more urgency.

'I've waited days to kiss you,' he said, touching his forehead to hers, his breathing as ragged as her own.

'I thought you didn't want me in that way,' she murmured, as his lips brushed hers again and again. 'I was starting to doubt what this was.'

'I want you in more ways than you could possibly imagine. But most important, Delphine, I want you in my bed, and I have from the very first time I laid eyes upon you.'

Her breath caught as he stroked his hands up and down her back, his eyes searching hers as if trying to gauge her answer. But instead of saying anything, she simply slipped her hand into his. Florian didn't need further encouragement this time, for he clasped her hand back and led her towards the stairs.

It appeared that their night wasn't over, after all.

14

GENEVA, AUGUST 1951

Delphine lay in Florian's arms, the sheets strewn around them, their limbs still tangled. She couldn't believe how different it was to be in bed with a man like Florian, how loved he made her feel, how alive. She also couldn't believe how quickly she'd fallen for him, or how desperately she wanted to spend every spare minute she had with him.

And now, as he propped himself up with pillows and she lay nestled in his arms, her cheek to his chest as he smoked a cigarette, she knew that this was how she wanted to feel for the rest of her life: loved and nurtured by a man who couldn't keep his eyes, or his hands, off her. Cherished in a way she'd never felt in her marriage, wanted in a way she hadn't even known was possible.

'I want you for longer than just stolen moments,' Florian said as he blew out a puff of smoke and offered her the cigarette.

She'd never smoked before Florian, but now whenever they made love, he'd taken to lighting one afterwards, and she found she liked to indulge, blowing the smoke up into the air. The way she was with Florian was different to how she was in almost every other part of her life, as if she became a version of herself with him that no one else had ever seen. As if she was finally, unequivocally, herself.

'I want that, too,' she eventually said. 'I hate that we can't be together all the time.'

'Would you want that? If I could find a way?'

She didn't hesitate. 'Of course, I would, Florian. There's nothing I want more.'

They lay there long after he put out his cigarette, his thumb stroking her shoulder as she traced circles on his chest with her fingertips. It wasn't unusual for them to lie in silence, content in each other's company, but today she couldn't stop thinking about what he'd said, because she didn't know how they would ever resolve that particular problem.

'Would you like me to bring dinner up for us?' he asked. 'I had the outside table set, but...'

'Dinner in bed sounds glorious,' she said. 'What did your cook prepare for us this time?'

'My poor cook must be starting to think I have a very large appetite, with the portions I've been requesting,' he said, kissing her on the mouth before sliding out of bed. 'Tonight was coq au vin I think, although I have to confess I was so busy trying to finish work before you arrived, that I didn't pay much attention to anything else.'

She watched his body as he bent to retrieve his underwear, laughing when he turned around and blew her a kiss. Delphine grinned and waited for him to disappear before wrapping herself in the sheet and standing. She walked around the room and looked at some of the photographs he had displayed, pausing at the familiar image of his son and wondering if they'd ever meet. It struck her that Florian must have been young when his son was born.

She heard him come back into the room, but kept walking, looking at another photograph that she presumed was of his family, when he'd been a young man. Arms encircled her from behind then, and Florian's lips brushed against her neck.

'My parents died almost five years ago,' he said. 'Within a few months of each other. I always thought my father died of a broken heart.'

Delphine turned in his arms, leaning against him, her head tilted up so that he could kiss her. Which he did. Florian very rarely missed an opportunity to touch her or kiss her, to love her and make her feel more alive than she'd ever felt before.

'It must be amazing to be married to a true love.'

He kissed her again, before she nestled tighter to his chest, listening to the steady beat of his heart.

'I wouldn't know how it feels,' he finally said, his mouth moving against her hair. 'My parents set a great example, their love clear for everyone to see, and yet I married because it seemed like the right thing to do.'

'You weren't in love? Even then?' She told herself not to be upset if he had been—they were talking about his wife, after all.

'I thought I was,' Florian said. 'But in truth, we were companions, and as our son grew we realised we had very little in common and preferred our own company to that of each other. We were nothing like my parents, and in hindsight I realised I wanted what they had.'

She sighed. It was hard to think about Florian and his wife, as she imagined it would be difficult for him to think about her and Giovanni. But she knew what he meant—the more time she spent with Florian, the more she wished she had married a love match, too.

'Speaking of our spouses, I had a letter from my husband today,' she said.

Florian's arms tightened around her, and she spoke quickly so as to reassure him.

'He wanted me to know that he'll be home for a handful of days at the end of summer. Even though he promised the children he'd be spending time with them, it seems he already has plans to travel with his mistress, if the staff gossip Martina has overheard is to be believed, that is.' Delphine hoped she didn't sound bitter, because she wasn't, not anymore. It was a relief to know he was going to be absent—it would give her more time to be with Florian, after all. 'I also heard that he returned to Switzerland recently, to attend business meetings.'

'He didn't come to see you or the children while he was here?'

She shook her head. 'It seems not. But I won't ever let the children know, it would break their hearts.'

Florian tucked his thumb beneath her chin then, and the way he looked into her eyes, the tender way he touched her, made her feel seen and loved by a man for the first time. Not even as a little girl had she felt so thoroughly cared for.

'He's a fool for not loving you the way you deserve to be loved,' he whispered. 'But his loss is my gain.'

Tears filled her eyes when Florian kissed her, not because she was sad for her husband not caring enough to even visit, but for the simple reason that Florian wasn't her husband. What a different life she would have had with him at her side.

'There are many advantages to us not being married,' Florian said, taking her hand.

Delphine used her other hand to keep the sheet wrapped around herself as she shuffled back to the bed and propped herself up against the pillows.

'I'm struggling to think of any,' she replied.

'Well, eating dinner in bed, for a start,' he said. 'I don't think that's something married couples do.'

She laughed. 'Oh really?'

'Yes, really,' he said, before joining her on the bed and putting a tray of food between them.

'Anything else?'

'I'm sure there's quite a list, I just haven't thought of it yet.'

They both laughed, and when Florian cut a piece of succulent-looking chicken and held it out to her on the fork, she gratefully opened her mouth and let him feed her, which only made them laugh all the more.

He reached over and stroked her hair back from her face then, his touch so tender it brought tears to her eyes. 'I love you, Delphine. More than I've ever loved a woman before.'

'I love you, too, Florian.'

And as the sky turned dark outside, they sat side by side in bed and devoured the meal between them, sharing laughter and kisses, and wishing the night would never end. She was particularly interested in his collection of paintings and other artefacts that he'd told her about, and she confessed to him as they talked that her dream had always been to study art history at university. It was a dream she'd rarely shared with anyone before, but Florian listened to her and made a point of telling her more about how he chose the pieces he had, about the private collection he was so passionate about.

'One day, when we're free to be together, perhaps you can take over the curation of my collection for me,' he said. 'My godfather has done an excellent job, and I must introduce you, but the job is yours whenever you want it.'

Delphine imagined him to be joking, but when she looked into his eyes, she didn't see humour, only kindness, and she realised that she loved him so much that it hurt. If she had to live her life without Florian... Delphine blinked away tears. Giovanni had hurt her heart, but Florian had the power to shatter it into tiny little pieces.

15

GENEVA, SEPTEMBER 1951

Four weeks later, Delphine stretched out beside the pool, her silk robe slipping from her shoulder and leaving it bare as she lay in the sun, smiling as she heard Florian's footsteps coming closer. She held out her hand for the drink he'd promised, but instead of a glass, he slipped his palm against hers.

She opened her eyes, sitting upright when she saw his serious expression and turning to face him. In the distance the lake shimmered, the late sun reflecting off the water.

'You look worried,' she said, reaching out her other hand to cup his smooth cheek as he lowered himself to the seat beside her, his dark hair falling forward as he leaned in. 'Tell me—what's wrong?'

'Nothing's wrong,' he replied, smiling as he squeezed her hand. 'On the contrary, I have something to show you.'

Delphine smiled back, only too happy to play along. Their stolen moments together brought her such joy and made her forget all the heartbreak that had come before, and she patiently waited for him to continue.

Her curiosity was piqued when she realised he was holding

a box in his other hand. 'What do you want to show me?' she asked.

'This,' Florian said, letting go of her hand in order to take the lid off the box, 'belonged to the former queen consort of Italy. I have a feeling you might be familiar with it?'

'The pink sapphire tiara,' Delphine said, her breath catching in her throat as she looked up at him, hardly able to believe what she was looking at. 'I know it well. In fact, I admired it when the queen wore it to a wedding I attended after the war. I don't think there's a woman in Italy who wouldn't recognise it.' She shook her head, leaning forward to better see the stunning jewels. It took her back to her time in Italy, of the years she'd spent going to glittering parties and rubbing shoulders with Italian nobility during the early years of her marriage. 'How has it come to be in your possession?'

'The family discreetly sold some unique pieces from their personal collection after they left Italy, and my personal curator made certain I was the successful buyer. Most of the other pieces were entrusted to the Bank of Italy in Rome for safekeeping, which makes the few pieces they sold even more special,' he said, holding it up between them so Delphine could look at it more closely. 'I've collected many beautiful diamonds and pieces of art over the years, but this tiara? There is nothing in the world to rival the history and the beauty of such a piece.'

It was certainly unique, and the fact that he'd been able to purchase it reminded her just how well-connected Florian was. The stones caught the light as Florian turned the tiara in his hands, the sapphires appearing the most vivid pink one moment, and then almost purple the next, made even more brilliant as the sunshine reflected against them. He was right that it was perhaps one of the most coveted and special pieces of jewellery he could have invested in.

'This tiara was held in the Italian royal family from the 1800s,' Florian said. 'And now it shall remain in my family for generations to come. This is one of those stunning pieces that I never intend to part with.'

'I hugely admire the former queen,' Delphine said. 'I recall her saying that her only regret during the war was not killing Adolf Hitler herself when she was in the same room as him, and I've always presumed she was capable of it. She's one of those rare women who is both feminine and forthright, so it's fitting that you've chosen her favourite tiara. I imagine it's absolutely priceless.'

'I couldn't agree more,' Florian said. 'And you're right, it is priceless. It is to be the jewel in my personal collection, for want of a better expression.'

'It's stunning, Florian. Thank you for showing it to me.' She tucked her legs up beneath her as Florian smiled at her, his expression hard to read.

'I showed it to you for a reason, Delphine,' he finally said, placing the tiara beside him and reaching for both her hands. 'I would like you to choose one of the sapphires so that I can have an engagement ring made for you.' Florian kissed her knuckles, his dark brown eyes never leaving hers as his voice lowered to a whisper.

'Florian—' she began.

'I want us to spend the rest of our lives together, Delphine. I don't want to hide any more. I want the world to know you are to become my wife, and this is my way of showing you what you mean to me.'

Tears filled her eyes, a solitary drop sliding down her cheek as she looked away, wishing it were so easy, wishing she was free to make her own decisions in life. The tiara caught her gaze, and she wondered what heartbreak it had seen, what love it might have been witness to; what sorrow.

'You know it's not so easy as my simply saying yes. If it were...' She couldn't bring herself to finish the sentence. When they were together like this, it felt as if they were the only two people in the world. But outside the walled gates of his compound, of the beautiful, secluded property by the lake that had been their private oasis these past few months, they couldn't be seen together freely.

Florian nodded, his hands guiding her closer until she was curled on his knee, her arms around his neck, tucked tightly to his chest. The tiara would be nothing without one of its sapphires, its value hugely diminished if it were ever to be offered for sale with a missing stone, but she knew that was what he was trying to tell her: that he would break up the most valuable piece in his collection, the piece that meant the most to him, for her. It was abundantly obvious that he had the funds to buy her the most expensive diamond from Tiffany's, and yet he was willing to sacrifice one of the precious sapphires as a gesture of his love.

'I am nothing without you,' Florian murmured into her hair. 'Please, say yes. Let me find a way for us to marry.'

Neither am I, Florian. Without you, I too am nothing.

Delphine looked up at him, her fingers grazing his cheek as she pressed her mouth to his in a long, slow, warm kiss.

'Yes,' she eventually whispered against his lips. 'I will marry you, Florian. If you can find a way, then I promise you. I will marry you.'

His dark eyes shone as he stood and held out his hand to her, leaving the tiara on the chair as he looked down at her.

'May I have this dance?'

Delphine laughed, but slipped her palm against his anyway. 'We have no music.'

'We don't need music,' he murmured, as he placed his other hand to the small of her back and nudged her towards him.

They began to sway together, just the slightest of movements side to side, and Delphine tucked her cheek to his chest. She loved the way she felt against him, how safe and loved; warm in a way she'd never experienced before.

'I have never loved anyone the way I love you, Delphine,' Florian whispered against her hair.

She lifted her head, their eyes meeting for the briefest of seconds before she stood on tiptoe and kissed him, a single tear sliding down her cheek as their lips met.

I love you, too, Florian. More than I could ever love another human being.

When their lips parted, his thumb gently erased another tear as it escaped from the corner of her eye.

'You are my heart, Florian,' she murmured.

'And you, my darling, are mine.'

16

PRESENT DAY

It had been a very long time since Georgia's stomach had danced with butterflies because of a man. She'd been so focused on work during her twenties, that other than the odd date, she'd barely had time for a relationship. She smiled to herself as she checked her appearance and reached for her necklace, admiring the diamond G as she clasped it. *It's also been a very long time since I smiled at myself in the mirror.*

She sprayed some perfume to her wrists, as well as a little spritz over her hair, and then looked at her phone. Luca would be there to pick her up in fifteen minutes, so she decided to head down to the lobby in case he was early. She was wearing a simple sleeveless dress and white sneakers, and she grabbed her blazer on her way out in case it was cool, and put the strap of her bag over her head so she could wear it cross-body.

Just as she was stepping out of her room her phone rang, and she grinned when she saw it was Sam. She swiped and pressed the phone to her ear as she checked the door had locked behind her.

'Please tell me your Sunday is shaping up to be better than mine?'

Sam laughed. 'Well, from the sound of your voice, I'm fairly certain mine is *definitely* better than yours. I've had room service for breakfast and I'm just heading out.' She omitted the part about *where* and *with whom* she was heading out.

'Harry's family thought I loved yesterday so much, they've arranged another day out for us.' Sam groaned. 'It's a disaster, and the worst part of it all is that Harry *loves* it! I've never seen him happier than when he's trudging around in the mud.'

Georgia grimaced. It was *so* no surprise to her that Sam was hating it—they were both city girls through and through. 'You could either feign a headache or just tell them the truth.'

'And how exactly would I do that?'

'Look, if you love this guy, then you need to be honest with them about who you are. Otherwise? You'll dread every time you have to see them.'

'So, you're suggesting I tell them that I hated yesterday?'

'I'm suggesting you tell them that you're more city than country, and that you'd like to sit this one out. Tell his mother you'll have dinner ready for them when they come home, and wow them with your culinary skills.' Georgia smiled as she pressed the button for the elevator. 'All you need to do is show them the real you, Sam. If you do, I promise they'll love you. And I have a feeling you might love them if you're not pretending to be someone you're not.'

Sam groaned again. 'Fine. You're right. But why is it so hard to be truthful?'

Georgia didn't know how to answer that, because she hadn't figured it out herself. 'How about I tell you something to cheer you up?'

'Oh my God, you wore the dress, didn't you?'

Georgia laughed, hoping her phone reception held while she was in the elevator. 'I did wear the dress, and I'm seeing him again today.'

'Business or pleasure?'

The elevator doors opened and to Georgia's surprise, Luca was standing there, wearing jeans and a white T-shirt, one hand hooked into his pocket as his face broadened into a wide smile.

'Ah, Sam? I'm going to have to call you back.' She ended the call as Sam begged her not to, her eyes meeting Luca's. 'Good morning.'

Luca stepped forward and kissed her cheek, his hand grazing her waist. '*Bonjour*,' he said, before kissing her other cheek. 'It's lovely to see you again.'

She inhaled the scent of his cologne, not moving until he stepped back slightly.

'Have you had breakfast?' he asked.

'I have. But I'd love a coffee.'

His smile touched his eyes as he indicated towards the door. 'I know just the place. We can stop there on the way.'

His car came as a shock to her, although given his love and knowledge of fine things it probably shouldn't have. It was a grey Aston Martin, and she couldn't help but admire it as he held open the door for her. Sam's parents had always driven nice vehicles, but she'd never sat in anything quite like Luca's car before.

'This is quite the car.'

'It's extravagant, I know,' he said, as he put his seat belt on and started the engine, which rumbled loudly to life. 'But cars are my love language.'

She felt her cheeks heat as he placed his hands on the steering wheel, his fingers dancing lightly over the leather. He was talking about his car, but somehow she couldn't stop staring at his hands, imagining him touching her so intimately.

'We'll stop at my favourite café on the way for coffee, and perhaps an Aprikosenwähe,' he said, glancing at her as he drove. 'I wouldn't want you to be hungry while we're exploring the museum.'

'After all the food we ate last night, I don't think I'll be hungry for days.'

He laughed, and she sat back deeper in the seat, turning her head slightly to study him. There was something about Luca; he drove an expensive car, yet still seemed impossibly down-to-earth, and there was an ease about the way he held himself, completely comfortable in his skin.

'What would you be doing today, if you weren't taking me sightseeing?' she asked.

He took his eyes off the road for a second to look at her again. 'I would be having brunch with a friend, or perhaps my mother, and then I'd go into work for the afternoon.'

'So you're a workaholic?'

'I am,' he said, glancing at her. 'You were the same, when you had your business?'

She nodded and shifted slightly to look out of the window. 'I was.' Georgia sighed. 'I'm starting to go crazy with nothing to do.'

'Do you have any new thoughts? For what you want to do next?'

She chewed on the inside of her mouth. 'That's the problem. I've been so focused on the work I was doing, on getting our company ready for sale, that I didn't give myself time to foster any new concepts.'

'Well, perhaps you will think of something while you're here, in Geneva?' he said, pulling into a car park and turning off the engine. 'Sometimes we come up with our best ideas when we're least expecting them.'

She nodded. 'Perhaps. I just, well, I want to love what I do next,' she said. 'If I'm completely honest, it was Sam who wanted to sell the business. We agreed at the very beginning that we would launch it and grow the company with the purpose of selling it, but in the end I would have preferred to keep growing it and have a majority shareholding.'

Luca turned to her, the space in the car suddenly making their conversation feel very intimate now that he wasn't driving. 'Then find another company to invest in or start, and don't compromise. Perhaps you don't need a partner this time?'

Georgia sighed. Perhaps he was right. But Sam had done so much for her; could she really tell her that she was going into her next venture on her own? Her friendship meant the world to her, and she wouldn't do anything that might jeopardise it.

'Coffee,' Luca announced, getting out of the car and coming around to open her door. 'And no more business talk, for either of us.' Luca's eyes twinkled as he spoke, surprising her when he took her hand.

She pressed her palm to his as they walked down the footpath and into a bustling café, the barista calling out Luca's name when he saw them. *No business talk.* She loved it. The only other person in her life confident enough to tell her that was Sam.

When they arrived at the museum, Georgia was taken aback at its size. It was enormous, and appeared as if it were an artefact of architecture itself, with big columns guarding the entrance and impossibly tall windows on each side.

'For some reason I imagined it would be much smaller,' she said. 'More intimate.'

'This is one of Europe's most extensive museums,' Luca said. 'Although given my penchant for watches and jewellery, I did almost take you to the Patek Philippe Museum instead.'

'I love a well-designed watch, but that might have been a little...'

'Boring?'

She laughed. 'You said it, not me.'

They walked inside, through the entrance area and straight into the first display, which was Ancient Egypt, filled with vases, jewellery and even an Egyptian pharaoh and tomb. Everything was incredibly well set out, and Georgia quickly became lost in her own little world of discovery. It wasn't until Luca placed his hand on her back that she spun around, realising they'd hardly spoken as she walked about, intrigued by the collections.

'How many times have you been here?' she asked.

'Hundreds of times. And every time I see something I didn't notice the time before.'

'It's amazing. It's been a long time since I came somewhere like this.'

'Can I take you upstairs to show you the collection of fine arts? It's my favourite part of the museum.'

She liked the way he kept his hand just touching her back as they walked, ascending the stairs and eventually arriving in a hall that was entirely different to the area where they'd just been downstairs.

'This is all relatively new,' he said. 'Much of the artwork shown here has come from the reserves, meaning art that hasn't been exhibited in many years is now here for everyone to enjoy. There is also more French, Italian, and Dutch artwork than ever before.'

'I can tell you're passionate about it,' she said, as they walked slowly past each piece.

'I am. I studied art history at university, and spent some time working as a curator in a smaller museum before returning to the family business.'

She smiled up at him. 'I have to confess that I knew that already. I googled you before I came to Geneva.'

He laughed. 'You did? Well, then it's time to confess that I did the same of you, before we met.'

She laughed with him. 'Well, now that we've made our confessions, how about you tell me why you didn't stay in a museum, as a curator?'

They began to walk slowly again.

'Because I was always going to take over the family business. My father simply wanted me to get experience elsewhere, so I could decide if it was truly what I wanted to do.'

'Was it a hard decision?'

Luca touched her shoulder to stop her, turning her around. 'You must see this painting,' he said. 'It's dated 1414, and is called *The Miraculous Draught of Fishes*. It's one of the most famous pieces of artwork displayed.'

Georgia turned to look at it, sensing how close Luca was behind her. If she turned ever so slightly, she would bump into him.

'It's incredible to think it was painted such a long time ago,' she said. 'Is this your favourite piece?'

'No,' he said quietly, taking her hand and leading her away. 'My favourites are by the Swiss artist Henry Fuseli.'

'I have to confess that I know very little of art history, and I haven't heard of him.'

'Once you see his paintings, they are very hard to forget.'

Luca stopped walking in front of three paintings, and Georgia couldn't take her eyes from them. They were the most haunting depictions she'd ever seen, ghoulish and terrifying, but at the same time so incredibly magnetic that she didn't want to turn away from them.

'The most famous is perhaps *The Nightmare*, which is in the collection at the Detroit Institute of Arts, but almost all his pieces are quite amazing.'

'How old are they?' Georgia asked.

'The late 1700s,' he replied, guiding her forward and pointing to the third of the paintings. 'There is a nightmarish restaging to many of his pieces, and I can't help but imagine what his state of mind was like.'

They stood in silence, both staring at the piece of art. 'It's somehow so eye-catching, even though it's terrifying.'

'Almost all his works are held in museums around the world, for the enjoyment of all, but there are a small handful of collectors who've been able to keep them in their private collections.'

She turned and looked up at him. 'Why do I have a feeling you know these collectors personally?'

'You asked before whether I wanted to work for my family's business, and that is the reason why,' he said. 'My family has been entrusted with the curation of private collections for the wealthiest Swiss collectors for generations, so it's not just our physical store that I was taking over, and that was something I knew I could never walk away from.'

Georgia stared into his light blue eyes as his fingers caught hers, swallowing as his gaze dipped to her mouth.

'But sometimes, those private collections can become all-consuming. It can feel impossible to achieve what is being asked of you.'

'Is that how you felt searching for the sapphire?'

Luca nodded, just a slight movement of his head that she wouldn't have noticed if she hadn't been watching him so intently.

'I refused to become as obsessed as my father became, but at the same time I didn't want his work to be for nothing.'

Georgia moved her fingers against his, and Luca let go, touching his hand to her face instead.

'It's hard to believe that the same stone that has brought you to me, was the end of my father.'

Luca's fingertips stroked her cheek as he dipped his head, hesitating slightly as if to give her the chance to pull away, before pressing his lips gently to hers. It was a soft, lingering kiss that she wished would go on forever.

'Do you bring all your dates to the museum to kiss them in front of your favourite paintings?' she whispered, knowing her cheeks would be in full flush as he smiled down at her.

'Only the ones with priceless sapphires in their possession.'

They both laughed, and Luca tucked his arm around her as they walked, pointing out the next collection he wanted to show her. Georgia pressed herself to his side, her head dropping to his shoulder, listening to what he was saying but also not really listening at all.

'This is much more modern,' she said, when they stopped in front of a collection of art that was in black and white, as if it had all been drawn by pencil, but nonetheless was somehow still vibrant. Georgia lifted her head from Luca's shoulder.

'This is by Marc Bauer,' he said. 'He's probably one of our most recognised artists. I'm very fortunate to have one of his paintings in my home. It was the last gift my father gave me before he passed away.'

She turned to him, saw the way he was staring at the art, as if lost in his own world.

'I can tell your father meant a lot to you.'

'He did,' Luca said, glancing back down at her. 'But it was a complicated relationship.'

She tucked her arm around his waist as they began to walk again, and he slid his arm around her. Georgia dropped her head to his shoulder again without thinking, as if it were the most natural thing in the world, nestled against him as they moved through the hall.

'You were close?' she asked.

'We were very close, and in some ways, he was the most incredible father. He was passionate about his work, devoted to his family, and he loved nothing more than taking me out sailing on Sundays. Those were probably the best memories from my childhood, being out on the water with him when it was just the two of us.'

He paused and she didn't push him, and they came to stand in front of some more modern art that didn't particularly catch her eye. But she sensed that Luca was waiting, thinking through what to say, and she looked over it as they stood.

'When my father was good, he was great,' Luca said. 'But when he became obsessed with something, he turned into a different man. Unfortunately, those episodes increased as he got older, and my mother couldn't live with him anymore. Eventually, he drove himself mad, and took his own life.'

'I'm sorry,' Georgia said. 'I know what it is to lose a parent.'

He turned to her, sighing as he gently touched his forehead to hers. 'Ah, *mon amour*, you lost both your parents when you were a child. I imagine it was much worse for you.'

Tears filled her eyes then and he caught them with his thumb, carefully brushing them away.

'I didn't mean to make you cry.'

'Hearing you talk about your father, it's—' She took a breath to steady herself. 'None of my friends have lost a parent, so they've never truly understood what I've been through, what the depth of that loss is like.'

'It's as if a dark hole opens that can never be filled, no matter how many months or years pass,' he whispered, dabbing away one last tear from her cheek. 'Just like not a day goes by that you don't think of something you wish you could tell them.'

Luca opened his arms to her and she stepped into his embrace, her cheek to his chest as they stood and stared at the paintings before them. She felt safe in his arms as they wrapped around her, warm in a way she hadn't felt in such a long time, and she wished they were in London, that she wasn't simply embarking upon a holiday fling.

In a way, she knew nothing and everything about Luca. On the one hand, they'd opened up to each other, but on the other she knew absolutely nothing about him and his life.

'I think we should go to a winery for lunch,' he said, his mouth moving against her hair as he kept hold of her.

She nodded, indulging in one more breath against his chest,

one more moment feeling as if she were cocooned against the pain and uncertainty of the outside world.

'Luca, can I ask you something?' she finally said. She kept her cheek to his chest so she didn't have to look at him when he answered. 'If I sold you the sapphire, if this all came to an end, would it give you and your family some closure? To know that the mystery was solved and the tiara was whole again?'

'Georgia, for all we know, the tiara might belong to you. We won't know any more until we see the lawyer tomorrow.'

She nodded. He was right; she needed to wait until they'd talked to the lawyer, to see if it helped her piece together any more of the mystery.

Luca ran his hand the length of her hair, stroking down her back. 'My father searched for years, most of his adult life, actually, for the sapphire. But it wasn't about seeing it whole again that he yearned for. It was understanding how it had become separated in the first place. It was the mystery that he couldn't solve that drove him to madness.'

'So, you're saying that we need to solve the mystery to complete what he started?' Georgia asked. 'That that's what would have been important to him?'

Luca stepped back and took her hand, lifting it and pressing a kiss to it. 'If we do that, if we can solve the mystery, then yes. I will have a sense of fulfilling my father's legacy.'

Then that's exactly what we'll do.

17

LAKE GENEVA, SEPTEMBER 1951

Delphine felt like the entire restaurant was staring at them when they walked in. She leaned into Florian, her arm through his, her head tilted ever so slightly to his shoulder as they made their way to their table. It was tucked in the corner near the kitchen—private and romantic—with a single candle on the table. Once he'd outlined his plan for them to be together, as the two of them lay tangled in the sheets of his bed the night before, she'd agreed that she would go out in public with him. Although now that they were actually doing it, she was wondering if she'd made a terrible mistake. There had been something so intimate about seeing each other in private, about not sharing what they had with anyone else, and she almost wished they'd left it that way. But according to Florian, the announcement of both of their divorces, or at least their formal separations, would be imminent. He was a powerful man with more money at his disposal than she could comprehend, and she believed him when he said that he could make the impossible happen.

'Is it just me, or is everyone watching us?' she whispered.

He laughed as he pulled out her seat and bent to kiss her cheek. 'They're not staring at us, they're admiring you.'

She blushed. Florian was always telling her she was beautiful, that he couldn't take his eyes off her, but after so many years with a man who never seemed to find her attractive, she still found it hard to believe he was telling her the truth.

'So, what do you feel like tonight, future Mrs Delphine Lengacher?'

Warmth spread through Delphine as he said her name. She was under no illusions that her divorce from Giovanni was going to be straightforward, but she knew that once it was done and she was legally married to Florian, she would finally be happy.

'Shall we have steak to celebrate our first night out in public? Or would you like the fish?' Florian continued.

Delphine laughed. 'We're hardly in public. We scurried around the corner here as if we were movie stars not wanting anyone to see us.'

Florian laughed with her. 'That might be so, but it's a start. Soon we'll be able to go anywhere without a care in the world.'

'Well, steak it is,' she said. 'And we might need champagne.'

He raised a brow. 'Champagne? What's the occasion?' Florian grinned. 'Or is us being together the occasion?'

A shiver ran down Delphine's back as she stared at Florian from across the table. She'd been wanting to tell him as soon as she realised, as soon as she'd woken up that morning and understood why she felt different. No one else knew. Not even Martina, who had been her confidante for so long now, and who was the only person in the world who knew the details of her relationship with Florian. It had been two months since she'd last had her monthly courses, but she'd been caught up in such a whirlwind of excitement with Florian that she hadn't even noticed.

Florian began to talk then as he held up the menu and pondered the best meal to go with champagne, and she gave her best impression of listening, even though her mind was a million miles away.

She trusted him more than she'd ever trusted a man in her life before, even her father. She'd grown up thinking her family loved her more than anything else in the world; she and her sister had had a wonderful upbringing, filled with love, and all the things a child would need. But now she was a grown woman, she realised she had been nothing more than a pawn that had been used to further her father's business arrangements. It was the same reason Giovanni had married her—to further his business interests and those of his family. No one had ever cared about how she felt, no one had ever let her make her own decisions, until now. Florian listened to her, he made her feel alive; he made her feel as if her opinion mattered. Florian was the man she had been waiting for her entire life.

'You seem distracted,' Florian said. 'Do you have something on your mind? If you're truly uncomfortable being here, we can always just leave and wait until...' His voice trailed off. 'Delphine?'

Delphine looked down at her hands, fingering the edge of the tablecloth, as her nerves got the better of her. They'd talked often about what their lives might look like when they were free to be together. He told her that he would always treat her children as if they were his own, and that she would be able to run the household as she saw fit, and make the decisions for her children without his interference. But one thing they had never discussed was whether they would have children of their own. She'd presumed it was something he would want, but now she was hoping she hadn't made a mistake in that regard.

'I, well...' She swallowed, nervous about his reaction as she stumbled over her words. 'I have something to tell you.'

Florian leaned forward and took her hand in his, their fingers interlinked as he leaned forward. 'Let me guess,' he said. 'You've decided which sapphire you want for your ring. If you're worried about the tiara, I've told you, I want to take the stone for you. It's the only thing I can think to do, to make you understand how important you are to me.' He lifted her hand and kissed the spot where her new ring would go.

She'd purposely left her engagement ring at home on her dresser these past few months, wearing only her gold wedding band when she was out in public. But tonight, she'd even taken that off, and she felt strangely bare without it.

'No,' she said, sucking her bottom lip against her teeth as she tried not to smile and give away what she was about to tell him. 'It's not about the sapphire, but thank you.'

'Don't leave a man in suspense then,' he said, his brows pulling close together. 'What is it you have to tell me?'

'Florian, I'm pregnant.'

He stared back at her for a long second, unblinking, before a smile lit his face. 'You're pregnant?'

She laughed, unable to hide her joy even as she saw his surprise. 'I'm pregnant. Can you believe it?'

He immediately called for the waiter and ordered champagne, and for a second she feared he might announce their news to the entire restaurant, he appeared so excited. But instead, he leaned forward and showered her hands with kisses as he held them, his face alive with excitement, telling her she'd been wrong to doubt his feelings for even a moment.

'Delphine, this is the most wonderful news. We can start our new lives together with our first child on the way.'

They both knew the divorce proceedings would have to be hurried along, neither of them needed to say it, but Florian did settle her nerves by bringing it up.

'I've already hired the best lawyers in Switzerland, and I have a meeting with them the day after tomorrow. You have nothing to worry about, Delphine. You just look after our little miracle, and I'll handle the rest. You'll be divorced in no time. We both will be.'

The champagne arrived then and the waiter poured them

both a glass. When they were alone again, Florian held up his glass and she did the same, clinking them together carefully.

'To our little one,' he said.

'To our little one,' she repeated, placing her free hand flat to her stomach as she took a small sip, the bubbles cascading all the way to her belly and making her feel as if there were butterflies there. She was pleased she'd had a taste, but she wasn't sure whether she'd be able to stomach the entire glass.

'You've made me the happiest man in the world, Delphine,' Florian whispered.

She basked in his affections, still not used to the way he loved her, the way he made her truly feel as if she were the most important person in the room. His eyes never left hers as they sat in their little corner of the restaurant, tucked out of sight.

Delphine was worried about how her family would react to her news, about how the divorce might affect her children, but she knew that Florian would stop at nothing to protect the three of them. All she had to do was trust him. Giovanni had always made her believe that he was important, especially in the business world, but now that she was with Florian, she was no longer scared of his influence. She doubted anyone could rival Florian and his wealth.

'Here's to spending the rest of our lives together,' Florian said, lifting his glass again.

Her heart skipped a beat. It was as if she'd waited her entire life to feel like this, glowing from the attention of a gorgeous man who would move mountains for her. And the little miracle growing inside her was only going to bring them closer together.

Later that night, as they sat in his car, Delphine kissed Florian one last time, lingering with her lips barely parted from his. She wished she could have stayed with him one more minute, one more hour, but she knew she needed to leave him and go inside before they were seen.

'Come to the lake house tomorrow?' Florian whispered.

She nodded, stroking her fingers down his cheek before reluctantly pulling away. 'I would love to.'

'I'll have a picnic prepared, and we can spend the entire time deciding what to call our little one. And you can finally tell me which sapphire you'd like.'

She smiled and leaned in for one more kiss, before groaning and reluctantly opening her door. She stepped out, poking her head in at the open window to smile at him. 'Until tomorrow,' she said.

'Until tomorrow,' he repeated.

Delphine walked away, slipping through the gate to her flat, looking over her shoulder one last time and giving Florian a little wave even though she couldn't see him in the dark. She heard the engine start once she was at the front door—he always waited with his headlights on to make sure she made it safely into the house—before driving away.

She listened to him go as she quietly shut the door behind her, leaning her back against it, her heart racing and her smile wide. Being in love with a man like Florian, it took her breath away sometimes, made her wonder what the future would hold. She only wished they'd met years earlier, before life had become so complicated for both of them, so difficult to untangle themselves from without hurting others in the process.

And if they had, they wouldn't have had to spend so much time apart, and she wouldn't have to keep her special news a secret. Her fingers danced across her stomach as she smiled, imagining all the names they would come up with.

Tomorrow can't come soon enough.

18

'Delphine! Signora Delphine!'

Delphine woke to someone frantically calling her name. Bleary-eyed, she rose from bed and went to the door. She felt as if she'd only just fallen asleep, and a cursory glance at her wrist-watch in the dim light told her that she was correct.

'What is it?' she asked, as she pulled open the door. 'Is it one of the children?' *Did I sleep through Tommaso calling out, in the throes of one of his nightmares?*

'There's been an accident.'

When she saw Martina standing there, her hair loose about her shoulders and in her nightdress, she knew that something was horribly wrong. What had roused Martina from her slumber?

'What type of accident?' Delphine asked, wrapping her arms about herself as she stared back at Martina. 'The children are safe, are they not?'

Martina walked past her and shut the door, taking Delphine's hand and walking her back to the bed. Delphine knew it was terrible news when she saw the tears in her confidante's eyes, when she pulled her down to sit with her.

'Martina, you're scaring me,' Delphine said, her breath catching as they whispered in the near darkness to one another. 'Tell me what's happened. What type of accident?'

'It's Signor Florian,' Martina whispered. 'He was involved in a car accident.'

Delphine's body went cold and she froze. No, not Florian. It couldn't be Florian. Not her darling Florian. 'A car accident? How badly was his vehicle damaged? Was Florian hurt at all?' It was so unlike him to be involved in something like that, when he was such a confident driver. There must have been a mistake. Florian would be home by now, asleep in his bed. Wouldn't he?

'Signora, Florian, he was, he's—'

'Stop.' Delphine gasped as she saw the pain etched into Martina's face. 'Please, that's enough.'

Martina began to cry; big, fat tears slipped down her cheeks, making it impossible for Delphine to look away, making it impossible for her not to know in her heart what had happened. *Not Florian. Please, God, not my Florian.*

'Signor Florian, he's gone,' Martina eventually whispered.

'No,' Delphine said, shaking her head. 'No, that can't be. We just spent the evening together, he brought me home, he was fine, he was alive, he—'

Martina blinked back at her, her face falling as Delphine's eyes met hers, as she saw the pain in the other woman's gaze. She was the only other person in the world who knew the truth about their relationship, the only person who could possibly imagine the depths of her pain.

'How?' she eventually whispered, as her body froze, as she asked the question she didn't truly want the answer to, as she tried to fight the words she was hearing.

'I don't know. All I know is that the police have confirmed that it was him, and that there was another car involved.'

Delphine's body began to shudder then, every part of her

trembling as she tried to process what she was hearing, news that was impossible to absorb. *He can't be gone. I was only just in his arms, looking into his eyes, feeling his warm breath against my neck as he held me and whispered in my ear.*

'You're certain he's...' She couldn't even bring herself to say the word.

'I'm certain. One of the maids came home with the news, she came across the scene on her way home. The lights from the ambulance were still flashing.'

Delphine couldn't believe it. Florian couldn't have left this world. They'd just had dinner together, she'd told him her news, they'd made plans for the future. Her generous, darling Florian simply could not have died, and not in a car accident.

'There must have been a mistake,' she said, standing up and beginning to pace. 'The girl must have it wrong. Had she been drinking? How would she have recognised his car?'

When Martina opened her arms, it hit Delphine like a punch to her stomach. She fell forward, a sob lurching from deep inside her as she let herself be held, as her world came crashing down around her. She'd gone to sleep dreaming of their wedding, imagining what it would be like to spend the rest of her life with Florian, to be adored by her husband rather than forgotten.

'It cannot be true,' she whispered, as Martina rocked her and rubbed her back in big circles, in the same way she would have comforted her Isabella. 'I cannot believe it.'

'Delphine, there will be time to grieve, but you need to think whether there's anything at his house that could be found. Any personal effects that you might have left there, that could be discovered to be yours. If your husband found out...'

She blinked, wiping away her tears as she sat up straighter. Martina was right; she did need to think about that. Giovanni had been very clear about how careful they were to be, how mindful of being discreet. If there was anything that was obviously hers at Florian's house, it could be found by his family. Or even the police.

'Also, is there anything he'd want you to have? Anything special that you'd like to keep to remember him by?' Martina asked. 'You have a very small window of time to let yourself into his house before anyone else goes there.'

Delphine swallowed what felt like a tennis ball in her throat, her eyes burning as she pushed her pain from her mind, knowing she had to stay strong, had to focus.

The sapphire. He wanted me to have the sapphire.

She stood, suddenly filled with fear as she realised what she had to do. If anything happened to her, if Giovanni ever discovered what she'd done, she'd need something of value. Florian wanted her to have the sapphire—he'd told her it was for her, and she knew he'd want to do anything necessary to keep their unborn child safe.

Delphine summoned a strength she hadn't even realised she was capable of and reached for her dressing gown, turning to Martina.

'Can you drive?'

Delphine would have been lost without Martina. She'd become so much more to her than just a lady-in-waiting: she was her confidante, her friend; as close to her as a sister or mother even. She would never have been able to turn to her own mother, but Martina was there for her no matter what, and tonight she'd proven that there was truly nothing she couldn't trust her with. But there was one thing, despite it all, that she chose to keep secret from even Martina.

They sat outside Florian's house, Martina behind the wheel and Delphine in the passenger seat. Driving there, they'd taken the long way so they didn't have to pass by the scene of the accident, and she'd managed to keep her composure the entire journey there, but now that they'd arrived, it was almost impossible.

'Will all his staff be asleep?' Martina asked.

'He only has day staff,' she replied. 'He liked to have the house to himself at night, to enjoy the privacy.'

'Then go quickly,' Martina said. 'I'll wait here, but you never know when the police might come. Get in and out as quickly as you can.'

Delphine nodded, took a deep breath and then got out of the car. She let herself through the gates and ran up the long driveway, her breathing shallow as she stopped at the front door and took the key from her pocket. Florian had tied a small piece of ribbon to the end, part of his desire to present it to her as a gift, and she thought then of the times she'd sneaked around to his property to enjoy the solitude, waiting for him to come home, ready to surprise him when he did.

She wiped at her eyes with her knuckles and stepped into the house, listening out before closing the door behind her to make sure that no one else was there. Every movement she made sounded loud to her ears, so she kicked off her shoes and walked barefoot in an effort to seem even quieter.

Delphine walked down the hallway to Florian's office, nudging open the door to find his lamp still on. She turned, half expecting him to saunter back in with a brandy in his hand, or to be sitting in the big leather chair, his feet up on the desk as he made his way through a stack of paperwork.

But, of course, the room was silent. She was the only one there. There was no Florian waiting with his easy smile, holding out his hand to her to clasp, setting down his papers and making her feel as if there were truly no one more important than her.

She took a deep breath, balling her fists and digging her nails into her palms. *I'm here to do a job. Find it and go.*

Delphine crossed the room and took one of the paintings off the wall to reveal his hidden safe, which she'd opened before for

Florian when he'd needed her to retrieve something. She carefully recited the correct turns in her mind, before opening it. Inside, she found cash, his passport and other documents, and the tiara. It was only there because he'd kept it at home for her to look at—he'd intended for her to choose which sapphire she wanted that very weekend. All of the other items in his collection were kept elsewhere, other than some of the paintings that he'd chosen to hang in the house, with many pieces held by Andreas, his godfather and most trusted curator.

She took out the box, carefully took out the tiara, and stared down at it in her hands. Even though she knew she was the only person in the house, she still found herself looking over her shoulder, as if expecting someone to catch her. She knew she had nothing to feel guilty about; Florian had intended this for her—he had made it clear that she was to choose any sapphire she liked for her ring—but still, she was uneasy taking it now that he was gone.

She carried it to his desk and sat down, gazing at the tiara. The former queen of Italy was here in Switzerland, separated from her husband as Delphine was from hers, the same woman who'd once worn the prized sapphires during her husband's short reign as king, and hers as queen consort. They'd once rubbed shoulders at the same soirees, moved in the same circles, with Giovanni always eager to elevate his family's standing in society. If only she'd known then that her queen was as deeply unhappy as she, most likely living in the same type of loveless marriage, despite their four children.

Delphine took a sharp letter knife from the desk and began to prise her favourite sapphire out. She'd spent hours looking at them all, lying in bed against Florian's chest and turning the tiara over in her hands, her fingers playing across each stone. Many of them were identical in appearance, but there were two on each side that were slightly different; more oval where the others were round, and larger in size. She turned the tiara and slid the knife beneath the sapphire, wiggling it back and forth, worried the pressure she was using might damage it or even break the stone. It was loose but still not falling out, and she tried again, this time managing to slip and slice the tip of her finger. Blood dripped almost immediately but she didn't stop, wedging the knife harder until the sapphire finally fell out.

Delphine used the edge of her dressing gown to wrap around her bleeding finger, thankful that she hadn't left any evidence of her wound on Florian's desk, and placed the sapphire in her pocket. Then, having replaced the tiara in its box, she turned to put it back in the safe, before something stopped her, her fingers tightening against it.

This was for our children. My sapphire was to be reunited with it one day, to restore it to its glory. It is nothing without all the sapphires.

Delphine stood in the middle of the room, wrestling with her thoughts, before lowering the tiara and searching the room for a bag, placing the tiara in it when she found one. Then she went back to the safe and took out a small amount of money, just in case she needed it for their child, before closing it and restoring the painting to its position. Once she was certain the painting was straight and that there was no evidence she'd been there, Delphine hurried upstairs to Florian's quarters. All she wanted to do was fall into his four-poster bed and sob into the pillow, to roll around in his sheets and smell his scent, to remember him and all the nights they'd spent there together.

But she didn't have long to do what she needed to do.

Delphine ran to his wardrobe and took out a cashmere jersey, holding it to her face and inhaling. Tears filled her eyes; it was Florian. His unmistakable, woodsy cologne clung to the fibres, and she quickly put it in her bag before turning to leave. She'd left nothing that she needed to collect at his home, nothing she needed returned to her, and so she forced herself to walk from the bedroom without looking back, to go down the elegant staircase and put her shoes back on without looking into his office one last time.

Delphine's hand hovered around the front doorknob as she indulged in one final gaze at the home she'd likely never set foot in again; the house that was to have been her new marital home, the place they would have raised their child, and which Tommaso and Isabella would have been welcomed into, with Florian as their doting stepfather.

She swallowed her pain and locked the door, hurrying back down the driveway and finding Martina sitting exactly where she'd left her, her hands still planted on the steering wheel, knuckles visibly white.

'I'm sorry I took so long,' Delphine said, as she sat down and closed the door.

'Do you have what you need?'

She nodded. 'I do. But we need to make one more stop before we go home.'

Martina stared at her as if she were mad. 'It's going to be light soon, which means the children will be waking. We need to be home before the rest of the household rises.'

'We just need to do this one thing. I promise you, it won't take long.'

Bless her, Martina did as she was asked, and twenty minutes later they were outside another house, this one not quite so opulent. Delphine wasn't surprised to see lights on inside; Andreas was Florian's godfather, after all, which meant that as one of his closest friends in Geneva, he would likely have been notified by the police already.

After promising Martina that she'd be as quick as could be, she stood at the door and knocked. Within minutes it swung open, and she was faced with a man who looked nothing like what she remembered from the one time they'd met. Andreas's eyes were hollow, his usually immaculate hair sticking up as if he'd only just risen from slumber, and there was a pain bracketing his face that she imagined was reflected in her own.

'Delphine?' he said, looking her up and down, most likely as shocked by her unkempt appearance as she was by his.

'Andreas,' she said, as tears streamed down her cheeks. 'You've heard the news.'

'I have.' His face crumpled and she stepped forward to hug him. 'I can't believe he's gone.'

'I know. I've been saying the same thing to myself, over and over.'

She knew that Andreas was the only person Florian had told about their relationship, which was why she was standing there, ready to trust him.

'Why are you here, Delphine? Did you come to tell me the news?' he asked.

She held up the bag she was carrying, having left the cashmere jersey in the car. 'Before he died, Florian told me to keep this safe. There is a sapphire missing. You will understand when you see it, but the tiara can only be returned to the person who has the missing stone.' She watched as he looked into the bag, his eyes wide when they looked back up at her.

'What do you mean, there's a sapphire missing? I was the one who sourced this for him. It should never have been tampered with!'

'Which is why I'm trusting you with it,' she said. 'Please, you must keep it safe, you mustn't let anyone else try to claim it because it belonged to Florian, and he intended it for me.'

Andreas looked uncertain, but he took the bag when she pushed it into his hands.

'Just promise me, it must be kept securely until the missing sapphire is returned.' She stared into Andreas's eyes. 'Promise me.'

'I promise,' he said. 'But Delphine, this is a very valuable piece. Anything from the House of Savoy is highly coveted, and—'

'Is there not a confidentiality clause?' she asked. 'No one other than you, me, Florian and whoever sold it to him even knows that it's part of his collection. Am I right?'

There was a noise behind him and Andreas shifted somewhat uncomfortably. She doubted he'd know how to explain her presence to his wife if she suddenly appeared behind him.

'I can trust you?' she asked.

'Yes, Delphine, you can trust me. I'll make sure it stays hidden.'

She backed away, her tears beginning to fall again.

'He truly loved you, Delphine. He told me that he fell in love with you the very first time he set eyes upon you by the lake.'

A sob escaped her lips then and she turned and ran back to the car, barely able to breathe as she fell into the passenger seat. Martina stayed silent as she cried, reaching for her hand and holding it, as if they didn't have to hurry back to the house, as if her world hadn't just fallen apart.

'I'm going to have to get us home now,' Martina said, gently. 'You can cry all the way back, but when we get there, you'll have to hold your head high and pretend as if everything's fine. You can have a day in bed if you need, I'll tell the children you're unwell, but they must not see your eyes red and puffy. We don't want them saying anything to their father when he returns.'

Delphine nodded, leaning her head back against the headrest and staring out of the window.

'Delphine?' Martina said, as if to make certain she'd heard her instructions.

But Delphine's head was a million miles away, thinking about what she'd do next, about how she was going to navigate the coming months. Puffy eyes were going to be the least of her problems.

'There's something else I need to tell you,' Delphine whispered, turning to Martina as they sat in the car, as the woman she trusted more than anyone else in the world raised her eyebrows in question.

'You can tell me anything,' Martina said. 'Nothing could be more complicated than what we've been through tonight.'

Delphine looked into her eyes, her voice quavering. 'I'm pregnant.'

19

PRESENT DAY

Georgia met Luca at the lawyer's office. He'd offered to collect her, but she'd decided to walk down to the café they'd passed the previous day, and she'd had a Swiss croissant and a strong coffee to prepare for the meeting ahead. She couldn't stop thinking about the afternoon they'd had the day before. After the museum, Luca hadn't taken her straight back to the hotel, but had instead driven them to the lake, where a boat had been waiting to take them for a romantic ride. He'd initially suggested a winery, but then told her he'd changed his mind and wanted her to experience an outing on the water. She blushed as she thought of the way he'd kissed her as they'd toured the lake, the way he'd looked at her. She didn't ever recall any man looking at her with the same kind of heat in his gaze that Luca had, or the way his hands skimming against her arms and hips had made her feel. She needed to fan her face just thinking about their time together.

When Georgia saw him already waiting in the lobby, she announced herself to the receptionist at the front desk and made her way over to him, wondering if he was as consumed with thoughts about their time together as she was.

'Georgia!' He stood and kissed both of her cheeks, and she kissed him back, her hand on his shoulder as she leaned in.

'Is it strange that I'm nervous?' she asked.

He indicated for her to sit first, and he pulled his chair slightly closer as he sat. 'It's not strange. I'm hoping the lawyer has some of the answers. That way, perhaps we'll both have some closure.'

'Luca, about the sapphire,' she began, before being interrupted by a well-dressed older gentleman with a full head of grey hair.

'Luca, Ms Montano,' he said, coming over to shake their hands. 'Please come with me.'

They both fell into step behind the lawyer, but as they walked Luca's fingers brushed against hers and he whispered in her ear, 'Everything will make sense after this,' he said. 'I'm certain of it.'

She squeezed his fingers in reply, before stepping into the office and sitting across from the lawyer. He asked them both if they'd like coffee, sending his assistant out to get their orders, before placing a file in front of him and looking first at her, and then to Luca. She couldn't help but think that he looked relieved, and she wondered how long he'd been waiting to meet someone with a connection to the missing sapphire.

'It's good to see that you've made each other's acquaintance,' he said. 'I'm not sure what Luca has already told you, but my law firm was instructed many years ago by a Mr Andreas Kaufmann to preserve the sapphire tiara, and manage any claims in regard to it. Over the years, we've dealt with some challenges to ownership, however, in recent decades, we've had no clue as to whom we are preserving the tiara for. We were starting to think there was no possibility of ever solving that particular mystery, as was the Kaufmann family. Until now, that is.'

Georgia swallowed and glanced at Luca before continuing. 'You believe that it's been held for me?' she asked.

'I believe it was being held for a woman in your family, of whom you are a descendant. So, yes, in answer to your question, I believe it is, in fact, being held for you.'

'I just... I have no idea why it was left for my grandmother, so please excuse me if I don't seem to comprehend any of this,' Georgia said.

'You've determined the authenticity of the missing sapphire?' the lawyer asked Luca.

'I have. It is, without a doubt, the missing stone,' Luca said. 'And it's being held for safekeeping at our premises.'

'Good,' the lawyer said. 'Now, in the absence of adoption records that show your family lineage, I've discussed with my colleagues and we've determined that, subject to confirming with the lawyer for Hope Berenson, you are indeed the intended recipient of the box that contained the sapphire. We will be attesting your ownership of the tiara, as well as presenting you with a key to a safety deposit box here in Geneva, where we believe a letter is being kept.'

'I'm sorry, a key?' she asked, trying to comprehend what he was telling her. 'And the tiara, doesn't that belong in a museum, or—'

'We can discuss the tiara, Georgia,' Luca said. 'There is no rush for you to decide what to do with it.'

'I agree with Luca,' the lawyer counselled. 'It would be imprudent to make a rash decision on the fate of the tiara without considering all your options. It's worth a great deal of money, so it would be wise to receive advice first.'

Georgia couldn't believe what she was hearing. How could a priceless Italian tiara have been left to her grandmother? It simply didn't make sense.

'Are you able to tell me more, about who left the key? About how you became involved?' she asked.

'Unfortunately, I cannot. I've inherited this file from my predecessor, and having not known Andreas personally, all I know is what's been left for me. The primary purpose of which was to give you the key.'

Georgia took a deep breath. 'And there's no possible way this is all a misunderstanding?'

'This is most definitely not a misunderstanding. Let me make a call to the late Ms Berenson's lawyer, and if everything is confirmed, I'll have the key for you within the hour. Are you free to wait? The coffee shouldn't be far away.'

Georgia nodded, shifting in her chair as she glanced over at Luca.

'Such a shame this didn't all happen in your father's lifetime,' the lawyer said, clapping Luca on the shoulder as he passed. 'I can only imagine the look on his face when he saw the sapphire after all those years.'

If she hadn't been watching carefully, she might have missed the way Luca's smile faded, the sadness that haunted his eyes, because by the time he looked over at her, his usual expression had returned.

'Luca, about the tiara,' she said, once they were alone again.

Luca leaned forward in his chair, his elbows resting on his knees.

'It doesn't feel right, the decision of what to do with it resting on my shoulders,' she said. 'Your family has protected and stored the tiara all these years, and I don't—'

'Georgia,' he said, reaching out and clasping her hands. 'Just breathe.'

'But—'

'No *buts*,' he said. 'I will help you decide what to do with the tiara. If you decide you want it exhibited in a museum, I will take care of the details, but not yet.'

She nodded, knowing that he was right. 'Did you know about the safety deposit box?'

He shook his head. 'I did not.'

'So, you have no clue what it might contain? Other than a letter?'

'A tiara from another fallen dynasty?' Luca teased.

As Georgia groaned, the assistant arrived with their coffees, and she gratefully took the cup and slid deeper into her seat. As much as she enjoyed spending time with Luca, she was ready for this part of the journey to be over. She wasn't sure if she could handle any more surprises.

20

LAKE GENEVA, OCTOBER 1951

'No one needs to know,' Martina said, rubbing Delphine's back in big circles as they sat on her bed, the door closed to stop anyone else from listening. 'We can keep this hidden.'

'There's no way we can keep this hidden!' Delphine cried. 'I'm going to lose my children. When he finds out, if anyone breathes so much as a word of this, I'm going to lose Tommaso and Isabella.'

Martina tucked her finger beneath Delphine's chin and made her look up, her gaze stern. 'No one is going to find out. I've found somewhere for you to go.'

Delphine's eyes widened. 'You have?'

It had been weeks since Florian had gone. So many long, painful weeks of mourning in private, of feeling as if her heart had been ripped in two, of having to pretend as if the love of her life hadn't been stolen from her. Some days she could barely breathe, couldn't comprehend that the world could just continue as if nothing had happened; and then there were the days like today, where panic set in, and she realised that she could lose everything. The only thing worse than losing Florian would be losing her beloved children.

'The place I've found is in London,' Martina said. 'You can travel there when you're six months along, and we can keep your condition hidden until then. Remember how long it took you to show with Tommaso and Isabella? Your stomach was barely even rounded at four months, so we have at least another month before we'll have to conceal it.'

'But if anyone were to suspect, if—'

'We will let some of the staff go now that we're moving back to your marital home,' Martina said, her voice low and calm. 'I will be the only one to attend to you, and you don't have to worry about Giovanni.'

'Because when was the last time he even tried to come to my quarters?' Delphine said, not even attempting to disguise the bitterness in her tone. But she'd long since given up keeping things from Martina. 'You're right that he wouldn't notice, unless he comes home and expects me to accompany him to something.' *Why couldn't Giovanni have been the one to die? Why did it have to be Florian?* The moment she thought it she felt ill to her stomach, though; Gio might not have been a good husband to her, but he didn't deserve to lose his life any more than Florian had.

'If Giovanni returns or does seek you out, you shall be sick,' Martina said. 'He will not question me if I tell him you're unwell, and he certainly wouldn't come to investigate the matter for himself. I actually believe that it will only help strengthen our story when you need to disappear for an extended period.'

'But what of the children?' Delphine asked. 'How will I hide this from them? Isabella may only be six, but she's smart. She'll notice the change in my appearance. And Tommaso, he's such a sensitive boy. What if the children figure it out? What if they suspect something?'

Martina took her hand and looked into her eyes. 'For this to work, you're going to have to leave the children for a period of time. We will need to devise a story about you being very unwell and needing treatment. We have to have a reason for your disappearance, a reason for you to be isolated or to seek specialist care instead of returning for them.'

'You expect me to leave them?' Delphine gasped. 'With who?' She'd never left her children for more than a night; couldn't stand to be parted from them.

Martina's eyes were soft, her expression caring, and Delphine knew she only had her best interests at heart. 'You must leave them with Giovanni in London, or with your sister here in Geneva. But wherever you choose to leave them, I promise you I'll stay with them the entire time. I'll be able to write to you and tell you everything that you're missing, and when you're back, they'll forget that you were ever gone.' She paused. 'This is only a short time, Delphine, and it will protect them and you.'

'I couldn't,' Delphine murmured. 'I couldn't leave them, not for so long. I—'

'It's leave them for three months, or lose them forever,' Martina said in a no-nonsense tone, the way Delphine might speak to her children when she was cross with them. 'There's no other way. I've thought of everything. If you want to make sure no one can take them from you, then this is what you have to do.'

'There is another way,' Delphine said, her voice barely a whisper now. 'The way we discussed. The way that could put an end to this immediately.' She shivered as she said the words, the very fact that she was even discussing such a thing making her feel nauseous. 'I'm prepared to do anything to keep my children safe and with me, even... that.'

Martina shook her head. 'No. I asked, and the risk is so high, you could bleed to death. And if someone saw you going there...' She patted Delphine's hand, hard. 'No, Signora Delphine. I cannot allow you to even think about it. It's much too dangerous.'

Delphine placed her palm to her stomach, feeling the slightly rounded curve. She could never have done it anyway; even as she'd said the words, she knew it was not something she could ever do, even to protect her children, but she was ashamed to admit she had considered it. At one point, when she'd lain awake in the night, she'd thought it might be her only option, had thought that she'd have to sacrifice her unborn child for the ones she could already hold in her arms and love; the legitimate children that could be taken from her if someone discovered her pregnancy or her affair.

'Tell me where I'd be going,' Delphine finally said. 'If your plan was to work, what type of place would I have to stay? Where would you have me go?'

'There is only one suitable place, and it's called Hope's House,' Martina said. 'It's a home run by a kindly woman, and she arranges adoptions to suitable parents. You would be able to trust her to look after you and your baby, and she's very discreet.'

'We would pay her for this...' Delphine hesitated. '*Service*?'

Martina nodded. 'It's not necessary, but I would suggest a generous donation.'

'You're certain this is the place for me?' Delphine asked. 'You don't think we should try to find somewhere here in Switzerland? Or even in Italy?'

'This is the place. I've been very discreet in my search, and I know this is the right home for you.' Martina had tears shining in her eyes as she spoke. 'For you *and* the baby. You will be safe there, and you will be treated with the dignity you deserve.'

'They are used to situations like mine?'

'It is primarily a home for unmarried mothers to give birth, but the woman who runs it does not discriminate. I've already written to her on your behalf.'

A fresh wave of tears threatened, but Delphine did her best to hold them back. She would not cry. She needed to be strong; she needed to do everything she could to keep her children, to survive without Florian, to find a way forward. If this was the only way to do that, then so be it. She would have to accept her situation, that she was now being lumped with unmarried mothers and their illegitimate children. Because that's what her unborn baby was, and she was worse than unmarried; she was an adulteress.

'You said this place is called Hope's House?' she eventually asked. 'Hope is the name of the woman in charge?'

'Yes, Signora.'

She nodded. If Martina said this was the best place for her, then she would go there. Delphine only prayed she was right and they could keep it hidden from everyone; most especially from Giovanni. If he discovered she was pregnant by another man... She shuddered. He would have no qualms about taking the children and making sure she never saw them again, about turning both of their families against her, about leaving her with nothing.

'Begin telling the staff that we will be making some changes,' Delphine said, clearing her throat as she regained her composure. 'We will make them slowly. I won't begin to show too obviously for some weeks, and during that time we will start to limit contact with me, until you are the only one permitted in my personal quarters.' She paused. 'And I'd like to ensure that we give generously to Hope's House, to help other women in need. I'll use my own money, so Giovanni doesn't find out and ask any questions.'

'Of course.'

'Can I leave all the arrangements regarding our trip to London in your capable hands? I don't think I have the nerve to deal with it all right now.' Her hands were shaking just thinking about how she'd execute her plan, how she'd make sure her children felt loved and cared for while she was gone. Martina was kind and thoughtful; she could run a household and ensure her children were fed and nurtured, but it wasn't the same as having their mother. Their father had already left them; the last thing she wanted was for them to feel that she'd abandoned them, too.

'Yes, Signora Delphine,' Martina said. 'I can handle everything other than your husband. I promise.'

'Thank you. I'll write to him in the morning and tell him that I'm becoming restless, that I would like to spend a short time with him in the spring, so that the children can see London and broaden their horizons,' Delphine said, thinking as she spoke, knowing that she would have to appeal to Giovanni's ego if she were to convince him of her plan. 'I shall invent an old school friend that I wish to see, and perhaps that can be the catalyst for my disappearance. I can become ill, write to him, even forge communication from a doctor to him. Perhaps he will even allow us to rent a house in London for a period, so he doesn't have to have us in his flat. That would be even more convenient, for me and for him, too, I suspect.'

Martina nodded. 'I think that's a perfectly sound plan. All he has to believe is that you're tired of being in Geneva alone, make him think that you'll be content so long as you get to broaden your horizons and travel.'

'Once we decide to do this, there will be no going back,' Delphine said, as much to convince herself as Martina. 'You and I, as well as this Hope woman, will be the only people to know of my pregnancy. We shall make the trip an adventure for the children, and so long as I can convince Giovanni, there's no reason that it won't work.'

There's no other way. This is what must be done. It simply has to work. I've pretended before, I've made him think I was happy when I was deeply miserable. I can do this.

As Martina squeezed her hand before walking away,

Delphine sat straight-backed on the bed, telling herself over and over that she was doing the right thing. Her grief over Florian was unbearable most days, leaving her breathless and with a pain inside her that was impossible to heal, but today she knew she needed to be strong. She needed to make keeping her secret and delivering this baby safely her greatest priority; it was all that mattered right now. *I have the rest of my life to grieve for Florian, to beg his forgiveness in what I have to do. I will love him forever, remember our child together, birth our baby with the utmost love, but there is simply no way that I can keep him or her.* The path ahead was going to break her heart all over again, for how could it not? But she didn't want to think about parting with their baby, not now. Losing Florian had almost broken her, but thinking about losing their baby? She shut her eyes, the pain too great.

Without Florian, she was nothing, had no power, no ability to change her destiny. She was at the mercy of her husband now, and that wasn't something she found easy to comprehend, especially given her condition.

When she heard the sound of children's laughter rising from outside, she stood and padded over to the window, looking out and seeing Isabella and Tommaso in a rare show of sibling affection, their heads bent together as they whispered about something. They were playing together, kicking a ball back and forth, the sun shining brightly after days of rain, but right then, Tommaso was passing the ball to his sister and saying something to her that brought a big smile to her face.

I am doing this for them. She touched her stomach once more, guilty all over again at the thought of the life growing inside her. But she didn't know this child; this baby, it was conceived in love, but she had a choice to make, and she had to choose the children she already loved, whom she already held so deeply in her heart, who were the only reason she rose each morning, instead of wallowing in her grief.

If there was another way, she would have chosen it, but there was not. She was a woman with nothing to her name, no way of surviving if she asked her husband for a divorce or chose to leave him. Her family would turn their backs on her, her husband's family would shun her and petition the court for her children, which she had no doubt they would succeed in doing, and she had no way to provide for them.

Except for the tiara. But she knew that if she tried to sell it and failed, if Florian's family knew of its existence and tried to challenge her ownership, that her fate could be even worse. She could be arrested, accused of stealing from him, and she had no way to prove that it was intended for her. The only thing she had was Florian's word, and without him there to confirm his intention, it meant nothing. It might help her in the future, but it would be too risky to try to sell it now.

Tommaso looked up then, as if sensing his mother standing by the window, and she held up her hand to wave. His smile broadened and he nudged his sister in the ribs, which made her look up, too, Isabella's smile bright as she jumped up and down and waved back, before holding up the ball as if to make sure her mother could see what they were doing.

She wasn't sure if their love in that moment made her decision harder or easier to live with, but she knew what she had to do. The only choice she could make was the one that guaranteed that Tommaso and Isabella remained with her.

I'm sorry, Florian.

Forgive me.

21

PRESENT DAY

Georgia held the key, closing her palm around it as she stepped into the room, looking at the boxes around her. They were all a dark bronze gold, stretching across three walls from the floor to the ceiling, with an ornate engraving on the front of each one, and she imagined they'd been there for the better part of the last century.

The banking assistant had escorted her into the room, after she'd shown her the key and the requisite paperwork from the bank, and now that she was alone, Georgia wasn't so certain she wanted to see what was inside the safety deposit box. It would have been different if it had been something left for her personally, but whatever was in there belonged to her grandmother, not her.

Here goes nothing.

She stepped forward and put the key into the keyhole above the number 526, turning it and carefully sliding out the box. It was much heavier than she expected, and Georgia carried it to the table, sitting down as she opened it.

Inside was a black-and-white photo of a man and a woman sitting beside a pool. The woman wore big sunglasses and had a mane of thick dark hair, and the man was equally handsome, but instead of looking at the camera as the woman was, he was gazing at her. Georgia turned it over and found cursive handwriting that stated: *1951, Delphine and Florian.*

Florian. Florian was the name in the newspaper article. She put down the photo and reached into the box again, finding a letter in an envelope as well as a delicate gold chain necklace with a diamond hanging from it.

Georgia held it in her hand, staring at it as she wove the chain between her fingers, the better to look at it. It was very pretty, and when she put it down, she picked up the photo again and held it closer to her face, squinting at the faded people looking back at her. And there it was: the woman in the photo, Delphine, was wearing the very necklace that was beside her now on the table.

She sat looking at the two new clues in front of her and wondering what it all meant. The fact that this man, Florian, was in the photo, told her that perhaps there was more to his family's claim over the tiara than Luca or even the lawyers involved had realised.

Georgia turned to the envelope, sliding her finger beneath its flap and carefully taking out the matching cream sheet of paper folded inside. She was taken aback by the weight of it, and even more surprised to find that it was written in English. Georgia sat back, her hands shaking as she began to read the letter.

July 1991

To my darling daughter,

My dark-eyed, raven-haired little girl, whose tiny hands I have never forgotten. My deepest regret is placing you for adoption, and I've thought about you every day since we parted. As I sit here, trying to imagine what you look like now, the type of young woman you've become, I wish for nothing more than the opportunity to turn back time and make my decision all over again. I was so deeply afraid at the time, grieving the love of my life and terrified of the repercussions if anyone discovered I was pregnant. My only wish is that you've lived a wonderful life with the family Hope chose for you, and that you haven't missed out on anything. Every birthday, every Christmas, every rainbow that shone in the sky, my heart was with you.

When Hope asked me to leave something behind for you, I couldn't think beyond my grief, for you and for your father. Your father, Florian, was a wonderful man who would have been an even more wonderful father to you, and at the time all I could think was to leave the sapphire that was to be made into an engagement ring for me. But in my haste, I neglected to leave any further information that would help you piece together the past. I wish for you to know why I did what I did, and why there was one solitary pink sapphire left for you. It was always meant to be mine, and because of that, I wanted it to be yours.

If you're reading this, you will know that the Italian sapphire tiara, not just the single sapphire, is your inheritance. It was the most unique piece in your father's collection, and I hope that it brings you some peace to know that it belonged to him. You may choose to do with it as you wish—whether you decide to keep it or sell it, the decision is yours alone. Your father told me of his intention before he died, that I was to select a single stone to wear for evermore, and it pains me to think he never lived to see it made into the ring he'd imagined. The tiara's value diminished greatly without all of the sapphires, but that was Florian's love language, to show me that I was more important to him than his most prized possession, that there was nothing more precious to him in the world than me. Whatever anyone says, whatever claims are made, you must know that the sapphire I took was always intended for me, and for any children we had together. It was never to be taken by another, and no matter what you're told, no matter what happens, you must understand that. Your father would have showered you with love and gifts, you would have been his world, so do not let anyone take this one thing away from you.

I was a married woman at the time of your conception, but you must know that it was a marriage in name only. Please do not think it was a great scandal or that we caused an aggrieved spouse any heartache due to our actions, and if anyone tries to tell you otherwise, it is simply not true. My husband was a man full of his own importance who wasn't interested in a partnership, and who had already taken a mistress. I was a vessel for his children, our marriage nothing more than a union of convenience for both our families, one that I was simply collateral damage to.

Florian and I planned to spend the rest of our lives together, and the night I told him that I was pregnant with you, the night he died, was the happiest I had ever seen him. I am a woman broken, even after all these years, from the loss first of Florian, and then you. It seems a miracle to me that I am yet to die of a broken heart, although my other children have given me a reason to live, to keep fighting for each day. When someone asks if love at first sight exists, I am the first to say yes, because the moment Florian and I saw each other, we knew that we were destined to be together. Nothing, not our respective marriages or the views of society, not even our children, could stop us.

No one knows of your existence, not my family, nor Florian's, but it doesn't have to be that way. If you want to tell them about our romance, about the great love we shared, then that is your decision to make. It was a secret I chose to keep, but not one that you are bound by. I cannot guarantee their reaction, and I fear that they will not be open to the truth of the past, but that is up to you.

My darling, my greatest wish is for you to live the life you want to live, for you to make your own decisions not from fear, as I did, but because you have the ability to follow your heart. I hope the jewels your father and I were able to leave behind for you allow you to live a life on your own terms. My greatest fear is that you will feel the weight of your mistakes in the same way as I have.

You may wonder why I wrote this letter so long after we parted ways, and I regret to tell you that I'm unwell and only have months to live. If there was just one thing I could do before I pass away, it would be to find you, as I have tried to do for so many years, but instead, this letter will have to suffice. I've fought this illness for so long, but I know that there's only so long I can keep fighting.

With all my love, and with my deepest regret, your mother, Delphine.

Georgia wiped tears from her eyes as she stared at the letter in her hand. She'd read it twice now, her heart breaking both times as the pain of this woman, from her own great-grand-mother, echoed so loudly from the page. She'd known there would be a story to go with the tiara, but she had never imag-ined the depths of sadness that would be attached to it, the tragedy that would hit so hard as she read the words of a woman grieving so deeply despite the years that had passed.

So, it had been a scandal of sorts, a pregnancy that had been hidden from one family to protect another. Georgia reached for the necklace and put it around her neck, fumbling with the clasp and then checking to make sure she had the diamond hanging squarely at the front. Perhaps this was why she'd never fallen in love with any of the jewels at the auction she'd been to with Sam? Perhaps it was the universe telling her that she was about to come into possession of something truly special? That this was the one piece of jewellery that was to be hers.

Georgia stood and put the safety deposit box back in place, turning the key to secure it even though there was nothing left inside. She went back to the table and gathered up the photo and the letter, sliding it back into the envelope before dabbing at her cheeks and letting herself out of the room. It was over. She'd uncovered the mystery, and now it was time to go home.

When she walked back out into the lobby after thanking the assistant who'd helped her, Luca was pacing back and forth, his hands in his pockets and his head down. But he stopped walking and looked up when he heard the click of her heels. She could tell he was as invested in this whole mystery as she was, and that he would be waiting to hear what she'd found. She only wished she had a happier tale to share with him.

Georgia saw the crease in his forehead as he watched her, as if he had a question to ask, but he waited for her to speak first. He'd been insistent that she go into the room alone, and even though at the time she wouldn't have minded him accompanying her, she was pleased she'd made the discovery by herself.

Luca was silent until he saw her tears.

'What happened in there?' he asked, reaching for her and gently touching the back of his fingers to her cheeks. 'Hey, what's wrong?'

Georgia blinked, not wanting him to see her emotion. She thought she'd cried her only tears in the safety deposit room, but seeing Luca's concerned face had made her realise how truly alone she was in the world. Coming to Geneva, a part of her had thought she might meet members of her father's family she didn't know about, that she might find a family to welcome her with open arms. Instead, she'd found out that no one even knew about her grandmother's existence, so there were certainly no long-lost relatives waiting to be reunited with her.

'Do you remember the newspaper clipping I showed you?' Georgia asked.

Luca nodded. 'Of course. It was about Florian Lengacher, the businessman who died in a car accident. I think I told you it was his wife who made a claim against the tiara.'

She nodded, finding it hard to believe what she was about to say. 'It turns out that he was my great-grandfather.'

Luca's eyes widened. 'But your great-grandmother...'

'Wasn't Florian's wife,' she clarified. 'It's why my grandmother was placed for adoption. She was born out of wedlock, the result of an affair. Which means that perhaps Florian's family did have a legitimate claim after all.'

'How do you feel?' he asked.

'I don't know. Angry, heartbroken, sad,' she said. 'It's a lot to take in. But ultimately my great-grandmother was a woman in love, and the man she loved with all her heart was taken from her. It was a scandal, yet it wasn't, from what I can understand.' Georgia took a breath. 'And this necklace was hers, a gift from the man she loved.' She touched her hand to the piece of jewellery.

Luca placed an arm around her shoulders and she leaned into him.

'Well, it's beautiful. It suits you.' He touched the diamond, as she dropped her head to his shoulder. 'Would you like to try to connect with any members of the Lengacher family?' he asked. 'Would you like to find out more about that side of your biological family?'

'No,' she said firmly, even as her heart leapt at the thought of having a blood relative out there. 'I don't think that would be appropriate, not given that it was an affair. None of this is turning out as I'd imagined it might.'

'What about your great-grandmother's family, if you could find them?'

Georgia swallowed. 'Maybe. I just need time to process it all, I think.'

Luca's eyes searched her face. 'Does this mean it's time for you to return to London?'

She tried to avoid his gaze, but he touched her chin and gently tilted her face towards him.

'Yes,' she whispered, wishing she didn't suddenly feel so tearful. 'I think it does.'

The mystery was solved, her heritage discovered. There was no longer any reason for her to stay in Switzerland. Not a legitimate one, anyway. She wasn't going to search for blood relatives, there was no one waiting to meet her; in fact, it seemed as if her family had been cursed with tragedy.

'Georgia, before you leave Geneva, I'd very much like for you to meet my family,' Luca said. 'Would you join us for dinner before you go?'

Georgia looked up at Luca, her stomach twisting as she stared into his eyes. Part of her wondered if it would be easier to simply walk away now and try to forget that he even existed, but the other part of her wanted to enjoy every last minute with him. Part of her even wondered if it was Luca she'd been supposed to cross paths with, not descendants of her great-grandmother, but she knew that was just fanciful thinking on her behalf.

'I would love that.'

'Tonight then,' Luca said, brushing a warm, toe-tingling kiss to her lips. 'Let me make your final night in Switzerland one to remember. You don't have to end your trip feeling sad.'

'Luca, there's still the matter of the sapphire,' she said, as she tucked herself into his side and walked from the building. 'And the tiara.'

'We can discuss that tonight,' he said. 'But there's no hurry.

My family has kept the tiara safe for decades, and we will continue to do so until you instruct us otherwise. The worst thing you could do after all these years would be to make a rash decision about what to do with it.'

She appreciated his advice, and she knew he was one of the only people in the world who could truly have an opinion about what she should do, about the right decision to make. 'Luca, I'd like to give you the letter to read,' she said, reaching into her bag and taking it out for him. 'I know you must have so many questions about how the tiara ended up in your family's possession, and I think this letter is as much for you and your family as it is for me.'

'You're certain you want me to read it?' he asked. 'If it's private...'

She passed it to him, closing his fingers around it. 'I'm certain.' She went to let go of the letter, now that Luca was holding it, but something about the way he was watching her made her stop. 'Why are you looking at me like that?' she asked.

'I just...' He cleared his throat. 'You need to know that Florian had a son. I met him when his mother was contesting ownership of the tiara, but he passed away some years ago. I'm only telling you because I have a feeling you still don't believe this tiara belongs to you, but Florian had no other descendants, and his son never had children of his own. There is truly no one else who could have a legitimate claim to it.'

Georgia inhaled, listening to his words. He was right; that was precisely how she was feeling. How could it possibly belong to her? She hadn't known Delphine, it was supposed to be her grandmother's tiara, a grandmother who hadn't even wanted her in her life. But if Florian had no other children, then technically she was the only person who could claim it, and she wasn't sure she liked the responsibility being bestowed upon her.

'If not you, Georgia, then who?' Luca said gently. 'You are a direct descendant of Florian Lengacher. I have seen the paperwork confirming that he himself purchased the tiara all those years ago, and you now have a letter explaining how the missing sapphire was separated from the main piece. That means that you are absolutely the legitimate heiress to anything he left behind.'

'You truly believe that? I thought your family would hate to find out that this is the end of the story. That the mystery ends with me, that there's nothing more to it after all those years of searching.' She sighed. 'Should it not be returned to the descendants of the House of Savoy?'

'No, because it was sold by their family to yours. And you couldn't be more wrong about how my family will feel.' Luca's gaze never left hers. 'Once you meet my mother, I think you'll understand.'

She stared into his eyes and knew he was telling the truth.

'What time do you leave tomorrow?' he asked. 'Or haven't you booked your flight yet?'

'I leave at midday,' she said.

His expression gave nothing away, and she wished it had. She wished he'd immediately asked her to stay longer, that he'd looked disappointed. But instead, he only raised a brow in surprise and smiled.

'Well, then we'd better make the most of things until then.'

22

Georgia looked at Luca as he reached for the front door to his family home, which was a large, extravagant-looking residence in Cologny, on the outskirts of Geneva. His grin was infectious, despite how nervous she was. Technically it wasn't a date, but she couldn't help thinking that she'd never been taken to meet a man's mother before, and no amount of trying to tell herself it was a business dinner was working to calm her nerves.

'You look scared.'

'I am scared!' She didn't return Luca's laugh.

'Scared of what? My mother can't wait to meet you.'

Georgia sighed. She hoped he wasn't just saying that. But when Luca knocked lightly and then opened the door, and they found a very attractive woman rushing out into the hallway, an apron tied around her waist and a smile as big as her son's, Georgia realised he hadn't been trying to make her feel better. He'd clearly been telling the truth.

'Georgia!' his mother said, taking her by the shoulders and kissing both her cheeks, her English heavily accented. 'I'm Marj. What a pleasure it is to meet you. Luca! Take her coat and make us a drink, my love.'

Luca grinned, kissing his mother before moving past her, as Georgia was led into a room that looked as if it had just been completed by an interior designer, with throw cushions covering the sofas and soft cashmere blankets folded at each end.

'Please, take a seat. I'm so happy to have you and Luca here tonight.' His mother sat across from her, and Georgia couldn't help but admire her thick dark hair, the same nearly black shade as her son's, only hers was peppered with silver. 'He's told me so much about you.'

'He has?' She hadn't expected his mother to know anything about her, other than that she was in possession of the sapphire.

'When I saw him yesterday, I asked him who the woman in his life was.'

Georgia felt her eyebrows lift in question, although she didn't know what to say.

'Only a woman can make a man smile in that way.'

'Mama, your drink,' Luca said, entering the room at just the right time and passing first his mother, and then Georgia, a glass. 'Champagne, since it's a celebration.'

Georgia was surprised for the second time in as many minutes. 'Celebration?'

'After all these years, all these generations, we have finally solved the mystery of the missing sapphire,' Luca said. 'I think I speak for my mother, too, when I say that it was about time.'

Luca's mother laughed and shook her head. 'It was about time. Although I can see that perhaps everything has happened precisely when it was supposed to.'

'*Mama*,' Luca cautioned.

She held up her hands as Georgia took a little sip of her champagne.

'I'm sorry your husband spent so many years of your marriage obsessed with the sapphire,' Georgia said. 'Luca explained to me that the mystery of it all caused some difficulty—'

'Ah, my husband,' his mother said, putting down her drink and standing. Georgia watched as she crossed over to a large side table adorned with photo frames, taking one and walking back across the room with it. She sat down beside Georgia and passed it to her. 'This was my husband, and his father beside him.'

Georgia could see the family resemblance—Luca looked just like his father.

'My husband was a brilliant man, with an eye for rare items and jewels that few possessed. But it wasn't only your sapphire that drove him to madness. There were many things over the years that he became so focused on, that we almost lost him to.' She sighed, and when Georgia glanced at her, she could see she was still staring at the photo, as if becoming overtaken by the memory. 'It would have been a wonderful thing for you to meet him, for him to finally solve the mystery, but you mustn't blame yourself or your family heritage for what happened.'

'I feel as if so much about my family's past was hidden, and yet it still managed to cause you and your family so much pain.'

'The past,' Luca's mother said, firmly, 'is in the past. What I'd like to know is how you've enjoyed Geneva. I do hope my son has taken you for dinner by the lake.'

Georgia glanced over at Luca, who was looking at her as if to say, 'I told you so'—his smile was so smug.

'He did take me for dinner. He's been the most obliging host I could have wished for.'

'Well, that's not hard, when he's clearly smitten with his guest.'

'*Mère, s'il te plaît. Assez!*'

Georgia laughed, not needing an exact translation to understand that Luca was reprimanding his mother. But Marj couldn't seem to care less, shrugging and taking a sip of her champagne, with a twinkle in her eyes that reminded Georgia of Luca.

'Luca, I'm not sure if I've ever told you, but your father knew there was a woman involved in the mystery.'

Georgia saw the way Luca stiffened. 'You're certain he knew that?'

'I am. He told me that his grandfather had told him that a woman had given the tiara to him. That's when he started to become obsessed with the mystery all over again.'

'That woman was my great-grandmother,' Georgia said, her voice barely a whisper. 'Delphine. The woman your husband was obsessed with finding.'

'Georgia, if you're uncomfortable discussing this—'

She watched as Marj rose, wondering what the noise was as Luca stopped talking. 'Please excuse me, I need to let our visitors in.'

'Visitors?' Luca asked.

'You didn't think it was going to be just the three of us, did you? I asked your sister and her husband to join us.' She smiled as she passed Luca and patted his shoulder. 'They couldn't *wait* to meet Georgia.'

'I'm so sorry,' he said, moving closer and sitting down beside her. 'I promise I knew nothing about this.'

'It's fine,' Georgia said with a shrug. 'I can very much see from the look on your face that this is a surprise to you, and it'll be nice to meet your sister.'

'But it's not just my sister we have to contend with—'

Before he could finish what he was saying, there was a shriek of delight, followed by two little blonde whirlwinds screaming, 'Uncle Luca!' at the very top of their lungs.

'The twins,' he said, passing her his drink just in time as they ran across the room and leapt into his arms.

Georgia could barely stop laughing to greet his sister, who looked as if she could have died when she walked into the room and saw what her two children were doing to their uncle.

'Georgia! I'm so sorry, they think their uncle is a toy to play with,' said a voice that sounded remarkably similar to Luca's mother's. 'I'm Elin and this is my husband, Nathan. And those are our wild girls, Stella and Luiza.'

Georgia put down both drinks and stood, holding out her hand. 'Lovely to meet you.'

'I have so much to ask you, but first of all, what have you done to my brother?' she said, leaning in with a grin. 'You're the first woman friend of his we've ever met.'

Georgia knew she was blushing, but she couldn't help it. 'This is just business,' she said. 'Closure for your family, given the circumstances.'

'You're talking about the tiara?' she asked, as Luca's mother came back into the room. 'Luca was the only one crazy enough to still be searching for that sapphire. The rest of us were more than happy to relegate it to the past.'

'So, Mama hasn't told you? The mystery has been solved, Elin, and if it hadn't been for me being *crazy enough* to keep searching, Georgia would never have discovered her family secrets.'

The girls shrieked again and launched themselves at Luca, and Elin took Georgia by the arm and led her away, gesturing for Luca's mother to follow. 'Let's leave the men with the girls, and you can tell us all about these family secrets. I'm dying to know how you ended up here in Switzerland.'

Georgia glanced over her shoulder at Luca, but no matter how much he might have wanted to join them, he was most definitely otherwise engaged.

'Have you asked her yet?' Luca's mother said, as she tucked her arm through Georgia's and led her into the kitchen.

'Asked me what?'

'Whether you play backgammon,' Elin said.

Georgia looked between them, realising how serious the expressions were on their faces. 'I do, actually. Although I haven't played for quite some time.'

'Perfect,' they both said in unison, as if they were exhaling on the same breath.

'You all play?'

'We're all fiercely competitive, it's an after-dinner tradition,' Elin explained. 'We've dreamed of Luca meeting a woman who can beat him, because he's so arrogant when it comes to backgammon. If you can beat him...'

Marj laughed, finishing Elin's sentence. 'You'd have an instant invitation to join the family!'

'He's that good?' Georgia watched as the women exchanged glances, realising that he was clearly *very* good at the game.

Deep laughter echoed behind them, and they all three spun around to see Luca standing there, his arms folded across his chest as he stared his sister down.

'Yes, he is that good,' Luca said, unfolding his arms and reaching for Georgia's hand, drawing her back towards him. 'Especially when he's playing against his sister. It's unfortunate that she didn't inherit our family's exceptional talents for the game.'

They all laughed and Luca winked at her, and in that moment, Georgia thought of her parents, imagined how they would have treated Luca if she'd been the one to bring him home for dinner. It was one of the many times she'd thought of them and wondered what it would be like, how different her life might be. And even though she'd only been a girl when she'd lost them, she knew they would have been just as welcoming.

'Thank you,' she whispered, as Luca leaned in and kissed her cheek.

'For what?'

'For bringing me for dinner, for letting me be part of this. Your family are wonderful.'

Luca's smile lit up his eyes, and she knew that if she stared into them for too long, she'd never want to stop.

'Georgia, I know you came here hoping to find your own family, but I want you to know that you are always welcome here,' Marj said, embracing her warmly at the door, her arms wrapped tightly around her as she spoke. When she stood back, she placed her palms to Georgia's cheeks and looked into her eyes, her smile genuine. 'Perhaps we were the family you were supposed to meet? At least I'd like to think so. It's been very special getting to know you tonight.'

'Being with you all, it's been wonderful. Thank you for inviting me into your home.'

'Have you decided what to do with the tiara?' his mother asked. 'It's none of my business, but after all these years...'

'Mama,' Luca warned. 'It's a big decision.'

'My inclination is to donate it to a museum, or at the very least exhibit it so that everyone can see it,' Georgia said. 'But there's so much to consider. I think I'll engage the law firm who held the information for all these years to advise me.'

'Well, whatever you decide will be the right way forward,' his mother said. 'There's nothing wrong with choosing to keep it, or selling it and putting the millions to good use. The decision is yours.'

'Thank you. I'm certainly feeling the weight of it.'

'You're welcome any time, Georgia, don't be a stranger.'

'Good night, Mama,' Luca said. 'Thank you for a lovely dinner.' He hugged her.

Georgia kissed the older woman's left cheek, and then her right, as well as Elin's, before raising her hand to wave good night in return. Luca surprised her by taking hold of her hand as his family watched them go, and they held hands until they reached his car.

When they did, he stopped and lifted her hand, kissing her knuckles, their fingers interlinked. 'I was thinking we could go back to my place for a drink?' he said. 'Since it's your last night here?'

She met his gaze and stepped closer, refusing to be embarrassed. This was her last night to be bold, to say yes to what she wanted. She also realised that she hadn't seen his house and she wanted to know everything about him, so she could remember him when she'd returned to London.

Georgia stood on tiptoe and kissed him, looping her arms around his neck as he slipped his hands around her waist.

'I take it that means yes?'

23

LONDON, 1952

Delphine heard Hope coming down the hall. She dabbed at her eyes before standing, holding on to the bedframe as a contraction tightened her stomach.

'How are you progressing?' Hope asked.

She grimaced. 'Not as fast as I'd like.'

'Would you like to go for a little walk, or we could always just sit?' Hope said.

Delphine nodded. 'I think I'd very much like to walk. It might hurry things along.'

Hope held out her arm and Delphine slipped her hand through it, happy to have her to lean on as they walked down the stairs and then out the door. Another contraction stopped her for a long minute, before they continued on.

'You know, you're the only woman I've had here who's had a baby before,' Hope said as they strolled. 'Would you like to tell me about your other births?'

'The first one was fast, much faster than anyone expected, which meant that the doctor only just made it in time to catch him.' Delphine laughed. 'I always whispered to my son that he was in a hurry to meet his mama, because when he was born his little eyes fixed on mine, as if he'd been waiting to see me.'

'And your second child?'

'Took her time,' Delphine said. 'It was absolute agony. I was pushing for hours.' Delphine paused again, her fingers tightening around Hope's arm.

'Have you,' she asked, catching her breath once it was over, 'ever given birth?'

Hope didn't say anything straightaway, walking Delphine around the garden, but when she finally spoke, her words were much quieter than before.

'It seems that you're not only my first mother who's birthed a child before, but also the first to ask me that question,' Hope said. 'I've been asked whether I have children of my own, to which the answer is no, but no one has ever asked me whether I've given birth.'

Delphine squeezed her arm. 'I'm sorry, I should never have asked you something so personal.'

'No, it's a perfectly understandable question, given that you're in the throes of childbirth yourself. I think my other girls have been so terrified of what's to come that they simply haven't thought to ask.'

Delphine paused again, realising that the contractions were closer together now. Hope had noticed, too, because she rubbed Delphine's arm and nodded before they eventually began to walk again.

'Many years ago, when I was a much younger woman, I was pregnant,' she said. 'I, well, I lost the baby. It simply wasn't meant to be.'

'And you never fell pregnant again?' Delphine asked.

'I had complications during the birth, and...'

Hope looked away, and once again Delphine wondered if the question had been too personal. She would never have usually asked such a thing, but she'd become so close to Hope in the time she'd been there. And Hope was guiding her through something deeply personal herself.

'Many young women, any women really, who find themselves unexpectedly pregnant, are not often treated with the respect and care they deserve,' Hope said when she finally turned back. 'I've met so many women over the years, and most of them share the same story.'

Delphine had a different twinge of pain in her side, and rubbed her hand there in an effort to relieve it.

'They don't want the baby?' she asked.

'No, oftentimes they do want the baby, or at least they would want the baby if their circumstances were different,' Hope said. 'But the one thing they all have in common is that they've been let down by men.'

Delphine nodded, knowing what Hope was trying to tell her. She guessed she was no different—Florian hadn't let her down, but Giovanni had. She would never have gone looking for comfort elsewhere if he'd treated her as a husband should.

'Some of my girls have been raped, and their parents don't want the shame of dealing with it, or perhaps they don't believe them. Others have been left by a man as soon as they discovered the pregnancy, and some have fallen for false promises. But at the end of the day, they've all had a man take something from them.'

'Is that why you started this place?' Delphine asked. 'To help those women?'

'I started this place because I knew what it felt like to be pregnant and unwanted. The doctor did things to me without asking first what I wanted, and he made a choice about my body that changed the course of my life.' Hope cleared her throat, and Delphine felt a sudden longing to comfort her, just as another contraction took over her body.

'I...' She groaned and bent forward, her hands on her knees, grappling with the pain. 'I think it's time.'

She would rather have heard more about Hope's story, to better comprehend how she'd come to do what she did, to have the resources to dedicate her life to women and babies, but suddenly she felt as if her insides were being torn in two, and she had the most overwhelming urge to push.

'That's it, let's get you back inside,' Hope said. 'I'll see if one of the other girls—'

'No,' Delphine said through gritted teeth. 'I don't want anyone else there. I've done this before and I can do it again.'

'Very well.'

Delphine clenched her teeth through the next wave of pain, hoping she didn't sound ungrateful, wanting to explain herself, but suddenly finding it hard to even put one foot in front of the other.

'I just, I want to do this on my own. It will be the only time I spend with my baby.'

'You don't have to explain to me. I'll only call someone for the doctor if he's needed.'

Delphine nodded and walked as quickly as she could. *In a hurry, just like my Tommaso.* Tears filled her eyes as she pictured holding another darling baby, kissing all their fingers and toes to celebrate the miracle of what she'd created.

'It's a girl,' Hope said, passing Delphine the tiny, crying bundle that was her baby.

'A girl?' Delphine's face was wet with sweat, her hair stuck to her forehead as she craned her neck to see her baby's face. 'I was certain it was going to be a little boy.'

'Well, she might not be a boy, but she certainly has a set of lungs on her.'

Hope had swaddled the baby tightly, but it was doing nothing to soothe her.

'Do you think there's something wrong with her?' Delphine asked. 'My other two were like little kittens mewling.'

'I think she'll be fine once she feeds,' Hope said. 'I think the poor little darling is just hungry.'

Delphine froze at the thought of feeding her, not having expected to be doing that. She didn't know what she'd expected, or why she'd thought she wouldn't be nursing her, but the thought sent a cold shiver down her spine.

'If I nurse her, if—' Delphine knew her eyes would be as round as saucers.

Hope sat down on the bed bedside her, not saying anything, but her expression telling Delphine she understood.

'It will be so much harder to say goodbye,' Hope eventually said. 'You think it will make your bond stronger, that you won't want to part with her.'

'You don't think it will make it harder?' Delphine whispered.

'To the contrary, I think you're absolutely right, but there's going to be nothing easy about leaving her, no matter what you do. Your heart is going to be broken regardless of whether you feed her or not. You'll think about never seeing her again, question whether you're doing the right thing.' Hope patted her hand. 'But the one thing you can do is to make the next few days with your daughter special. You can give her every bit of love in your heart, nurture her and care for her the same way you have your other children, tell her all the things you want her to know.'

Delphine began to cry then, which only made her baby more and more upset. But she couldn't help it. Once the tears started, they were almost impossible to stop.

'I don't ever want to let her go,' she whispered. 'I don't want anyone else to hold her. I don't want her to be someone else's child.'

Hope opened her arms and embraced her and her daughter,

holding them both as Delphine cried. Once her sobs had given way to little hiccups of tears, Hope gently stroked her face and dried it, before looking into her eyes.

'Tell me why you're doing this,' Hope said gently. 'It will help to remind yourself, to say it out loud.'

'Because if I don't, my husband will discover that I've been unfaithful,' she murmured. 'I will lose my other two children.'

Hope's fingers were featherlight against her skin.

'I will have no means to provide for my baby. I will be alone, and I will never see Tommaso and Isabella ever again.'

'You need to decide what is most important to you, Delphine. Every woman I see here is faced with an impossible decision, although it does come more easily to some,' she said. 'But you, you're different. You know how quickly this baby will grow into a lovable child, a child who you will fight for with all your heart, just as you're doing for your other children now.'

'Then why do I feel as if I'm making the most horrible choice? Why do I feel as if Florian will never forgive me?'

'Because making the right decision is never easy. It's not supposed to be,' Hope said, gently. 'There's nothing easy about being a mother, or giving up a baby for adoption.'

'Or losing a baby?' Delphine asked.

'Or losing a baby,' Hope replied. 'Giving birth and then not having a baby to fill your arms with, it's the most painful thing of all. But you,' she said, her smile bright. 'You have two gorgeous children to hold, to cherish and love. You will mourn your baby, yes, but you will know every day that you've made the right choice as you watch your other children grow.'

'You truly believe that?'

Hope nodded. 'I do. And I think that in your heart, you know that, too.'

Delphine finally let her gaze rest on her baby daughter again, realising that she'd stopped crying and had gone silent, her tiny hand having wriggled free and now fisted to her chin.

Her face was perfect, her little lips dark pink and full, a smattering of dark hair covering her head.

'I keep thinking of my Florian. Of what a wonderful father he would have been, what it would have been like seeing him hold her.' Delphine blinked away fresh tears. 'I keep thinking that he would have done everything he could to protect her, and yet I'm letting her go without a fight.'

'But he's not here, my love. You're alone, and you're making the only choices you can.' Hope stood then, leaning over to kiss her forehead before walking away.

Delphine had half a mind to ask her to stay, but she knew she needed to savour these precious moments with her daughter, to soak up every second and commit them to memory, so she'd always be able to close her eyes and remember.

'Hope?' she said, looking up from her daughter.

Hope stood at the door, her hand raised to the handle as she looked over her shoulder.

'I'm sorry about your baby,' Delphine said. 'I'm sure you would have been a wonderful mother.'

Hope brushed at the corner of her eye as she slowly nodded. 'Thank you. I'd like to think I would have been, too.'

And with that, she disappeared and shut the door behind her, leaving Delphine and her baby alone. She stared at her perfect little face, forced herself to kiss those tiny red fingers with even tinier half-moon nails, inhaled the smell of newborn baby. And when she was ready, as her baby started to cry again, she adjusted herself so she could feed her, taking only a few attempts to get her suckling.

The tugging sensation wasn't unfamiliar to her, but it was so intimate, her tiny infant drinking from her, that it brought tears to her eyes.

I wish I could feed you for a year, as I did my others. I wish I could kiss your little downy head every morning, give you my finger to hold as you drink, swaddle you and comfort you whenever you need your mama.

'I wish your father could have met you,' she whispered. 'He would have loved you so much. You would have had him wrapped around your little finger, his beautiful daughter.'

Her tears fell and dropped onto the baby's cheek, but Delphine didn't try to wipe them away because more kept falling, impossible to stop.

I wish I was there to see your first smile. To cut your first lock of hair, to whisper to you in the dark to soothe your nightmares. I wish I was there to see your first tooth; I wish you could meet your brother and sister.

I wish we could have had just one moment as a family, to both hold you in our arms.

I wish Florian could have lived long enough to see you, long enough to mean that I didn't have to make this decision.

Delphine closed her eyes as she cried, wishing above all else that she wasn't sad right then, because even though her daughter would be too young to ever remember her, she wanted the sound of her voice to be soothing, her breast to be nourishing, her touch to be loving. She wanted the first moments of her life to be wonderful ones, to be cherished ones.

'I love you, daughter,' she murmured. 'I want you to know that you were loved from the moment you were conceived.'

The tugging stopped then, and Delphine was surprised to see that her baby was looking up at her. She'd expected that she might have fallen asleep, but instead she was gazing back at her as if she understood what was being said.

'If there was any other way...'

But there wasn't, and there was no use trying to pretend otherwise.

24

PRESENT DAY

Georgia couldn't have been more surprised when they walked in through the door of Luca's home. She'd expected a town-house, something modern and very much a bachelor pad, but instead she'd walked into a two-storey chalet that truly felt like a home. Art was placed strategically on the walls, and as he rushed ahead to turn on some lamps, she was able to admire the deep cushioned sofas and pieces of antique furniture. It had been stupid to expect anything less, given his penchant for collecting rare and unique pieces in his work life, but she certainly hadn't expected such a *home*.

'It's incredible,' she said, turning around slowly to take in the architecture and the way he'd furnished it. She could almost guess that he'd bought it with a family in mind—the only things missing were the wife and children, and it made her wonder about a life she'd never imagined for herself before. She'd spent her entire adult life trying to prove herself, to show that she could do everything off her own bat, but suddenly she could see that perhaps that wasn't enough. She pushed those thoughts away and walked to the windows on the other side, peering out even though it was almost dark. 'Can you see the lake from here?'

Luca smiled and walked back towards her. 'You can. Perhaps you can admire it in the morning?'

Georgia swallowed as he stroked her face and leaned in for a kiss. Another man saying those words might have sounded conceited, but something about Luca saying it just made it sound tempting.

'Champagne?' he asked.

She took his hand and followed him through the living area and into the kitchen, where he went to the fridge and took out a bottle of Mumm. He wasted no time popping the cork and taking down two glasses, filling them and moving back around to her.

'Why do I get the feeling you had all this planned?' she asked, as he gently clinked his glass to hers. 'Or do you always have champagne chilling, just in case?'

'I'm not going to lie,' he said. 'I've been wanting to ask you back here since our very first day together.'

'You have?'

'I have. Only I didn't want to come across as too forward, which is why it's taken so many days.'

Georgia stayed silent. If she were braver, she would have told him that she'd wanted that, too. And now here they were with only one night left. One final evening to be with Luca before she left and never saw him again.

'Can I ask you a question?' he asked, placing his hand on her hip.

She took a sip. 'Of course. Anything.'

'Would you stay another few days, if I asked you to?'

'Here?' she asked, glancing around. 'With you?'

Luca nodded, and as he did, she reached up to touch his face, her fingers grazing his stubble.

'I think I can manage an extra couple of days,' she replied, as his lips met hers. *What harm would it be to extend her stay?* 'But only until the end of the week.' So much for just having one night with him and then leaving. But after a few days, she'd *have* to return to London, to her real life. There was only so long she could justify playing make-believe.

Or perhaps she was scared of how hard it would be to leave Luca behind if she spent any more time with him.

Somehow their glasses ended up on the table as Luca's arms went around her, his mouth hungry against hers, kissing her as if he'd been waiting a lifetime to claim her. Georgia ran her hands across his shoulders, down his back, pulling away, and looking up into his eyes.

She'd never imagined falling fast and hard for a man, but it seemed that this time, she'd fallen head over heels just when she was least expecting it.

25

LONDON, 1952

Delphine stared at the perfect little wooden box Hope had placed on the table in front of her. Her hands were trembling as she picked it up and studied it, listening to what Hope was telling her.

'Many of the young women who come through my door never want to speak of or think about what happened here ever again, but there are some, like you, who feel differently. Who will never, ever stop thinking about the child they were forced to part with.'

Delphine put the box down. 'You want me to think of something to leave for her, in this little box?'

Hope smiled. 'From experience, I believe that the moment you set eyes on that box, you thought of something to put inside it. Perhaps even more than one something.'

She was right. Delphine had thought of something, knew exactly what she'd leave in there for her daughter. In the beginning, she wasn't sure whether she'd keep it for herself or tuck it into her daughter's blanket, but now that Hope had given her the box, she knew what she needed to do.

'I'm going to leave you for a while, let you think about it, and when you're ready you can simply tie the string around it and I'll store it for when she's older.'

Delphine reached for the box again, but this time she looked up at Hope. 'You'll make sure she gets this? That it won't sit forever collecting dust, never to be discovered?'

Hope nodded. 'I promise. My intention is to have the boxes delivered to the children when they're adults, or, of course, if they ever come to me looking for adoption records or answers.'

Delphine thanked her, waiting until she was alone to open the box. It was only small, but she knew that she could fit in what she wanted. First, she took the pink sapphire from the inside pocket of her jacket, placing it into the box and staring down at it. The light caught the reflection and shone back up at her, catching her eyes in a prism of colour, and she knew without a doubt that it was the right thing to leave. And then she stood and went to her bag, taking out her copy of *Neue Zürcher Zeitung* that she'd brought with her. She cut out the newspaper article announcing Florian's death, and she decided to part with it, so that her daughter could read about the man who was her father.

She wanted to write a letter, to tell her how she felt about leaving, about how loved she was, but she couldn't. She'd told her a thousand times now how much she adored her, told her how life could have turned out if things were different, and she simply couldn't bring herself to write those words on a page.

The sapphire will give her financial independence if she needs it, and the article will tell her who her father was. That's all she needs to know.

One day, she would see her again; she could feel it in her heart. And that's when she would explain to her why.

By the time Hope returned to see if she was finished, Delphine had tied the string tightly around the box, ready to give it back to her.

'Whatever gave you the idea to use little wooden boxes?' Delphine asked.

'Because a similar little box meant the world to me many years ago, so I understand the power of leaving something behind.'

Delphine wasn't sure she knew what Hope was saying—had she herself been left a box? But Delphine didn't want to ask, not after the personal questions she'd already posed to her when she'd been in the latter stages of labour, being far more inquisitive than she would ever usually be.

'Delphine, in the morning, when the family arrive...'

She forgot all about the box as she looked up at Hope. Her three days of caring for her daughter were almost over. A pain that easily rivalled her labour stabbed deep inside of her at the thought of giving up her darling little baby, but she also felt another pain, from not seeing her other children in so long.

Delphine nodded and left the room, going quickly upstairs and to her bedroom, to find the baby still sleeping soundly, tucked up in her crib. When she'd had Tommaso and Isabella, she'd been surrounded by others helping her. In the night, someone would bring her the baby if it needed feeding, and someone else would take the baby from her during the day if she needed some time to herself, but her experience with her third child couldn't have been more different. Delphine had barely been parted from her for so much as a minute, other than to go downstairs to prepare the box. She'd placed her crib right beside her bed so she could leave her hand dangling into it, fingertips brushing against her daughter as they both slept. She'd nursed her and kissed her, sung lullabies to her and rocked her to sleep in her arms, and walked with her around the gardens, tucked in a little blanket with just her face peeping out. She'd made sure to soak up every single moment with her, showing her as much love as she could, making space in her heart for her little daughter, even though the pain of what was to come terrified her.

'Tomorrow, we have to say goodbye,' Delphine told her as she saw her little eyes blink open, scooping her up into her arms. 'But tonight, we will be together. Tonight, I will stare at you and kiss you all night long, little one.'

Her baby held out one little arm, her tiny pink mouth stretching into a yawn as she listened to her mother. It was the most innocent, normal little movement, but just seeing that made a sob rise and then choke in Delphine's throat. She forced herself to clear it, looking down at her daughter as tears filled her eyes.

'Why don't I tell you all about your big brother and big sister?' she said, walking over to the window and kissing her daughter's forehead as she stood in the dappled sunlight. 'If your father was here, we would have moved into his lake house by now. Your sister would adore you—I think she'd take on the role of second mother. And your brother is the sweetest, most thoughtful boy. He would have doted on you from the moment I arrived home with you.'

The baby was silent, staring up at Delphine as if she could understand every word. Delphine bent to kiss her again, this time gently placing her lips to her cheek, and then to her little hands.

'If only your papa could have met you,' Delphine whispered. 'He would have loved every inch of you.'

She stood for a while longer, but when the sun began to fade, she walked back to her bed and propped herself up against the pillows. She knew she would never sleep tonight, not when they had only hours left together, not when she would have to say goodbye in the morning. Tonight, she would tell her daughter a lifetime of stories, and she would also tell her the story of the sapphire and why she'd chosen to leave it behind for her to discover one day.

.   .   .

The next day, Delphine got into the car and huddled in the back seat as the driver took her bags. Her breath was coming in sharp pants, her shoulders hunched, and she felt as if her heart was bleeding into her chest.

'Delphine,' said a warm, familiar voice.

It was Hope. Of course, it was Hope. The woman had soothed her and counselled her during her three-month stay. She'd been like a mother to her, a trusted friend who could feel her pain, and quite possibly the most selfless person she'd ever met. But now, after the agony of saying goodbye to her daughter, Delphine could barely lift her head to look at her.

'I saved this for you,' Hope said, passing her something as she leaned in through the door. 'I thought you might like to keep it.'

She realised what it was the second Hope placed it on her lap, and she immediately reached for it and held it up, burying her face against the little cardigan that her baby had been wearing. The soft wool still smelt of her, made Delphine's breasts begin to leak as she remembered the weight of her little girl in her arms, as she yearned to feed her one last time.

'And you left this behind by mistake,' Hope said. 'And I was certain you'd want it.'

She took the piece of paper Hope held out to her, her heart breaking for another reason entirely as she stared down at the brightly coloured drawing. Isabella had drawn it for her and Martina had sent it, Delphine pinning it to the wall in her room at Hope's House. It was a picture of a pretty house with a bright yellow sun high in the sky and a collection of flowers sprouting up all around. Then, to the side, there were two people holding hands, women or girls with long hair, and she knew that Isabella was drawing a picture of them together.

'Remember why you did this, Delphine. Don't ever let yourself forget why you made this decision.'

Delphine nodded and clutched the picture in one hand and

the item of clothing in the other as Hope stepped back and closed the door, before the driver got in behind the steering wheel and drove them away. Delphine looked over her shoulder at Hope as she left, wishing she had the strength to lift her hand in a wave, but she couldn't. Her body felt numb, her eyes felt raw, her heart felt broken; but as she looked down at the picture, she tried to remember Hope's words.

I'm going to see my children. Today, I get to hold my two children in my arms.

Hope had called ahead to speak to Martina, advising her that her medical treatment was over and that she was ready to return to her family, so she knew that everyone would be expecting her. Her only saving grace was that she was supposed to look unwell or as if she were still recovering from an illness, and she knew that it would be only natural for her to cry and become emotional after not seeing her children in three months. There would be nothing unusual about her tears, which at least meant her puffy eyes would go unnoticed.

The closer they got to the house she'd rented for her and the children, the tighter she held the item of clothing, but when they were within a few blocks, she tucked it down into her brassiere, wanting to keep her baby's scent as close to her skin as possible.

When the car finally pulled up, she knew it was time to gather herself. The children would be waiting for her, Martina would be waiting for her; her husband could even be waiting for her.

She stepped out, smoothing down the creases in her skirt and thanking the driver for his assistance with her bags. He carried them up the few steps and she held her hand to knock, hesitating before finally tapping her knuckles against the timber.

It felt strange to be knocking at the door of the home she'd rented. Part of her had wondered about just letting herself in, but she felt that it would be better to wait than give anyone inside an unexpected surprise.

'Mama?' The boy standing on the other side of the door when it swung open looked far too grown up to be her son.

'Tommaso?' she cried. 'Look at you! How did you grow in such a short time?'

Her son threw his arms around her and hugged her, not letting go as she peppered his head with kisses.

Soon there was someone else standing there. Isabella was watching them, her back straight as Martina placed a hand on her shoulder. Delphine's first instinct was to run and envelop them both in a warm hug, but instead she nodded politely to Martina and held out her hands for her daughter.

'Isabella, my sweet Isabella,' she said, bending low so that she could encourage her forward, into her arms. 'You've grown as much as your brother has, and look at your long hair!'

It took a moment for Isabella to come forward, but when she did, she crashed into Delphine's legs and wrapped her arms around her.

'You look different,' Tommaso said, studying her as she hugged his sister. 'Are you still sick?'

'No, my love, I'm fine now,' Delphine said, forcing a bright smile. 'I'm just so glad to be home with the both of you.'

'Papa says that we're moving soon,' Tommaso said. 'He said it's ridiculous to still have this house here, that we should be in Geneva.'

'Then we shall return there,' Delphine said. 'So long as the three of us are together, that's all that matters.'

The children jumped up and down and proceeded to tell her hundreds of stories all at the same time, speaking over one another, each sibling clearly trying to outdo the other. But she didn't mind; these children were her life and soul, the children she knew she'd been destined to have. But in that moment, as she smiled and nodded, as she tried so desperately to be present, a tear escaped and slid from the corner of her eye, down her cheek.

'Mama?' Tommaso asked, his voice husky with concern. 'Mama, what's wrong?'

'I'm fine, I'm just so happy to be back with you both. It's been so long since I got to hear your lovely voices or see your beautiful faces.'

Martina stepped in then, her smile wide as she addressed the children. 'Come along now, my loves. We need to let your darling mama get changed. It will have been a long drive for her.'

Tommaso didn't look convinced about leaving, but when his sister skipped off, he reluctantly followed her. She watched them go, waited until they were both outside before dropping into the closest chair as she began to cry.

'We need to get you up to your bedroom and changed into something more comfortable,' Martina said. 'Come, let me help you. Perhaps you might want a bath first?'

Delphine didn't say a word as she let Martina lead her, as she took her upstairs and sat her down on the bed. Next, Martina took out clothes and touched up her make-up, before leaning forward and reaching for her hands.

'I'm sorry,' Martina said. 'I can't imagine the pain you're in.'

'Thank you,' Delphine whispered. 'But she's gone now, and I have to do my best to forget about her.'

'It was a little girl?'

Fresh tears clung to her lashes. 'A little girl. A gorgeous little girl who looked so much like her big sister that it made it all hurt even more.'

'Would you like me to tell the children you've gone to bed for a rest?' Martina asked. 'I can always—'

'You will do no such thing,' Delphine said. 'If I'm to accept my decision, I need to make the most of every day I have with them. I'm going outside to play whatever they want.'

'To play with them?' Martina repeated, as if she were positively mad.

'Do you know where Giovanni is?' Delphine asked, changing the subject.

'I believe he's at his place. He's had the children to visit but—'

Delphine shut her eyes, trying to ignore the pain of what she was hearing. His children were right here in London, without their mother, and he still hadn't bothered with them.

'Send word to him that we'll be returning to Geneva. Switzerland is our home, and I intend to buy a property by the lake just as soon as we return.'

'Of course. I'll have word sent immediately,' Martina said. But as she spoke, she held out her hand and took Delphine's palm in hers, tears spilling from both their eyes as they stared at one another. 'They're very happy to have their mother home,' Martina whispered.

Delphine nodded. 'And she's very happy to be home with them.'

Or at least I would be if I could find a way to accept what I've done. She just had to keep telling herself that she'd made the only decision available to her, and trust that Hope had found a loving, wonderful home for her baby daughter. Because if she couldn't believe that? Then she knew there was no way she could ever live with herself.

26

LONDON, PRESENT DAY

Georgia opened the door to her flat and dragged her bags in behind her, pushing the door shut and walking over to her sofa. She flopped down into it, closing her eyes and hating how silent her home was. It wasn't so long ago that she'd loved the solitude, especially when she was trying to focus on her work, but suddenly all she wanted was to be back in Geneva, exploring the city and going back to the restaurant Luca had taken her to on the lake.

Luca. It wasn't just the city she missed. If it was, she could go downstairs and take a taxi to her favourite part of London. She could go out for lunch and shop to her heart's content; she could go to the National Gallery even. There were many things she could do to replicate her time in Switzerland; the only thing she couldn't do was conjure up the man who'd made her time there so special.

Georgia reached into her bag and took out the little wooden box. It had lost some of its meaning without the sapphire inside, but she still didn't want to part with it. She turned it over in her hands and studied it; pictured her great-grandmother holding it, trying to decide what to put inside. Had her tears fallen on the wood? Had she held the little box to her chest, her heart broken as she imagined her daughter one day discovering it? She retrieved the photo from the safety deposit box from her bag—the necklace still around her neck—and she stared down at the contents, wishing it didn't hurt so much to think about a past that she hadn't even known existed. Of the family out there somewhere who didn't know her grandmother had even been born.

She blinked away tears and took out the newspaper clipping, toying with the necklace that she hadn't removed since she'd returned home, the diamond nestled just below her collarbone. Even though she couldn't read it, it didn't make it any less important. Delphine had given birth while grieving for the man she loved, forced to give up her baby in order to save the children she already had. If ever there had been a heart-wrenching decision to be made, she couldn't think of a worse one, and as she stared at the photo, looking at their faces, at the happiness that was so clear in their expressions, it truly broke her heart. They'd been in love and had to hide it from the world.

Georgia couldn't stop wondering if her grandmother would have been different if she'd known the truth about her past, if she'd been the one to receive the wooden box and discover the clues. Perhaps it would have changed the way she felt about her daughter-in-law, or made her want to reconnect with her son. She also couldn't stop wondering about why the sapphire had never been sent to her grandmother. Delphine had clearly expected that she would receive it, but as far as Georgia understood, no one, not even Mia, knew why those boxes had remained hidden for all those years.

And now here Georgia was, home, with her own decisions to make. She'd spent so much of her life focused on her business, looking no further ahead than to the sale they'd set their sights on, and for the first time in her life, she didn't have a goal. She didn't know what she wanted.

As a teenager, she'd been focused on school and exams; as a young adult she'd been consumed by her achievements at university; and as a young woman, she'd poured her energy into her business. It was almost as if she needed to find herself again, to understand what she wanted from life, and she had Luca and her great-grandmother to thank for showing her that success in business wasn't enough to create true happiness.

There was a gentle knock on her door then. Sam was the only one who had her codes and keys, and before Georgia could rise, her best friend was opening the door, nudging it with her hip as she held out a tray containing coffees, with brown paper bags perched on top.

'I had a feeling you were going to need this,' Sam said, placing the tray on the table and taking out one of the coffees.

'I'm so lucky to have you,' Georgia said. But as the words came out of her mouth, as Sam looked at her, tears began to stream down Georgia's cheeks.

'Hey!' Sam set down the coffees and sat on the sofa, wrapping her arms around Georgia and holding her in a tight hug. 'If I'd known you'd get this upset over a flat white...'

Georgia laughed despite her tears, nestling her head on Sam's shoulder. 'I'm sorry, I just, seeing you—'

'No need to explain. I think you've been holding back tears for a decade, so it's high time they came out.'

Sam was right. She'd spent years reining in her emotions, refusing to be the victim when she knew she had so much to be thankful for, but after the past week, all her emotions seemed to be bubbling to the surface. Her grandmother, her parents, the love she'd been given by a family with whom she shared no blood ties, and then the way Luca's mother had welcomed her with open arms. Despite the love of Sam's family, she was suddenly acutely aware of what she'd lost, of what she'd grown up without. There was nothing easy about being an orphan, and the most difficult part to wrap her head around was that it was her grandmother who'd been left as a baby. Perhaps she'd known about the adoption, found out somehow, and that had turned her into the difficult, bitter woman she'd become.

'I just... going on this journey, finding out more about my family's past, it's brought it all back,' she said, dabbing at her eyes as she pulled away from Sam. 'I can't stop thinking about how much loss my family has endured.'

'Are you also thinking about a certain handsome Swiss man?'

Georgia laughed. 'I've barely thought of anything else.'

Sam sighed and reached for the coffees. 'Well, I have croissants and pastries, so I'm ready to sit back and hear all about him.'

'Honestly?' Georgia said. 'He's perfect. He's successful, warm, fun to be around, and he adores his mother. There was nothing not to like about him. I might even go as far as saying that I've never felt this way about a man before.'

'But?' Sam asked.

'But he's in Geneva and I'm in London,' she said. 'My home is here, and his home, his family, and his business, they're all in Switzerland. It just wouldn't work.'

Sam reached for her hand and squeezed it, keeping hold of her fingers. 'G, I'm going to point out the obvious here, and I don't mean to be blunt, but there's nothing keeping you in London. I can see what's keeping Luca in Switzerland, but why can't you relocate there and give this a real chance? If he was truly that special, if you can see yourself with him, if you've fallen in love...'

Georgia stiffened. *Love? Had* she fallen in love with him?

'Do you love him?' Sam asked gently.

'I haven't known him long enough,' Georgia said. 'I mean, can you fall in love with someone that you've only known—'

'Do you *think* you could fall for him?' Sam asked. 'Don't overthink it, just say what's in your heart.'

Georgia knew the answer, she just didn't want to admit it. 'I'm not going back there, Sam. Imagine how he'd react if I just turned up in Geneva again.'

Sam shrugged. 'Think about it, that's all I'm saying. If he could be the one, then why not spend some time there? You've always said you'd love to travel.'

'Tell me about your weekend,' Georgia asked, ready to move the conversation on. 'Did you take my advice?'

Sam grinned. 'I did. And you were right. I think they were relieved to spend some one-on-one time with their son, and I relaxed at the house and cooked for them all. I don't think his mother had ever had someone do that for her, and we got along brilliantly after that.'

'Well, I'm pleased to hear it.'

'You might also like to see this,' Sam whispered, holding out her left hand.

Georgia's eyes widened as she looked at the diamond nestled on her friend's finger. 'He proposed and you didn't tell me?'

'I wanted to show you,' Sam said. 'And ask if you'd be my maid of honour. We're going to get married next summer.'

'You know the answer is yes.' Georgia opened her arms, her tears replaced with happiness. 'I'm so happy for you, Sam. This is wonderful news.'

'But you know I'm not going to be barefoot and pregnant once we're married, right?' she said. 'If you want to talk new business concepts, or start-ups we could invest in...'

'You know what,' Georgia said. 'I'm confused about a lot of things right now, but the one thing I'm certain of is that I want to start another company from the ground up. I've realised that's what makes me happy, only this time I don't want to start it with a sale in mind.'

'What are you thinking?'

'I want to grow something that we keep,' she said. 'I want to retain ownership, grow something long term. I've been thinking about our last business, whether I should have said yes to staying on as a creative director, but I've realised that wouldn't have made me happy, either.'

'Well, I'm in,' Sam said. 'There's no one else I'd rather be in business with.'

'The question is, what?' Georgia said. 'I wanted to come back from my trip re-energised and with some new ideas, but I don't have anything yet.'

'Perhaps you need to take some more time off and travel. Let yourself be open to new concepts.'

Georgia raised her eyebrows at Sam.

'No, I'm not pushing you back to Switzerland, although I'm all for that decision if you want to take a sabbatical there. But, honestly, why not travel? You've always wanted to, and maybe it's what you need?'

'That's not your worst idea,' Georgia said. 'I'll think about it.'

'But can you promise me that you might stop in Geneva at *some* point in your travels?'

Georgia ignored Sam completely and reached for one of the paper bags. 'You said you had croissants?'

Sam snatched the bag from her. 'Only if you start at the very beginning and tell me all about Luca,' she said. 'I want every last detail.'

Georgia rolled her eyes, but this time Sam didn't stop her from taking the bag.

'Oh, and where's the sapphire?' Sam asked.

'It's a very long story,' Georgia replied, breaking off a piece off the flaky croissant and savouring the buttery taste. But as soon as she swallowed, all she could think about was Luca, and the breakfast they'd shared that morning on the way to the museum.

'You're thinking about him, aren't you?'

Georgia took another bite, not wanting to answer Sam's question. Perhaps going back to Geneva in the near future wasn't such a bad plan after all. Perhaps she should have stayed longer in Switzerland, should have made more of an effort to connect with the descendants of her great-grandmother. If she had family out there in the world, shouldn't she at least try to meet them?

'Before you tell me the story about the sapphire, can you promise me one thing?'

Georgia waited, taking a sip of coffee as she studied the earnest expression on her friend's face.

'Just promise me that you'll be open to love. With Luca. Or any other man, for that matter,' Sam said. 'You deserve love, G. No matter what happened in the past, or how afraid you are of losing someone else you care about. Please don't push him away for the wrong reasons.'

'You're presuming that Luca feels the same way about me as I do about him,' Georgia said, taking another bite of croissant and sinking back into the cushions. 'He's a handsome man who had fun with a woman who was only in town for a week or so. I hardly think he had love in mind.'

'Didn't he take you to meet his mother?'

'It was business. She knew about the sapphire. Like I said, it's a long story.'

'Well, how about you start telling me these long stories, so I can better understand what part of him taking you to meet his mother was just business?'

Georgia knew Sam wasn't going to stop asking questions, so she settled in with her coffee to tell her everything, ready to share the events of the past two weeks with the person she loved more than anyone in the world.

27

LONDON

Georgia couldn't help herself. It had been six weeks since she'd returned from Switzerland, and every few days since, she'd gone online and searched to see if there was a news report about the tiara, and every day the only hits were years old. But today, there was one that appeared at the top of the search engine results.

She clicked to translate it into English, and then clicked through to read more. Her heart skipped a beat when she saw a photo of Luca, her eyes stalling for at least a few seconds on his image as the nights they'd shared together came back to her, remembering what it had been like to be in his arms, to feel his breath against her skin, before moving down to read the rest of the article, which had only been posted a few hours earlier.

Generations of the Kaufmann family have searched for answers over the disappearance of the missing stone from the famous Italian sapphire tiara, and now they are pleased to confirm that it has been returned. It is understood that the existence of the sapphire has only recently been discovered, however, it was being held by the rightful owner throughout the past decades. 'It is with great pleasure and excitement that I can confirm that the missing sapphire has been authenticated and returned to the tiara. This development solves one of the great mysteries that my family has been involved in for many, many years, and indeed one of the great mysteries of the Italian monarchy. I would like to thank our anonymous client, who contacted us with the purpose of returning the sapphire, and I would also like to confirm that the sapphire has been held legitimately since it was purchased from the royal family, following their departure from Italy.'

Although Luca Kaufmann has today confirmed he will not be giving any more information about this recent develop- ment, he has shared that the tiara has been loaned to the Museum of Art and History under a long-term agreement, to ensure that it can be shown in perpetuity. The donor received the blessing of the former Italian royal family to do so, and who agreed to the display that will be part of a wider commemoration to past and current European monarchs.

According to Kaufmann, the tiara has an estimated value of €4 million, which makes it one of the most expensive items of jewellery to be owned by a private individual.

Georgia read the article again. She knew all the details; she'd been the one to issue the instructions, after all, but some- thing about reading Luca's quote kept drawing her attention. She missed him. She couldn't stop thinking about him. And she couldn't stop wrestling with the thought that she should have stayed longer, that she should have asked him if he wanted her to stay instead of simply leaving.

As if he knew that she was thinking of him, an email popped up in her inbox.

From: Luca Kaufmann

To: Georgia Montano

Dear Georgia,

Just in case you haven't seen this, there was a press release this morning. I hope you don't mind that I gave them a brief interview. Perhaps you could come to see the display later this month? I would be more than happy to be your host if you do decide to come. The exhibition launch is on 10 September, and you could attend anonymously as my guest, or officially as the donor. The choice would be yours.

With my love, Luca

Georgia groaned. What did that even mean, *I would be more than happy to be your host?* Was he extending a professional courtesy, or did he *want* her to go? They hadn't spoken since she'd left Switzerland, even though she'd picked up her phone so many times to call him, and she wondered if he felt the same, or if he'd simply forgotten about her. At the same time as she was telling herself not to overthink the invitation, she opened a new browser and searched for flights from London to Geneva. The event was in five days' time, and there were flights every day between now and then on British Airways and Swiss.

She hesitated, her hands shaking as she tried to decide what to do. *Just do it. If it's purely business, then so be it. But if it's more...*

Georgia checked her calendar and booked the flight for Thursday, deciding to arrive in town the night before the event. She'd email Luca back and tell him when she'd be there and at which hotel, leaving the ball in his court. If she were braver, she would have called him, but she wasn't.

She stood and went straight into her bedroom to search her wardrobe and see if she had something appropriate to wear.

He'd already seen the little black dress, and she didn't exactly have an endless supply of evening wear. Georgia got out her phone and searched her emails again, looking for the invitation she'd been sent weeks earlier from the museum to the exhibition opening. The dress code was black tie.

After riffling through everything for the better part of thirty minutes, she knew there was only one thing left to do.

Two rings later, she was on the phone with Sam.

'I have a fashion emergency,' she said. 'I think we need to go shopping.'

'Music to my ears,' Sam said, her voice rising an octave. 'Occasion?'

'I've just booked a flight back to Switzerland. I'm going to the exhibition opening.'

'I'll call you when the car's outside your place,' Sam said. 'And Georgia?'

'I'm here.'

'I'm so proud of you.'

Georgia flopped onto her bed, wondering if she'd just made the best decision of her life, or the worst.

28

LAKE GENEVA, 1991

There was something about knowing that she didn't have long to live that was making Delphine question every decision she'd ever made. The hardest of all, even forty years later, was knowing that she'd chosen to give up her own flesh and blood. Some days she forgave herself, and other days she simply couldn't accept what she'd done.

But most of all, she thought about what could have been. With Florian, her life would have been full of love and laughter; there would have been a lightness that had been missing from her life since he'd been taken from her. She knew it was mad, when she'd known him for such a short time compared to the course of her life, but no one had ever made her feel like he had. Her children had brought her love and selflessness, happiness in a different way, but only Florian had truly brought her to life. Only Florian had shown her the woman she could be; only he could have given her the life she'd come to believe she was destined to have.

But now, as her body began to fail her, the cancer slowly spreading and taking hold in ways that could no longer be stopped, she was ready to say goodbye to her children and be reunited with Florian. It pained her that she'd never found her missing daughter despite writing to Hope frequently over the years to ask for information. Hope had made it clear that she wasn't allowed to share anything, that the information had been sealed at the request of the adoptive parents, and she'd also never answered Delphine's questions about the box. Delphine couldn't help but wonder why the tiara was still in hiding, waiting to be claimed. Whether it was because her daughter was yet to be given the box, yet to open it, or simply because she didn't want to know what was inside, she would never know.

Delphine's hand shook as she took out the newspaper she'd saved, turning it to the second page so she could reread the article about the House of Savoy, the former Italian royal family —it had piqued her interest from the very first time she'd seen it.

Instead of sitting in her depressing room in the care facility, she'd decided to go for a walk and sit by the lake. Someone would start worrying when they noticed her gone, but Delphine wasn't a prisoner and she refused to be treated like one. She was an old woman with all her faculties; it was simply her body that was giving out on her. Her hand shook as she held the paper, reading the headline and then dropping her gaze to read the article.

Unlike many former royal families who sold all their jewels immediately after being sent into exile, the House of Savoy retained almost all of the pieces in their extensive collection. Although the family are in the throes of petitioning the state for access to the collection that was left behind in Italy for safe-keeping, many of the younger would-be royals have been seen wearing special pieces from the family's personal collection.

The tiaras are often the most coveted of a monarch's jewels, and although the former princesses have been photographed wearing the family's tiaras over the years, one notable tiara is missing from the collection. It is assumed that the sapphire tiara, previously held in the family since it was made for the then Italian queen in the late 1800s, was sold soon after the family fled Italy for Geneva. Although subject to a confidentiality agreement at the time, the tiara was owned by collector Florian Lengacher, and became the object of a dispute after his death. In a further twist, it is understood that the tiara is missing one of the pink sapphires that makes it unique, the location of which is unknown.

Florian Lengacher was a renowned collector of fine things. He was one of Switzerland's most successful financiers, and boasted a collection of vintage cars, paintings, and fine jewels that would have been worth an estimated forty million francs, had his estate still been intact at the time of writing. The tiara was entrusted to the Kaufmann family in Geneva, who were involved in the acquisition of rare pieces for notable Swiss collectors, and they intend to honour the instructions given to them confidentially many years ago. They are hopeful that one day the missing sapphire will be found, although after so many years it seems unlikely that it will be reunited with the tiara from which it was taken.

Delphine shut her eyes, wishing she'd left clearer clues all those years earlier. She hadn't been intentionally cryptic, but when she thought back about what she'd left, all this time later, she could see how hard it would be to understand what it all meant. Which was why, after all this time, she'd instructed the law firm she'd worked with for the past four decades to secure a safety deposit box. She intended to sit by the lake and write for as long as it took to pour her feelings from her heart onto the page. She'd already sent them the diamond necklace that Florian had given her. It wasn't an item of jewellery that her daughter Isabella had ever seen, so she knew it wouldn't be missed. She'd taken it out of her box of precious things every day since Florian had passed, wearing it openly only when she was at Hope's House, when no one from her day-to-day life would see her, so that she felt close to him. Once she'd given the baby up, she'd hidden it away, knowing that it would have to be buried along with her love for Florian and her heartache over their baby. But it hadn't stopped her from taking it out each night before bed and clasping it around her neck, staring in the mirror at the diamond resting beneath her collarbone, remembering the kiss that had been placed in the little hollow there before Florian had given it to her.

Even after so many years, it still only felt like yesterday that they'd been together. But in reality, it was a lifetime ago.

And so Delphine sat back and began to write, her hand steady despite her pain, remembering the happiest moments of her life and committing them to paper. But the happiest moments were also followed by the saddest, and her pen moved more slowly then, her eyes damp as she apologised to the child, the daughter, who'd had to grow up without her.

It may have only been forty-odd years ago, but times had been so different then. The expectation to stay married, the weight held by family to dictate who a young woman should be betrothed to—they all seemed such foreign concepts now. She could only imagine how hard it would be for Isabella and Tommaso to understand, especially when she'd spent so much time living apart from their father. Now, when she looked back, she wondered if she could have had the baby in secret and then pretended to adopt her; whether she could have made up a story or convinced her husband to make love to her, *anything* other than adoption. But, of course, hindsight was a wonderful thing.

She signed the letter and reread it, picturing her daughter opening it, wondering what she would think, hoping that she would discover it at all. And when she was content with what she'd written, Delphine addressed it and affixed the stamp she'd bought earlier, before rising on aching legs to walk to the post office.

An hour later, she was back at the same spot by the lake, her eyes watering from pain as she realised she'd done too much. She'd intended on going back to the care facility, but somehow she'd ended up right back where she'd started.

As she sat, her breath started to come in sharp, short pants, and the pain she'd felt earlier in her legs was suddenly everywhere. But she refused to cry, refused to feel sorry for herself. If this was to be her final moment, then at least Florian would find her. It's where they'd first walked together, first sat side by side under the moonlight and envisaged a time when they didn't have to hide what they meant to each other.

The piece of newspaper she'd been holding caught on the wind, and Delphine tried to hold on to the low wall she'd sat down on, her knuckles burning as she tried not to fall. She heard someone call out to her, but no matter how hard she tried to stay upright, she couldn't. When she fell, she hit her shoulder and it felt as if it shook the breath from her, and she was so, so tired.

She only wished she'd been able to say goodbye to those she loved.

Delphine tried to reach for the necklace, tried to feel for the diamond Florian had given her, but her hand wouldn't move. Then she remembered she'd already sent it away for safekeeping, that it had been left for her daughter, for the child she'd never had the privilege of meeting as an adult. For the child she'd never had the joy of raising.

I sent the letter. I sent the letter before I died, and that's all that matters.

Please God, let her find it.

29

GENEVA, PRESENT DAY

Georgia still hadn't decided whether going back to Geneva was a sensible idea or not, so instead of calling Luca the moment she arrived, or going to surprise him, she'd stayed in her hotel. She'd started consulting to a charity over the past weeks, and was working on a business plan for a non-profit concept she'd been toying with for some time, so she'd buried herself in work and ordered in room service rather than going out.

Which was why she found herself walking up the steps to the Museum of Art and History alone, and standing outside as if she were an imposter. Somehow, the most important detail of the trip had eluded her—she'd forgotten to RSVP.

'If you could just use your radio and tell June Meier that Georgia is here—' Georgia couldn't believe it when the security guard turned his back on her, ignoring her, and greeted another patron.

'Excuse me,' she tried again. 'If you could...' It was no use. For reasons unbeknown to her, it was harder to get into the museum than through security at Heathrow Airport. Perhaps making her donation anonymously hadn't been such a great idea after all.

'You came.'

Georgia's blood immediately ran hot. She turned around and saw Luca standing there, looking devilishly attractive in a black tuxedo paired with a crisp white shirt and a black bow tie. It made his features look even darker, his hair midnight black as he stood a few steps below her, impossibly handsome.

There were so many things she wanted to say, but nothing came out of her mouth.

'Georgia, you look stunning,' Luca said, closing the distance between them and making her feel far less awkward as he took hold of her shoulders and kissed one cheek and then the other. 'But what are you doing standing out here?' He looked around, before a dark cloud passed over his face. 'You're waiting for someone? Are you—'

'No,' she said quickly, not wanting him to think she was there with anyone else. 'I actually couldn't get past security. It seems that in my haste to get here I forgot entirely about notifying the museum I'd be attending.'

'Ah,' Luca said, his smile returning. 'If you'd only told *me*, I would have RSVP'd for you.' He shook his head. 'Did you prefer to give me a heart attack? Waiting on the steps like that? I nearly tumbled all the way back down again when I saw you.'

She laughed. 'Truly?'

'Truly,' he confirmed, his mouth still kicked up into a smile.

'I had every intention of calling you before I left London, and then going straight to your office when I arrived, but I just, well, I didn't know if you'd want to see me.'

He frowned. 'See you? Did you not receive my email?'

She glanced away, but he took her hand and then she couldn't help but look up at him.

'I wasn't sure if your email was business or...' She didn't finish the sentence.

'Pleasure?' he asked. 'You weren't sure if I meant business or pleasure?' Luca moved closer to her, standing one step below her, which put them on more of an even footing heightwise. He was a smidge taller than her, but with her heels and the step, he'd almost lost his height advantage.

'Georgia, what do I have to do or say to convince you that I very much want to see you, for reasons that have nothing to do with business?' he murmured, his fingers stroking through her hair and then playing down her spine as he kept his gaze fixed on her. 'As far as I'm concerned, any business we had together is finished now. Which means the only reason I want to see you is for pleasure.'

Something about his whispered French accent made every word he said even more appealing, and when she didn't answer he kept his hand to her back and drew her forward ever so slightly. She slung her arms over his shoulders, grinning as his mouth met hers, in a kiss very slow and gentle, their lips barely touching and yet somehow making her entire body tingle with anticipation.

'Now, shall we go inside before we miss the official opening?' he whispered in her ear.

Georgia went to take his hand, but he let go and strode ahead to the security guard, speaking to him in such rapid French, Georgia couldn't make out a word that was said. But she did understand the look that passed over the security guard's face, and when Luca indicated that she should come forward, she took his arm, keeping her gaze down as she stepped through the door.

'I apologise for the inconvenience,' the guard called out. 'Enjoy your evening.'

'*Merci*,' she said, knowing that he'd just been doing his job, but also annoyed that he'd taken Luca at his word and not hers. 'What did you say to him?'

'That this evening wouldn't be going ahead if it weren't for you, and that you could recall the main display piece with one phone call and end the night for everyone.'

Georgia laughed. 'Except I couldn't take it back even if I wanted to,' she said.

'But he doesn't know that, does he?'

Georgia held tightly to Luca's hand then, wishing she'd gone to see him before turning up at the event.

'Luca,' she began, trying to find the words she wanted to say.

He stared down at her, his expression difficult to read.

'I missed you,' she eventually said.

'I missed you, too,' he replied. 'More than I could have imagined.'

She tilted her head slightly to look up at him. 'I should have come straight to see you when I arrived, but I didn't know how you felt. I mean...' Georgia sighed. 'This is all new to me.'

'This is all new to me, too,' he said. 'I've been married to my work for most of my life, and then suddenly you walked into it.'

'But we're ill-fated,' she said. 'My life is in London and yours is here, and the longest relationship I've had is with a houseplant.'

'Mine is with my cat.'

She groaned. She didn't even know he had a cat. What was she thinking? They barely even knew each other. What they had was nothing more than lust.

'Where are you staying tonight?' he asked, his voice husky as he kept his fingers around hers and tugged her closer.

'The Beau-Rivage again.'

'We'll stay here long enough to be polite, and then you can get your bags and check out. You're staying with me.'

A shiver of excitement ran through her as Luca smiled and greeted someone from the museum, propelling her gently forward as someone cleared their throat to declare the exhibition open. She should have told him that *she* would decide whether or not she wanted to check out of the hotel, but he'd given her exactly what she wanted: proof that he felt the same way about her as she did about him.

Luca stood behind her still holding her hand, and she leaned back just a little so that she could feel his breath against her cheek, so her bottom brushed his hip as she stared at the tiara twinkling under the lights. The pink stones were radiant, and she shared in the collective gasp of those around her as it began to turn inside the glass display case, its beauty second to none.

'As soon as everyone starts clapping, we're leaving,' he said. 'How long are you in town for?'

'Two days.'

He whispered directly into her ear. 'Then we'd best make the most of it.'

What they had was nothing more than a holiday romance. Being with Luca was impossible; they lived in different countries for a start and she had no interest in a long-distance relationship, but that didn't mean they couldn't enjoy two more days together.

An hour later, the exhibition long forgotten, Georgia held Luca's hand as they walked along the lake. She had his tuxedo jacket slung over her shoulders, snuggling into it as he walked in his shirt. It wasn't particularly cold, but in the dress she'd been wearing she was grateful to have something else to put on.

'I can't believe you're back here,' Luca said as they strolled.

'Honestly? Neither can I,' she replied. 'I just...'

She didn't know what to say, and it seemed as if Luca didn't either.

They stopped and stared out at the water, and she tucked herself into him, his chin resting on her head as they stood together. Luca rubbed her arm and she finally felt brave enough to ask the question that had been burning inside her since she'd first realised she was falling in love with him.

'Luca, would you ever leave Geneva?' she asked. 'Could you ever see yourself living anywhere else?'

He didn't answer, but he did hold her tighter. 'My life is here. I want to say that I could, but I've always had a sense of walking in my great-grandfather's footsteps, of my father's footsteps,' he said, his voice growing deeper as he spoke. 'There was an expectation when I was growing up, knowing my destiny, knowing that I was being trained to take over the family business one day. And that was always fine with me, it's what I wanted.'

'And now? Is that still what you want?' she asked, too scared to look up at him, holding herself tightly against him instead.

'I want more than one thing, Georgia,' he said, kissing her forehead and drawing her even closer. 'I want to fulfil my family's expectations of me, that's not something I could ever walk away from, but what you and I have here?'

He didn't need to say anymore, because she felt it, too. But there was no easy answer to what was keeping them apart.

'And you?' he asked. 'Would you ever leave London?'

She hesitated. It wasn't so much that she wouldn't leave, it was more that she'd grown up thinking she'd never sacrifice her dreams, her future, for a man. Especially a man she barely knew.

'I don't know how to answer that,' she eventually said. 'I have a whole life in London, my friends, my home...'

He cleared his throat and looked down at her. 'Then we make the most of the time we have together,' he said. 'Whatever is supposed to happen, will happen.'

She swallowed, on the verge of changing her mind and telling him that she would leave it all behind. But that wasn't who she was. She'd fought to be independent, been determined to stand on her own two feet and prove that she was capable, that she wasn't defined by what had happened to her in the past.

'The time we've spent together, Luca...' she began.

'I know,' he said. 'You don't need to put it into words.'

So she didn't. Instead, she slipped her arms around his neck and let him kiss her. If they couldn't be together, then all they could do was enjoy what they had in the here and now. After that, she'd have to figure out a way to forget all about him.

Which would be much easier said than done.

Georgia stood beside the bed and looked down at Luca. He had one arm flung out, an arm that had only minutes earlier been across her body as she'd snuggled to his side, trying to commit the feel of him to memory, not ever wanting to forget him.

They hadn't left Luca's house since the night of the exhibition, staying in their own little cocoon and not wanting to think about her leaving. But her flight left in three hours, and instead of a drawn-out goodbye, she'd decided to let herself out of the house and make her departure less traumatic.

She leaned down and pressed the softest of kisses to his cheek, inhaling the smell of him one last time, before quietly picking up her bag and tiptoeing down the stairs. Tears streamed down her cheeks as she stopped in the kitchen and found a piece of paper and a pen. She took a deep breath, trying to think of what to say and struggling to know how to say it to the man whom she'd fallen for so hard and so fast.

In the end, she stopped thinking and wrote the truth.

I'm not good at saying goodbye. Thank you for everything.

She hesitated as a tear fell onto the page and blurred the last two words.

You have my heart. Georgia x

She left quickly before she could change her mind, slipping out the door and pulling her case behind her. The Uber she'd ordered was waiting for her and she got in, not daring to look back as they drove away. Because if she'd seen that Luca had been standing at his bedroom window looking down at her, she knew she would have asked the driver to turn around.

I barely know him. I can't turn my life upside down for a man. I cannot give up everything I've worked so hard for.

But no matter how many times she had these thoughts, they were becoming harder and harder to believe.

30

PRESENT DAY, SIX WEEKS LATER

'Why won't you just tell me where we're going?' Georgia grumbled, as Sam kept a firm hold on her hand and marched her down the footpath.

'Because that would ruin the surprise!' she said, sounding exasperated. 'Can you just walk without moaning, please?'

Georgia sighed, but kept walking as she'd been instructed. All Sam had told her was that they were going out for a special dinner, which she could only presume had something to do with her maid-of-honour duties. Although she was fairly certain that *she* was supposed to be the one organising pre-wedding get-togethers for the bride, not the other way around.

'Come on, it'll be fun,' Sam said. 'You've been sad ever since you got home from Switzerland.'

Switzerland. The one place she was trying her best to forget, and failing at miserably. She'd hoped that the more days and then weeks that passed, the easier it would be to forget about Luca, but instead, it had become harder. How many times had she taken out her phone, her finger hovering, ready to call him, or opened her laptop and looked at flights that would have her there within hours?

'Georgia?' Sam asked, as she stopped walking.

'Sorry, I know I've been a terrible friend since I got home,' she said. 'You're right, this will be fun. A night out is exactly what I need.'

'We're here,' Sam said. 'And you're right, this is *exactly* what you need.'

When they walked into the restaurant, she saw that there was a large table set for at least eight people across one wall, but Sam led her straight past that table, nodding to the waiting staff as she directed her to a much smaller table for two.

'It's just the two of us?' Georgia asked, as Sam fussed about and gestured for her to sit. 'What was the great surprise about this restaurant if it's just the two of us?' She looked around. It was a fabulous restaurant, and the food coming from the kitchen smelt incredible, but she wasn't convinced it was worthy of such a dramatic arrival. Had she been so hard to convince to go out, that Sam had had to pretend it was a special event just so she would say yes?

'I just need a minute,' Sam said, but Georgia didn't miss the deep-pink shade of her cheeks.

'Are you okay?' Georgia asked. 'You look—'

'I'm fine, I'll be back soon.'

'If you're going to the ladies', then I'll—'

'No!' Sam said, before lowering her voice. 'I mean *no*. Please, just sit there and don't move until I get back, okay? Can you, just this once, do what I ask without questioning me?'

Georgia nodded, taken aback by her friend's sudden outburst. Sam never spoke to her like that. She noticed Sam had gone in the wrong direction for the ladies', but not wanting to defy her orders by racing after her and telling her where it was, she stayed seated.

'May I take your order, ma'am?'

A deep voice laced with an unmistakable French accent filled her ears.

Luca? She turned slowly, telling herself how silly it was to even... *Oh my God.*

'Luca!' she cried, her heart feeling as if it were caught in her throat. 'What are you doing here?'

She leapt to her feet as he opened his arms, pressing herself against him, her arms wrapped around him, her head to his chest as she listened to the steady beat of his heart. She'd imagined this moment every day, every *hour*, since she'd left him, and now he was here, in London, in the very place she thought she'd never see him.

'I thought you were never going to come. I've been pacing out the back for the longest half hour of my life.'

She pulled back and looked up at him, smiling against his mouth as he kissed her. What on earth was he doing here?

'You could have just called and asked me for dinner,' she said, shaking her head as he guided her back to her seat. 'Or told me that you were coming to London. Why didn't you just, I mean...' She was lost for words.

'That would have ruined the surprise,' he said, and she noticed then that his cheeks were flushed, that something was different about him. She also realised that Sam hadn't come back.

'Why are you in London, Luca?' she asked, her excitement turning to suspicion as she looked around for her friend. 'And how did you—'

Luca's smile melted her heart, but when he pulled out her chair and asked her to sit, she forgot all about interrogating him. He cleared his throat and stood on the spot, not moving around to the other seat.

'What are you—' she began, before her voice died in her throat as she watched him go down on one knee.

'Georgia Montano, I've never believed in love at first sight, but as soon as I met you, I knew you were special,' he said, reaching for her hand and linking their fingers as he spoke.

'My father said to me many years ago that I would know when I met the woman I was supposed to marry. He said that when I met someone I couldn't live without, I would know without question, and Georgia, I know. I know that I don't want to live without you. I know that I'd be making the biggest mistake of my life if I let you go. I know that the last few weeks without you have been the most miserable weeks of my life.'

Georgia clutched tightly to his fingers, her breathing shallow as she digested his words. *This can't be happening.* Her heart began to pound as she watched him, as he searched her eyes for the longest of moments.

'What are you saying, Luca?'

'Georgia,' Luca finally said, letting go of her hand to reach into his pocket. He produced a little blue velvet box, and when he opened it she saw an enormous, oval-shaped pink stone surrounded by diamonds. 'Will you marry me?'

She opened her mouth, but she couldn't speak, the words evaporating in her throat as she stared at the ring looking back at her.

'I know your life is in London and mine is in Geneva, but I don't want that to be why we're not together. Is that really reason enough to live our lives apart?'

Georgia closed her eyes and when she opened them, she saw the way Luca was looking at her, knew how much he meant the words he was saying. And she believed them, because she felt the same.

'Georgia,' he whispered, taking the ring from the box, which he put back in his pocket, the ring in his other hand. 'Will you marry me?'

'Yes,' she whispered, as he slid it onto her finger. 'Yes, Luca, *yes* a hundred times over. *Yes.*'

She looked from the ring to Luca and back again. *What just happened?*

'How did... I mean, when...' She laughed. 'How did you plan all this?'

Luca stood and pulled her up with him, taking her face in his hands with such tenderness as he gently kissed her, not answering her question with words. It was like their first kiss all over again, as if everything was new, every part of her body alive as his lips moved against hers.

'I take it she said yes?'

A familiar voice made her pull away from Luca. *Sam*. Of course, Sam was in on it all. Dragging her out of the flat, telling her she had to get dressed up for a special event—only Sam could ensure she was perfectly prepared and yet also completely taken by surprise at the same time.

'I thought we didn't keep secrets from each other?' Georgia said, trying her hardest to look cross, but finding it impossible to wipe the smile from her face.

'I thought this was one secret you wouldn't mind me keeping from you,' Sam said, before opening her arms wide and embracing both of them. 'You make a gorgeous couple. Congratulations.'

'*Merci*, Sam,' Luca said, and Georgia watched as he kissed her friend's cheeks. 'I trust we can become great friends.'

Sam looked like she was swooning, a hand to her heart as she leaned in and whispered, 'If only you could see the way this man looks at you. He's divine, absolutely divine.'

Georgia blushed. There *was* something different about the way Luca looked at her; she'd felt it from the very first moment she'd met him. It was the first time in her life she'd felt as if the man she was with genuinely couldn't take his eyes off her, that a pretty girl walking past couldn't turn his head because he wasn't even looking.

'Luca, I know this is supposed to be a romantic dinner for two, but since Sam is here...'

She stopped talking abruptly when she saw Luca and Sam

exchange glances, and she knew then that there was more going on than just an unexpected meeting.

'What? Why are you looking at each other like that?'

'Because, my love,' Luca said, drawing her close again and dropping a familiar kiss to the top of her head. 'I invited your family to join us. We have the rest of our lives to be just the two of us.'

She looked back up at him. *Her family?*

'You told me that Sam's family had taken you in as if you were their own, so I thought you'd want them here to celebrate with us.'

Tears filled her eyes as Sam swept her arm out extravagantly to the large table behind her. 'The little table was in case you said no. I wanted to cover all bases just in case, but this one—'

'Was for if you said yes,' Luca finished, interlinking their fingers, her engagement ring unfamiliar against her skin as she tightened her hold on him.

'This is all too much, I just—'

The door to the restaurant opened then and Georgia was suddenly overwhelmed with emotion as she saw Sam's mum, dad, and grandparents coming towards them, as well as Sam's beau, Harry, all with big smiles on their faces.

'Georgia!' Sam's mother Marion cried, hurrying towards her, her hands to her face as she half laughed, half cried. 'Oh Georgia, what a wonderful surprise.'

'She said yes!' Sam declared, as her mum hugged Georgia first and then turned to Luca.

'Well, I can see why you fell for this one just from looking at him. What a gentleman. Can you believe he called Fred and asked for permission?'

Georgia was certain her jaw actually dropped open as she turned back to Luca. 'You called Fred?'

Luca shrugged. 'It seemed like the right thing to do. You

said he was like your father, and I wanted to go about things the right way.'

'Thank you,' she whispered, sliding her arms around his neck and kissing him. 'Thank you for listening, for seeing who I am and who is important to me. It means the world to me, truly it does.'

Luca kissed her back, touching his forehead to hers when their lips parted. 'I thought you were going to scold me for asking for permission.'

'Not at all,' she said, before whispering: 'Although I trust you still would have asked me even if he'd said no.'

They both laughed and Luca kissed her, but they'd barely touched lips when Sam parted them, grabbing hold of their hands on either side and marching them to the table.

'There's time for smooching later,' Sam said firmly, as if she were a schoolteacher scolding petulant children. 'Now it's time to celebrate with everyone who loves you.'

Georgia tilted her head and touched it to Sam's.

'Thank you,' she murmured. 'I have no clue how you did all this, how Luca even contacted you, but thank you.'

'You're very welcome,' Sam said, and Georgia couldn't help but notice the tears shining in her friend's eyes. 'Now, let's drink champagne. It's not every day your sister gets engaged!'

Georgia gave Sam a quick hug before turning back around, not knowing which way to look, but in the end, she moved from person to person, introducing them to Luca, seeing the smiles and love radiating from the faces of the people there for her. All this time, she'd told herself that she didn't truly have a family, had always referred to them as *Sam's* family, but in that moment, she realised that they were not just Sam's family. They were her family, too, her ride or dies, the people who loved her most in the world.

I'm not alone. I wasn't then, and I'm not now.

Georgia took her seat beside Luca as the waiters brought

two bottles of champagne to the table and began to pour them, barely hearing anything as everyone seemed to talk and laugh at the same time. But it was Luca she turned to, who smiled only for her, who made her feel for just a second that she was the only person in the room.

'Should I have made this a dinner for two?' he whispered, reaching out to stroke her hair. 'I'm starting to regret not having you all to myself.'

'No, this is perfect,' she said. 'Overwhelming, but also perfect.'

'Would you mind if I said a few words?'

She shook her head and smiled back at him. 'Not at all.'

He leaned in, his first words murmured into her ear, for her only. 'I know there's so much we need to figure out, where we'll live and what our lives will look like. But there's nothing I won't do for you, Georgia. If I have to commute to London every weekend for the rest of my life, I'll do it.'

She kissed him before he stood, reaching for her champagne glass as he took his, and taking a quick gulp to calm her nerves. He was right; London and Geneva weren't that far away. If they had to commute, if they had to take turns going between the two cities for as long as it took for them to decide where to live, then so be it. It was worth the sacrifice to be with him, she just hadn't been able to see that before.

'I know I'm a stranger to all of you,' Luca said, looking at everyone seated around them before glancing down at Georgia, 'so I would like to thank you for trusting me when I asked you all to come here tonight. Thank goodness she said yes!'

Everyone laughed and sipped their drinks, and Georgia let Luca take her hand as he spoke again.

'Marriage wasn't something I'd thought about before, but when Georgia left Geneva to return to London, I knew that for the first time, I'd met someone that I could spend the rest of my life with. It was as if I'd been let in on a secret, only it took me a little while to understand what I was supposed to do.'

'Luca,' she said, squeezing his hand, her eyes damp with tears again.

'I know we've only known each other a short time, but I've never felt this way about anyone,' he said, facing her now. 'You changed my life the day I met you, Georgia, and I cannot wait to spend the rest of our lives together.'

She stood as everyone raised their glasses.

'To Luca and Georgia!' Sam cried, visibly blinking away tears.

And as everyone cheered for them, Georgia slid her arms around Luca's neck, admiring her ring over his shoulder before staring into his eyes.

'It's not a sapphire from the royal tiara,' he told her, 'but I thought it would remind you of what brought us together.'

'I love it,' she said, as his lips met hers in a kiss that tingled all the way down her spine.

'It's an antique pink diamond,' he whispered. 'Similar enough to remind you of a sapphire, but different enough for—'

'It to be our stone,' she said. 'I love it. It's perfect.'

Was this how her great-grandmother had felt, looking at the sapphire that was to be her engagement jewel? Georgia had thought about Delphine a lot lately, but right now, knowing how desperately in love she was with Luca, imagining a life growing old together, she couldn't bear to think what it must have been like finding out that the man she loved had died. Before they'd even begun their lives together.

'Do you know who will never forgive me for not being part of this?' Luca said quietly.

She sighed. 'Your mother.'

He groaned. 'She is going to kill me.'

'Then let's have an engagement party at your home for her. Celebrate with your family, too.'

'She would adore that.'

Georgia reluctantly sat, wishing they could stay wrapped in each other's arms for the rest of the night. But she knew she needed to be grateful for everyone around her, not just for Luca. Because they'd been there for her through the happiest moments of her life, and also the saddest, and this was as much a celebration for them as it was for her. They'd raised her with the same love they'd shown to their biological family, taking in an orphan, Sam's best friend, and not hesitating in making her their own.

She reached into her bag then and realised her phone was vibrating. She'd just missed the call, but it was a number she didn't recognise, so she wouldn't have answered it anyway. But when a text came through before she put her bag back down, she quickly read it.

Dear Georgia, sorry to be putting this in a text, but I received your letter, and I'd like to meet. We had no clue our grandmother Delphine had had a daughter adopted, so the news of your grandmother has all come as quite a shock, but we're open to meeting you and hearing more. Any chance you're visiting Lake Geneva again soon? My daughter and I would love to meet you, so please do let us know if you're ever in town. Anna

Georgia's hand shook as she looked up at Luca and then Sam. They were in Geneva. All the time she was there, searching for answers, trying to understand her past, she was in the same city as members of her biological family. Family who were open to meeting her.

'What is it?' Sam asked, leaning across the table.

'Georgia, you look like you've seen a ghost,' Luca said. 'Is it bad news?'

She turned her phone around so they could read the screen.

'I reached out via a lawyer to the descendants of my great-grandmother, Delphine. I wasn't going to, but after I got home from my first trip, I was overcome by the feeling that I needed to at least try to tell them that my family existed, and about the story of my great-grandmother.' She shook her head. 'After all this time, I presumed they didn't want to communicate with me. I never thought I'd hear from them.'

'Maybe our wedding will be larger than expected then,' Luca said, his arm extended behind her chair, his thumb gently caressing her back.

'Are you going to say yes? To meeting them?' Sam asked.

'They're my family,' Georgia said, looking at the people around her. 'I love the family I have, but if there are aunts and cousins out there with a connection to my father? Then I think I'd never forgive myself for not meeting them.' She took a breath and watched as Sam's parents and grandparents laughed and talked, their happiness contagious. 'No one will replace this family, my *true* family, but I'm still curious, I suppose, just in case they're like my dad.'

She swallowed as she glanced back up at Sam and Luca. 'There's something else, too, another reason I want to connect with my family.'

They both looked back at her, expectantly.

'During my search, I came across someone who knew my grandmother. For the very first time in my life, I have some understanding of why she turned her back on my father and then me. I always knew she didn't approve of my mother, but it turns out that she held deep regrets for how she'd treated my father throughout his childhood and in the years before he married.' Georgia cleared her throat. 'Apparently, she never wanted to have children of her own, and felt that she wasn't capable of showing me the love and care that my parents had. She felt it was better to cut ties with me, rather than jeopardise the chance for me to find a loving family to take me in, and she knew that my mother wouldn't have wanted her to be the one to raise me in her absence.'

Sam put her arm around her, and Georgia leaned in. 'Well, maybe now you can start to forgive her. I, for one, am very grateful she made that decision.'

'So am I,' Georgia said, giving her friend a one-armed hug as she lifted her glass in her other hand. 'I'm very grateful for your family, or should I say *our* family.'

'To family, then,' Luca said.

'To family,' she repeated, clinking glasses with Sam before taking a long, slow sip of her champagne.

To family. To the one I lost, to the one I gained, and to the one I'm soon to be a part of. And maybe to the one I didn't even know existed.

31

LAKE GENEVA, 1991

Delphine tried to lift her head, but everything hurt. One moment she'd been sitting looking at the lake, lost in her memories, and the next she'd woken up on the ground, unable to move. Her body felt as if it no longer belonged to her as sirens blared and people leaned over her, shining lights in her eyes and touching parts of her body. She did appreciate the warm blanket that was tucked over her, and if she hadn't heard the sound of her daughter Isabella's worried voice, she'd have closed her eyes and surrendered to the overwhelming sensation she had to sleep. If she closed her eyes, the pain might disappear, that's all she could keep thinking.

'Please, I need to get past. She's my mother.'

Isabella. She'd always been a demanding child, and as an adult she never let anyone stand in her way. But what was Isabella doing here? How had she found her?

Delphine's eyes came into focus when Isabella's soft, warm hand touched her cheek. Her breath wheezed from between her lips as she leaned into her touch.

'Mama? Can you hear me?' Isabella asked. 'I'm right here.'

Her daughter reached beneath the blanket to take her hand, and Delphine used all her energy to squeeze back, to tell her that she could hear every word. The pain was bearable if it meant seeing her daughter one last time. She'd known this day would come, but she hadn't expected it to be so sudden, or marred with so much agony.

'My mother has stage four stomach cancer,' Isabella said. 'She's supposed to be in hospice care.'

Hospice care. The place she'd been sent to die, when all she'd wanted was to stay in her own home until the end. The doctor had told her the day before, when she'd said how full of energy she felt, that it was most likely the body's last hurrah, almost like a surge of adrenaline, and she hadn't believed him. But she certainly believed him now.

She heard her daughter sigh. 'Mama, you're not supposed to get out of bed. How did you even get down here on your own? What were you thinking?'

Delphine could hear the worry in her daughter's voice, knew that if she was able to sit up and look at her, that her eyes would be filled with tears, that her face would be stricken with fear. Isabella was yet to come to terms with her mother's diagnosis; that she was dying. Whether she'd got out of bed or not, nothing had changed. She may have turned weeks into days by exerting herself, but the outcome was still the same.

'Isabella,' she whispered, her voice barely a croak.

But Isabella heard her, leaning close to listen, holding her hand still. 'What is it, Mama? Are you in pain? Do you need morphine?'

She tried to shake her head, but everything hurt and she was suddenly so very, very tired. She did need morphine, but she didn't want her brain to be addled from the pain relief; she would rather have her last moments with her daughter lucid.

'Something,' she whispered, her breath rasping, 'to tell you.'

Isabella leaned closer, and Delphine couldn't help but wonder if her other daughter still looked like Isabella. They'd been so similar as babies, their features almost identical, with dark lashes and dark hair from birth, and perfect little pink Cupid's bow mouths that had stolen her heart. She had a feeling that both girls would have been as forthright as each other, both feisty in their own ways. It warmed her heart, because she knew that she hadn't been feisty enough; no one, not even her family, would have ever convinced Isabella into a marriage of convenience.

'Daughter,' Delphine murmured, trying to get the word out. But her mouth wasn't working properly, her throat constricting as she tried to speak, as pain ricocheted through every inch of her body.

'Yes, I'm your daughter,' Isabella said. 'I'm here, Mama. I promise I won't leave you.'

'Had,' she whispered. 'A daughter.'

Isabella's face showed that she didn't understand what she was trying to say, and Delphine knew she'd left it too late. All these years, all those decades when she could have said something, when she could have told Isabella the truth, but she'd been too afraid.

Afraid of what? Once her children were grown, once her husband had passed away and lost his power over her, she should have told them. She should have given her children, *all* her children, the chance to meet. She should have tried harder to find the daughter she'd lost, the daughter who'd occupied her thoughts from the second she was conceived. But now it was too late for anything. Now her daughter thought her mother was confused and didn't even know who she was.

Delphine's eyelids drooped then, and she tried hard to keep her eyes open, even though it was as if someone was standing over her and forcing her to shut them.

'Mama?' Isabella cried. 'Mama, stay with me! We just need to get you to the hospital. You're going to be fine.'

It's too late for me, my darling. It's time for me to be with the other love of my life. Florian is waiting for me, and I wished you'd had the chance to know him properly, as a stepfather. I wish he'd had the chance to be part of your life, so you could see what I was like with him, so you could have had an example of what it was for a man to truly love a woman, to see the way he seemed to light me up from the inside. I wish you could have seen the version of me when Florian was near, when his eyes found mine across a room.

You and Tommaso, you have given me so much joy. I always knew when I became a mother that I would do anything for my children, only I never knew I would have to choose between you, that my children would be parted.

'Mama?' Isabella cried. 'Mama! Please, help her! Somebody, do something to help her!'

Delphine would have opened her eyes if she could have, to reassure her Isabella one last time. But suddenly everything felt so heavy; her eyelids, her chest, her heart.

This time, she didn't try to speak. Instead, she used her last reserves of energy to smile, and suddenly she was able to open her eyes. But as her focus blurred, it wasn't Isabella she saw, but Florian.

He was standing outside his stately home, his hand outstretched, and he hadn't aged a day. His smile was just as she remembered it, and when he said her name, when she lifted her hand to take his, all the pain left her body. His palm slid against hers and their fingers intertwined, as he lifted their hands and pressed a warm, slow kiss to her knuckles.

Delphine could hear someone saying her name, but the pull to keep her eyes shut and keep hold of Florian's hand, to finally walk back into his embrace, was too strong to fight.

She only hoped he would understand what she'd done,

would forgive her for the decision she'd had to make, for the life she'd lived without him.

As her breath stuttered from her throat, as the pain she'd felt for so long finally disappeared, Florian's arms encircled her, drawing her close.

I'm finally home, my love. I'm finally home.

32

LAKE GENEVA, PRESENT DAY

'I've never been so nervous,' Georgia said, running her hands down the front of her jeans and looking over at Luca. 'How do I look?'

'Beautiful, as always,' he said. 'I only hope you're not this nervous when we get married.'

That made Georgia smile. 'I'm not nervous about our wedding. That, I'm excited about.' She went to speak again, but saw the way Luca was looking past her. 'They're here?'

He nodded. 'I think so.'

Georgia stood and turned, and as she did, she saw two women with dark blonde hair walking towards them. The older of the two women was perhaps thirty years older than her, but the younger one appeared to be of a similar age to Georgia. She knew instinctively it was them, and when they both smiled in her direction, she felt a huge sense of relief.

'They're going to love you,' Luca whispered, standing with his hand on her shoulder. 'How could they not?'

'Georgia?' the older woman said.

'Anna?'

She'd expected to feel uncertain, worried about what to say

and awkward about meeting someone with a shared biology, but Anna immediately grinned and hurried forward, embracing her in a hug.

'I can't believe we're actually meeting,' she said, standing back and gesturing to the other woman beside her. 'This is my daughter, Mara.'

'It's lovely to meet you both,' Georgia said, giving Mara a quick welcome hug. 'This is my fiancé, Luca. He's here for moral support.'

Luca laughed good-naturedly and shook both their hands, before disappearing to find a drinks menu. Georgia imagined it was his way of trying to give them a little space.

'I wondered if we might look alike,' Anna said. 'I had visions of meeting you, and realising you looked just like one of my daughters.'

'Me, too,' Georgia said. 'I kept thinking that I'd see you both and feel immediately as if you were family due to some weird physical resemblance, but I suppose we do all have the same blue eyes?'

Mara grinned. 'You're right, we do!'

They all looked up when Luca returned, to check they all liked rosé, and when they were settled again and seated around the table, Georgia took out the little box.

'I know you were probably sceptical about my intentions when I asked my lawyer to contact you, so please don't think that I expect anything from you at all,' she said. 'I started out on this journey trying to understand more about my grandmother's adoption, and that's all I'm trying to do.'

Anna nodded. 'As I said to you over the phone, we knew nothing about any of this. It was certainly a well-kept secret, from my sister and me, anyway. We had no idea that our grandmother was anything other than a devoted wife and mother, and my mother, Isabella, certainly never mentioned anything.'

Georgia held out the box. 'I was given this when I first

became aware of the adoption, and at the time it contained a sapphire as well as the newspaper clipping that's still in there. The photo I've added, after finding it in a safety deposit box.'

'May I?' Mara asked.

Georgia gave it to her and watched as she opened it, taking out the photo and passing it to her mother.

'Well, it's my grandmother, Delphine, without a doubt,' she said. 'And this is most definitely not my grandfather.'

Georgia grimaced. 'I have no intention of besmirching your grandmother's name. This is a secret that can exist purely between us.'

Anna reached for her hand across the table. 'From what you've told me, she was a woman in love, and, let's face it, if this were to happen now, she would have divorced her husband and been free to do as she pleased. There will be no judgement from us.'

Georgia met Anna's gaze from across the table. 'I hadn't thought about it like that. I mean, I didn't judge her, I felt her heartbreak more than anything, but you're absolutely right.'

'Do you think your grandmother ever knew?' Mara asked. 'Or do you think it was all a secret, hidden until the day you discovered the box?'

'Honestly, I can only presume she didn't know. Unfortunately, she was estranged from my father, but given the type of upbringing he described, I'd say that if she did know, it was a very closely guarded secret.'

'Do you have family, Georgia?' Anna asked, as Luca arrived back to the table, flanked by a waiter who held a tray with four glasses and a bottle of wine.

Georgia looked up at him, loving the way he sat down close to her, his thigh pressed to hers. 'Not in the traditional sense,' she replied. 'I'm an only child, and my mother and father passed away many years ago, but I'm very fortunate to have more than one surrogate family.'

Georgia felt a lightness talking to Anna that she wouldn't have felt even a few months earlier. Being with Luca, seeing the way he was with those around him, how he'd embraced the family who'd raised her and the way his family had in turn embraced her, had made her feel as if she truly belonged in the world.

'Did Georgia tell you we're going to be married soon?' Luca asked, as he began to pour the rosé into each glass.

'Here in Geneva?' Anna asked.

'Right here in Geneva,' Luca replied. 'We're splitting our time between here and London, but my mother would never have forgiven us if we didn't have our wedding here.'

'And I was only too happy to let her organise everything,' Georgia said with a grin. 'Planning a party holds very little appeal to me, and she seems to have been made for it. I told her that all I want to do is choose my dress and arrive at the venue on the day.'

They all laughed, at ease as they held up their glasses.

'To the family we didn't know we had,' Georgia said.

'Family,' they all said, before taking a sip.

Once they'd all set their glasses down, it was Mara who spoke first.

'Georgia, when my mother told me about you, the first thing I did was search your name online, and I came across the business you sold.'

She sighed. 'Ah, yes, my firstborn child. I'd be lying if I said I wasn't missing it.'

'Mara is also very interested in the cosmetics industry,' Anna said. 'She's been working on a small range of organic products for some time.'

'Is that so? Well, maybe it runs in our blood.'

'I was wondering,' Mara said, 'if you do any consulting work. I'm only a start-up, so I don't have a large budget, but—'

'I'd love to,' Georgia said. 'What stage arc you at?'

'Well, I've been through beta testing, and I'm close to finalising my packaging, but actually launching the product, it's all new to me. I'm passionate about what I've created, but I feel I need some direction. There are just so many organic products on the market, so I need to develop an innovative way to show that my brand is better than the others.'

Georgia glanced at Luca before answering, not able to disguise her grin. 'Your business is based here in Geneva?'

'Yes,' Mara said, smiling back at her and giving her a quizzical look in reply. 'What's funny about that? I feel like I'm missing something.'

Luca slung his arm around Georgia's shoulders. 'I've been looking for a reason to convince my fiancée to stay in Geneva for a little longer than she's been willing. Who would have thought I'd find it today?'

Georgia laughed. 'Well, I wouldn't say yes to just anyone, but I do miss being part of something new. How about we arrange a time to talk about it more, just the two of us?'

Mara's eyebrows shot up. 'So, you'll consider it?'

'I will,' Georgia replied. 'But only if you'll both come to our wedding. Luca, I'm sure your mother won't mind finding space for two more guests, will she?'

Luca pulled her close and kissed her temple. 'For the people who've found a way to tempt you to stay here?' he asked. 'She might just find them space at the bridal table.'

EPILOGUE

Georgia had never been the little girl who'd grown up imagining her wedding day. She'd never pictured herself in a big white dress, or having a brood of children, but now that she was standing in her wedding dress, her emotions were starting to get the better of her. Her life had changed so much over the past year, both personally and professionally, and she was suddenly finding it all very overwhelming.

She turned from the full-length mirror and walked away, dabbing at her eyes and wishing she wasn't feeling so emotional. Her parents had died when she was a teenager, and because of that she remembered them as young parents, their smiles wide and their eyes bright. Today, she wondered if her father's hair would be grey, whether her mother would be fretting over her appearance or happy in her own skin; if they'd both seem as vibrant and full of life as they'd been before they'd gone on that fateful trip. The truth was, she would never know; but she did know without a shadow of a doubt that her father would have been there to walk her down the aisle. *Nothing would have stopped you, Dad. I know that.*

There was a soft knock at the door then, and after dabbing

at her eyes again, she called out to come in, and Sam appeared. She was dressed in a blush-pink silk dress that clung to her figure, and Georgia smiled the moment she saw her. She looked beautiful.

'I thought we agreed no tears today,' Sam teased, immediately coming over to her and giving her a big hug, her palm warm against her back as she stroked in big circles. 'You are the most gorgeous bride, Georgia. Absolutely jaw-droppingly gorgeous.'

'Thank you,' Georgia said. 'Pity about my make-up. I can't seem to stop crying.'

'Let me take a look,' Sam said. 'Sit down over here. We don't have long.'

Georgia followed her and sat down, watching as Sam opened a bottle of champagne and popped the cork, before pouring two glasses.

'I thought we didn't have long?'

'We don't,' Sam said. 'But that gorgeous man of yours can wait a little. You need this.'

She wasn't wrong. Georgia did need time with her friend; she needed a moment to just sit and let her mind still.

'Are your tears because you're scared or because you miss your family?' Sam asked, as she dabbed some concealer gently beneath Georgia's eyes. 'Or both?'

'Family,' Georgia said. 'I just... I can't stop thinking about them. My dad walking me down the aisle, my mum fussing over me, the look on her face when she sees me in my dress for the first time. I've missed out on so many things with them.'

She watched as Sam looked up at the ceiling, her bottom lip quivering as she blinked away her own tears.

'I know we would have stayed friends no matter what, but when you came to live with us, G, you truly became my sister,' Sam said. 'I want you to know that I'll never think of you as anything less.'

Georgia reached for her hand. 'I know. I feel the same. You know I do.'

They both laughed as they wiped away fresh tears.

'Look at us! We're both a mess,' Sam scolded, just as there was another knock at the door.

'Knock, knock,' someone called out as it slowly opened.

Sam's mother and father appeared then, and Georgia and Sam both laughed at the looks of concern etched on their faces.

'Is everything okay here?' Sam's mum asked.

'Sweetheart, if you want to run, I'll drive you,' Sam's dad said, looking deadly serious. 'You still have time to change your mind.'

'She hasn't changed her mind!' Sam said. 'Dad, you're not driving her anywhere.'

Once Georgia started laughing, she couldn't stop. The image of Sam's darling father grabbing her hand and running out of the house to make a getaway with her was too much. Within seconds they were all hugging, the four of them with their heads bent, all either laughing or crying.

'Okay, how about you give me a few minutes? I'll meet you downstairs soon,' Georgia eventually said.

They hugged her again and kissed her, and Georgia took a deep breath as Sam's hand lingered on her shoulder.

'You're sure you don't want me to stay?'

'I'm sure,' she said. 'I'll be down soon. I promise.'

Once she was alone again, Georgia went to the mirror and touched up her make-up some more, before reaching into her bag for the familiar little box that she'd kept with her ever since she'd rediscovered the sapphire. She opened it and reached inside, taking out the diamond necklace that had been left for her grandmother and putting it around her neck. Then she picked up the photo and looked at the happy, smiling couple. They never had the chance to marry, never had the chance to be open about how they felt for each other. She lifted the photo and pressed a kiss to it, before folding it in half and nestling it back into the box and closing the lid.

I'll never forget you, Delphine. I only wish I could have had the chance to meet you.

Then Georgia checked her appearance one last time, before leaving the room and walking down the stairs. Sam was waiting and stepped forward to give her the simple bouquet of white flowers she would carry.

'You're ready?' Sam asked.

'I'm ready,' Georgia replied.

The music started then, a quartet playing as Georgia took her first steps outside, and with that, Sam's mother and father both stepped forward. She slid one hand through each of their arms, nodding to first her mum, and then her dad. It felt right to have them both walk her down the aisle in the absence of her own father. They'd both raised her, both chosen to have her join their family; both made her feel as if they were the second daughter they'd always wanted.

'Thank you,' she whispered. 'For everything.'

'Georgia, you have nothing to thank us for. You're our daughter, and daughters don't need to thank their parents.'

She knew there wasn't a dry eye between them as they both walked her outside and towards her waiting groom, but any sadness or melancholy she felt disappeared as soon as she set eyes upon Luca. He was standing there in a tuxedo, as handsome as the night they'd met at the museum, and the way he looked at her, the way his entire face lit up as she walked towards him, made her heart sing.

Georgia forced herself to look away from him as she walked, glancing at the intimate group of people gathered on each side of her. The rest of Sam's family, Luca's sister and her family, some friends, Anna and Mara, Hope Berenson's niece, Mia, Ella and her darling little baby, and most important Luca's mother, who was sitting at the front and beaming back at her as if she couldn't have been happier.

'*Belle fille*,' Marj said, standing as she passed.

Georgia stopped to hug her, kissing her on each cheek and seeing just how much it meant to her mother-in-law-to-be. She was positively radiant, smiling from ear to ear, her happiness clear for all to see.

'I promise to love your son with all my heart,' Georgia whispered before she pulled away.

'*Merci*,' his mother said, her hand to her heart. '*Merci*, Georgia.'

Georgia gathered herself and began to walk again, letting go of Sam's parents only when she reached her fiancé. They both kissed her before taking their seats, and suddenly it was just her and Luca. It was as if no one else was there once they faced each other. Luca took both her hands in his and stared into her eyes, as the celebrant stepped forward and began to speak, their ceremony underway.

Georgia barely heard a word, reciting what was told to her as she smiled at Luca, as she studied the face of the man who would become her husband. It was hard to believe that such a short time ago, she'd been googling him to understand what she was up against, convinced that the story about the sapphire was part of some elaborate hoax. And now, she was about to marry him.

Before she knew it, the ceremony was over and Luca was grinning as he stepped forward, as one hand touched her waist and the other her cheek, gently cupping it as he smiled down at her.

'Hello, wife,' he murmured, dipping his head slightly.

'Hello, husband,' she whispered back, just before his mouth met hers and the small crowd gathered erupted into a chorus of claps and calls of congratulations.

Georgia slipped her arms around his neck as they kissed

again, as Luca swept her into his arms and carried her back down the aisle despite her protests. Eventually she tucked her head to his collarbone and let him, unable to stop laughing as he twirled her in front of all their loved ones.

When he eventually set her down again, Luca kissed her.

'We should have just eloped, and then I could have carried you straight to the bedroom.'

Georgia swatted him away as his mother and Sam's family began to circle them and wish them well, everyone swept up in the love they shared. But it was Mia who caught her eye, standing slightly away from the others, one of the only people gathered who wasn't family.

Georgia excused herself and went over to her, enveloping her in a hug. 'Thank you so much for coming,' she said. 'Without you, I wouldn't be here. I would never have crossed paths with Luca.'

Mia's smile was kind. 'Well, I don't know about that. You may well have crossed paths without me.'

'We wouldn't have, and you know it,' Georgia said. 'And see those two over there? The mother and daughter?' She waited for Mia to see who she was pointing to. 'They are the only biological family I have, and I've met them because of you, too. What you did, finding the descendants of those boxes?' Georgia said. 'It was the most selfless thing a person could do, Mia. The contents of that box changed my life, and I will be forever indebted to you.'

Mia's smile was worth a thousand words; no matter what she tried to say otherwise, Georgia could tell that she understood what she'd done, how important her decision had been to reunite those boxes with their rightful owners.

'You mentioned you had a box of your own,' Georgia said. 'That you were trying to find out more about Hope? Or what might have once been in the box left for her?'

'Georgia!' Luca called. 'Come back over here!'

Mia took her hand and squeezed it. 'I'll tell you all about it another time, it will wait. Besides, I think your husband wants you.'

Georgia looked over at Luca then back at Mia, torn between the two of them. 'You're sure it can wait?' she asked.

'Of course, this is your wedding day. Go and enjoy yourself.'

Georgia nodded, giving Mia a quick hug again before going back to Luca and his family, caught up in their good wishes and embraces. And by the time she looked back for Mia, she was gone.

'Who was the woman you were talking to? I didn't recognise her.'

She glanced around again, surprised she'd left so soon. 'Someone very special,' Georgia said. She'd tell Luca about Mia once they had some time alone; now, it was time to celebrate.

But even as she was embraced by family, kissing cheeks and being kissed, revelling in the love and attention of those around them, she couldn't help but wonder what Mia would have told her if they hadn't been interrupted.

'Luca, I'll be back soon,' Georgia said, kissing his cheek as she squeezed past him.

They had the rest of the afternoon and evening to celebrate, but if she hurried, she might just catch Mia before she left. Because she didn't want to wait, she wanted to know what Mia had discovered; and if she needed help tracing her clues, then Georgia was ready to be there for her, and she was certain Ella would, too. In fact, she was starting to wonder if every woman who'd been at the lawyer's office that day might be prepared to help Mia; after all, she'd changed their lives with her decision to save those little boxes. And for that, Georgia would be always in her debt.

A LETTER FROM SORAYA

Dear reader,

Thank you so much for choosing to read *The Sapphire Daughter*! If you enjoyed the book and want to keep up to date with all my latest releases (including the next books in the series!), just sign up at the following link. Your email address will never be shared, and you can unsubscribe at any time.

www.bookouture.com/soraya-lane

I do hope you loved reading *The Sapphire Daughter* as much as I enjoyed writing it, and if you did, I would be very grateful if you could write a review. I can't wait to hear your thoughts on the story, and it makes such a difference in helping new readers to discover one of my books for the very first time. This was the fourth book in The Lost Daughters series, and I'm looking forward to sharing more books with you very soon. If you haven't already read *The Italian Daughter, The Cuban Daughter,* or *The Royal Daughter*, you might like to read those books next, and enjoy being swept away to Italy, Cuba, and Greece and falling in love with some truly unforgettable characters.

KEEP IN TOUCH WITH SORAYA

One of my favourite things is hearing from readers—you can get in touch via my Facebook page, by joining Soraya's Reader Group on Facebook, or finding me on Goodreads or my website.

Thank you so much,

Soraya x

www.sorayalane.com

Soraya's Reader Group:
facebook.com/groups/sorayalanereadergroup

 facebook.com/SorayaLaneAuthor

ACKNOWLEDGMENTS

There are parts of writing a book that are incredibly solitary, but there are also wonderful moments as an author when you're part of a team, and I'm so grateful for my incredible team at Bookouture!

First and foremost, I have to thank editor Laura Deacon for sharing my vision and taking a chance on The Lost Daughters series. Huge thanks, as always, also go to rights extraordinaire Richard King who, along with Saidah Graham, is responsible for selling the series into twenty languages around the world. In my wildest dreams, I could never have imagined my books finding their way into the hands of so many readers in so many languages, so I will be forever grateful to Richard for the way he passionately pitched The Lost Daughters!

Thank you to publisher Ruth Tross and her team for making me feel so well taken care of with Laura away on parental leave. I couldn't have asked for a better editorial team, and I'm hugely grateful to Natasha Harding for her excellent structural edits on this book. I'd also like to make special mention of editor Ruth Jones, who has recently joined the Bookouture team and is working closely with me on the next books in the series! I honestly couldn't wish for a more supportive, engaged team to work with.

Special thanks to Peta Nightingale, Jess Readett, Melanie Price, and everyone else at Bookouture who has worked on my series so far, and also to my amazing line editor Lauren Finger, copyeditor Jenny Page, and proofreader Joni Wilson. I also have to say thank you to my agent, Laura Bradford, who has been with me since the very beginning of my career. Thank you for your dedication to my work, and for always being there for me, no matter what.

My list of people to thank became a lot longer with the publication of The Lost Daughters series, and I'd like to acknowledge the following editors and publishers for their support. Thank you to Hachette; to my UK editor Callum Kenny at Little, Brown (Sphere imprint); my New Zealand Hachette team, with special mention to Alison Shucksmith, Suzy Maddox, and Tania Mackenzie-Cooke; US editor Kirsiah Depp at Grand Central; Dutch editor Neeltje Smitskamp at Park Uitgevers; German editor Julia Cremer at Droemer-Knaur; editors Päivi Syrjänen and Iina Tikanoja at Otava (Finland), Norwegian editor Anja Gustavson at Kagge Forlag; and French pocketbook publisher Anne Maizeret from J'ai Lu. I would also like to acknowledge the following publishing houses: Hachette Australia, Albatros (Poland), Sextante (Brazil), Planeta (Spain), Planeta (Portugal), City Editions (France), Garzanti (Italy), Lindbak and Lindbak (Denmark), Euromedia (Czech), Modan Publishing House (Israel), Vulkan (Serbia), Lettero (Hungary), Sofoklis (Lithuania), Modan Publishing House (Hebrew), Pegasus (Estonia), Hermes (Bulgaria), JP Politikens (Sweden), and Grup Media Litera (Romania). Knowing that my book will be published in so many languages around the world by such well-respected publishing houses is truly a dream come true.

Then there are the people in my day-to-day lives who are so supportive of my writing. I would be remiss not to thank my incredible family, who are always my biggest cheerleaders. Thank you to Hamish, Mack, and Hunter for never being surprised by my endless questions about whatever story I'm writing, and for just always being there for me no matter what. Thanks also to my parents, Maureen and Craig, and to author

Yvonne Lindsay (who also writes under the name E.V. Lind) for her daily support. Yvonne, I honestly don't know what I'd do without you. And I also have to say a very, very special thank you to my assistant Lisa Pendle, who this book is dedicated to. Not a day goes by that I'm not grateful for everything that you do for me, and I feel so fortunate to have you in my life.

Finally, my biggest thanks goes to you, my readers. Without you, I wouldn't be able to write the stories I love, and I appreciate every single book that you've bought, read, reviewed, and shared.

Soraya x

PUBLISHING TEAM

Turning a manuscript into a book requires the efforts of many people. The publishing team at Bookouture would like to acknowledge everyone who contributed to this publication.

Audio
Alba Proko
Sinead O'Connor

Commercial
Lauren Morrissette
Jil Thielen
Imogen Allport

Cover design
Debbie Clement

Data and analysis
Mark Alder
Mohamed Bussuri

Editorial
Ruth Jones
Natasha Harding
Melissa Tran

Copyeditor
Jenny Page

Proofreader
Joni Wilson

Marketing
Alex Crow
Melanie Price
Occy Carr
Cíara Rosney

Operations and distribution
Marina Valles
Stephanie Straub

Production
Hannah Snetsinger
Mandy Kullar
Jen Shannon

Publicity
Kim Nash
Noelle Holten
Myrto Kalavrezou
Jess Readett
Sarah Hardy

Rights and contracts
Peta Nightingale
Richard King
Saidah Graham

Made in the USA
Monee, IL
05 March 2024

54527160R00163